# My Reminiscences

## Rabindranath Tagore

## with an introduction by
## Andrew Robinson

Rupa & Co

First published by Macmillan & Co. 1917
This edition published in paperback 1991 by
PAPERMAC
a division of Macmillan Publishers Limited
London and Basingstoke

First in Rupa Paperback 1992
Second impression 1993

Published by
**Rupa & Co**
7/16 Ansari Road, Daryaganj, New Delhi 110 002
15 Bankim Chatterjee Street, Calcutta 700 073
135 South Malaka, Allahabad 211 001
P. G. Solanki Path, Lamington Road, Bombay 400 007

By arrangement with
Macmillan London Ltd., London

This edition is for sale in India only

Printed in India by
Gopsons Papers Pvt Ltd
A-28 Sector IX
Noida 201 301

**Rs 80**

# My Reminiscences

# Contents

# Contents

*Rabindranath in 1881 at the age of twenty by Jyotirindranath Tagore. (Courtesy Rabindra Bharati, Calcutta)*

# Introduction

As the twentieth century draws to its close, we hear talk on all sides of the need for cultural plurality. Rabindranath Tagore's apprehension of this need at the beginning of the century becomes ever more far-sighted. 'The most significant fact of modern days is this,' he wrote in *Creative Unity* (1922), 'that the West has met the East. Such a momentous meeting of humanity, in order to be fruitful, must have at its heart some great emotional idea, generous and creative.'

Bengal, where Tagore was born, was the world's first true laboratory of East and West, and Tagore was its greatest product. His 'memory pictures' written at the age of fifty and published in Bengali as *Jibansmriti* (My Reminiscences) in 1911, before the West had heard of him, offer a unique and charming insight into the interplay of two great civilisations.

No wonder W. B. Yeats described the memoir in its English translation as 'rich'. Reading it after *Gitanjali*, Tagore's prose poems that had so greatly stirred him, Yeats must suddenly have comprehended the complexity of culture that had given birth to such simplicity. By the time Tagore reached his late

twenties – the point at which *My Reminiscences* closes –
he had a deep and genuine appreciation of Sanskrit,
Bengali and English literature, a similar grasp of
Bengali and Hindustani vocal music and a wide knowledge of English and Irish songs, besides first-hand
experience of many aspects of life in England; all of
which had enabled him to produce poetry, plays,
stories, novels, essays, 'operas' and songs that are
still read and performed by Bengalis a century later.
And this was before he reached maturity as an artist.

He was not, of course, the first Bengali to demon-
strate striking sophistication of intelligence and imagination (nor the last). That distinction belongs to Raja
Rammohun Roy (1772–1833). Best known today for
his stand against *sati*, widow-burning, Rammohun
was colonial India's first reformer, who used his
phenomenal command of languages to examine the
world's great religious texts, including the Hindu
scriptures, and to apply what he found to be their
essence to contemporary Hinduism, in order to rid
it of inauthentic traditions. After years of debate
with Christian missionaries in Calcutta, he founded,
around 1830, the Brahmo Sabha, a Hindu movement
opposed to the prevailing idolatry and caste practices
that took its beliefs from Rammohun's interpretation
of the *Vedas*, Hinduism's earliest scriptures. Within
a few decades, this movement became the Brahmo
Samaj, the most influential movement of religious and
social reform in nineteenth-century India. One of its
pillars was the Tagore family.

Dwarkanath Tagore (1794–1846), Rabindranath's
grandfather, was among Rammohun Roy's greatest
admirers. He was also one of the wealthiest men of
his day. His combination of idealism and worldliness
made for a life of exceptional interest and lasting significance, despite his being almost forgotten today.

Dwarkanath's money came from business, the firm Carr, Tagore and Company he had founded. It covered indigo factories, coal mines, tea picking and sugar production and owned a fleet of cargo boats that plied as far as Britain, a bank that for two decades was the keystone of the commercial structure of Calcutta, and extensive agricultural estates in East Bengal (now Bangladesh) and Orissa – estates that would be managed by Rabindranath Tagore in the 1890s.

But if Dwarkanath was business-like, he was philanthropic too, and on a scale that had few equals. British and Indian alike, the celebrated and the unknown, practical works, charitable activities and religious institutions were all beneficiaries of his largesse. He also threw the most spectacular parties in Calcutta, attended by the British élite of the 'City of Palaces'. When he travelled to Europe in 1842 (in his own steamer), his reputation for munificence increased still further, and he became known as 'Prince' Dwarkanath Tagore, friend of both Queen Victoria and King Louis-Philippe. At the end of one party in Paris the 'Prince' draped a fine Indian shawl over the shoulders of every lady present as she left the room.

He had a vision of an industrialised India as a partner in Empire, with Indians collaborating on equal terms with Europeans, who would settle in India as they had settled in America, Australia and South Africa. Had he lived, he might have brought it to pass by sheer determination and energy. But the British rejected his vision in favour of short-term material gain, and his family rejected it in favour of spiritual and artistic gains. Astonishing as it is to record, Rabindranath Tagore refers only once, in the most passing manner, to his pioneering grandfather in *My Reminiscences*. In his forties he is said to have burned

most of Dwarkanath's correspondence. It is almost as if
he felt the memory contaminated him.

Perhaps he inherited this feeling from his austere
father Debendranath (1817–1905), known for the
last half-century of his life as the Maharshi, 'Great
Sage'. To the dismay of Dwarkanath, his eldest son
largely lost interest in the family firm in 1838 at
the age of twenty-one. Inspired by the example of
Dwarkanath's friend Rammohun Roy, Debendranath
revived the Brahmo Samaj and began a search for true
religion all over northern India. Upon Dwarkanath's
death (in London in 1846), his son scandalised the
rest of the family by refusing to perform the usual
idolatrous funeral rituals. For many years he made it
a point to abandon the family mansion at Jorasanko
in north Calcutta at festival time to avoid witnessing
the orthodox Hindu rites of his domestic circle. When
Carr, Tagore and Co. crashed, he insisted on giving
whatever the family owned to pay the creditors,
regardless of his legal obligations. So impressed were
they by his probity that the Tagores were permitted to
continue the administration of the firm and to receive
an allowance for the maintenance of the family. Within
ten years most of the debts had been paid off.

None of Debendranath's seven sons inherited a head
for business, but three of them, Dwijendranath (1840–
1926), Satyendranath (1842–1923), and Jyotirindranath
(1849–1925) were remarkable men, even when compared with Rabindranath, who was the youngest. Each
has a role in *My Reminiscences*. Between them they
performed with distinction in almost every branch of
the arts and humanities. They also helped to create
the national movement that in 1885 gave rise to the
Indian National Congress; and Satyendranath, ironi-
cally, became the first Indian to enter the Indian Civil
Service (ICS). Their examples, combined with those of

other gifted Tagores living in Jorasanko and the cream of the city's artists and intelligentsia attracted to the house, infused Rabindranath's childhood and youth (and hence the pages of his memoir) with a variety, vivacity and celebration of eccentricity virtually bound to nourish any seeds of talent.

The three or four decades following Tagore's birth in 1861 were the zenith of what is generally termed the Bengal Renaissance. They were also the high noon of the British Empire. Though the precise relationship between these two facts is controversial, there can be little doubt that they are connected. Tagore is the most dazzling instance of the benefits of this cultural collision; while others described by him in *My Reminiscences* adumbrate the damage that more typically resulted and has persisted in Bengali society ever since.

In his famous Minute of 1835, Macaulay had defined the aim of colonial education as the creation of 'a class of persons, Indian in blood and colour, but English in taste, in opinions, in morals and in intellect'. Many young Bengalis of the time embraced Macaulay's idea with passion. 'I can speak in English, write in English, think in English, and shall be supremely happy when I can dream in English,' quipped one of them (Raj Narain Bose, see chapter 22) about his deracinated youth before he joined the Brahmo Samaj and reverted to his own language Bengali.

At the other end of the gamut of cultural response, the orthodox refused to countenance any departure from prescribed Hindu rituals. One of Tagore's servants, a former village schoolmaster, is described as being like this (see chapter 4):

> The earth seemed too earthy for him, with too little water to keep it properly clean; he was engaged in constant warfare with its chronically

6

*My Reminiscences*

soiled state. He would shoot his water-pot into the
tank with a lightning movement so as to get his
supply from an uncontaminated depth. It was he
who, when bathing in the tank, continually thrust
away the surface impurities until he took a sudden
plunge, trying to catch the water unawares, as it
were. When he walked, his right arm stood out at
an angle from his body, as if, we liked to think,
he could not trust the hygiene of even his own
garments. Day and night he carried himself like
someone on perpetual guard against infinite kinds
of pollution that might slip through his defences
and infect his contact with earth, water and air.
The fact that his body had contact with the world
at all, seemed insufferable to him.

Rabindranath was drawn to neither religious orthodoxy nor crass anglicism. Even as a teenager he began
intuitively to borrow what he liked from English literature to enrich his Bengali writing. Other writers were
doing the same, with varying degrees of imitation,
but Tagore was the most creative. He absorbed not
the details but the spirit of the foreign work. In
chapter 21, for instance, he tells of how Chatterton,
the eighteenth-century boy-poet, inspired him when
he was sixteen to write his first worthwhile verse.
Chatterton had passed off his own poems as the work
of a fifteenth-century monk, been ostracised when he
revealed the deception, and committed suicide. What
Chatterton's poetry was like Tagore had no idea, but
the 'melodramatic element' in the story fired his
imagination: 'Leaving aside suicide, I girded my
loins to emulate young Chatterton.' He pretended
to discover the work of an old Vaishnava poet while
rummaging in the Brahmo Samaj library. The first
friend who read it was ecstatic and declared that it

must be published. When Tagore revealed the truth, his friend's face fell and he muttered, 'Yes, yes, they're not half bad.' In due course when the poems appeared in the family magazine *Bharati*, it was under the name of Bhanu Singh (Bhanu meaning 'Sun', as does Rabi). A Bengali then in Germany included Bhanu Singh in his thesis on the lyric poetry of Bengal, giving him a 'place of honour as one of the old poets, such as no modern writer could have aspired to'. And was then awarded his PhD – as Tagore informs us with wry amusement.

He lets us know what he himself thought of the poems – not much – but does not bother to spell out his point: we are left to make of it what we will, as with most of the anecdotes in *My Reminiscences*. Still it is clear that Tagore regarded the whole episode as typical of the 'multi-cultural' confusion of the time: the Bengali critic fell for the bogus because he did not know Bengali properly and saw his language through foreign eyes; and his German supervisors, not knowing Bengali at all, lacked the means to detect the mistake. Only genuine knowledge and empathy will do when attempting to analyse one's culture to determine what is wheat and what is chaff, Tagore implies. Furthermore, they form the only sound basis on which to hope to judge other cultures. This requires 'the great emotional idea, generous and creative' mentioned in *Creative Unity*.

Maharshi Debendranath, and before him Rammohun Roy, tried to treat Hinduism in this way, in order to purge it of excrescences like *sati* and, in his eyes, idolatry. But Debendranath was not prepared to go as far as his youngest son; he remained, in some ways, highly conservative. He arranged for Rabindranath to be invested with the Brahmin's sacred thread, for example – see chapter 13 – and insisted on his marrying a wife he had never

met, an almost illiterate ten-year-old of the right Pirali
Brahmin caste. Such was the custom then, even among
the enlightened Tagores. If Tagore objected he did not
reveal it in *My Reminiscences*, dutiful son that he was.

In other important ways, however, Debendranath
was liberal. In 1878 he sent Rabindranath to England
intending that he should train as a barrister like
many – too many – of his contemporaries. When his
son showed no inclination towards the law, his father
made no attempt to force him.

Tagore writes of his fifteen months in the heart
of the Empire (see chapter 25) with sympathy and
self-mocking humour, sometimes tinged with disgust.
His letters of the time, which he later regretted publishing, show that much of his stay was an uneasy
experience. He spent happy days with his elder brother
Satyendranath's family in Brighton and Devon, and
as a lodger with an English doctor in London, who
treated him as one of the family and whose young
daughter taught him many English and Irish songs
that he later adapted for his 'operas'. Otherwise, he
felt mostly dismay or indignation.

Unsurprisingly, perhaps, he hated the lack of light
and space compared to what he knew of Bengal and
the rest of India. As for human relationships and art,
he felt there to be a dearth of intimacy and a preoccupation with the superficial at the cost of the
essential. The very aspects of English society that
seem to have appealed to his fêted grandfather in
1840s London (so far as one can tell from surviving
letters and reports) repelled Rabindranath, not that
he ever made the comparison. It is as if he sensed
in the soul of mid-Victorian London a cold-hearted
despair of the kind that drove Robert Clive to suicide
a century before. As a boy, this story had shaken
him. 'How could there be such brilliant success

on the outside and such dismal failure within?' (see chapter 18).

But Tagore was too subtle an artist and judge of human beings ever to tar a whole nation or race; in fact, he specifically stated that 'human nature is everywhere the same', after observing in London the devotion of the doctor's wife to her husband, an attitude he admitted believing earlier to be the unique prerogative of the Indian wife. However tempted he might have been to generalise about the ruler or the ruled, he always knew that it was the individual, in all his or her lonely mystery, who mattered most. He was deeply shocked when his favourite sister-in-law Kadambari Devi killed herself when he was twenty-two, four months after his marriage (see chapter 42). Her motive is no clearer to us than Clive's. It would be easy to conclude from *My Reminiscences*, and especially from Tagore's paintings, and his moving novella *Nashtanirh* (The Broken Nest) filmed by Satyajit Ray as *Charulata*, that Kadambari was in love with Rabindranath and he with her, but we can never know the full cause of the tragedy.

Tagore eventually overcame it and found himself strengthened. Much less easy for him to accept was his lack of genuine appreciation by Bengalis. The applause for Bhanu Singh's poetry despite its artificial sentiments, is symptomatic of Tagore's lifelong reception in Bengal. Whenever he departed from convention in his work, which was almost always, he was attacked – often scathingly. When *Nashtanirh* appeared, critics asked why the author had shown an extramarital relationship. When *Jibansmriti* (My Reminiscences) was published, they questioned how Tagore could remember all these things he claimed had happened to him as a child. And in 1914, the year following the award of the Nobel prize, a Calcutta University exam paper asked candidates to rewrite in 'chaste and elegant' Bengali a passage from Tagore! Over and over, right until his death, Bengali critics discovered or invented some wart on Tagore's work or life and in the process missed his all.

He never allowed this tendency in his public to corrode him, but his natural aversion to it invests the final pages of *My Reminiscences* with some bitterness and poignancy:

In other parts of the world there is no end to the movement, clamour and revelry of life. We, like beggar-maids, stand outside and look longingly on. When have we had the wherewithal to deck ourselves and join in? Only in a land where an animus of divisiveness reigns supreme, and innumerable petty barriers separate one from another, must this longing to express a larger life in one's own remain unsatisfied. I strained to reach humanity in my youth, as in my childhood I yearned for the outside world from within the chalk ring drawn around me by the servants: how unique, unattainable and remote it seemed! And yet, if we cannot get in touch with it, if no breeze can blow from it, no current flow out of it, no path be open to the free passage of travellers – then the dead things accumulating around us will never be removed, but continue to mount up until they smother all vestige of life.

Who, looking objectively at the condition of modern Calcutta, can fail to feel the force of this diagnosis by the city's greatest son? It is a *cri de coeur*, wholly characteristic of Rabindranath Tagore. Break down the barriers! Let in the light and air! And let human beings truly sympathise!' he calls, both in his art and in his long, courageous life. 'I do not put my faith in institutions, but in the individuals all over the world who think clearly, feel nobly and act rightly. They are the channels of moral truth.' (*Creative Unity*)

*Andrew Robinson*

# A note on the translation

In the Translator's Preface to the 1917 edition of
*My Reminiscences*, the following comments appear:

> [These] memory pictures, so lightly, even casually
> presented by the author, [reveal] a connected history
> of his inner life, together with that of the varying lit-
> erary forms in which his growing self found successive
> expression, up to the point at which both his soul and
> poetry attained maturity.
>
> This lightness of manner and importance of matter
> form a combination, the translation of which into a
> different language is naturally a matter of consider-
> able difficulty. It was, in any case, a task which the
> present Translator, not being an original writer in
> the English language, would hardly have ventured
> to undertake, had there not been other considera-
> tions. The Translator's familiarity, however, with the
> persons, scenes and events herein depicted, made it
> a temptation difficult for him to resist, as well as
> a responsibility which he did not care to leave to
> others not possessing these advantages and there-
> fore more liable to miss a point, or give a wrong
> impression.

13

Surendranath Tagore, the translator and a nephew of Rabindranath, was undoubtedly correct on both counts: he was steeped in the atmosphere of the Tagore family, but he was also not entirely equal to the challenge of conveying that atmosphere in English. His translation has therefore been extensively revised. Its many appealing qualities – the period flavour not least – have been preserved, while its stiffness, unneeded archaisms and occasional obscurities have been removed. A small quantity of material in chapter 34, felt to be repetitious, has been omitted, and some references to details of Bengali life and culture, originally cut out on grounds of their unfamiliarity to foreign readers, have been restored, without attempting to add certain short passages of poetry rightly judged untranslatable. (The translations that do appear are by Rabindranath Tagore.) A glossary of Indian words used in the text has been provided, along with a Tagore family tree and notes on the people, places, events and works mentioned by Tagore. These notes, compiled with the help of Krishna Dutta, incorporate the footnotes printed in the original English edition, where they are required by and satisfactory to the modern reader.

A final word is necessary on spelling and transliteration of Bengali in English. Many of the places mentioned by Tagore, such as Chandernagore or Tipperah, have modern spellings closer to their original Indian pronunciation and spelling, for example, Chandannagar, Tripura. In spelling titles, such as *Sakuntala*, and people's names, such as Satyendranath, the generally accepted spellings have been employed. All other Bengali words have been spelt without diacritical marks, as they are rather cumbersome; instead a spelling has been used that tries to reproduce the sound and not the orthography of the Bengali. For example, Bengali has three letters for 's' but in pronunciation the distinction between two of them is so slight that the unaccustomed ear does not hear it. Rather than employing the conventional but confusing 's' and 'sh' to represent these three sounds, all three Bengali 's' sounds have been transliterated as 'sh' throughout, except where there is an established spelling, as in the word sari. However, no system of Bengali–English transliteration is entirely satisfactory.

A.R.

# 1. *Preamble*

I do not know who has painted the pictures of my life imprinted on my memory. But whoever he is, he is an artist. He does not take up his brush simply to copy everything that happens; he retains or omits things just as he fancies; he makes many a big thing small and small thing big; he does not hesitate to exchange things in the foreground with things in the background. In short, his task is to paint pictures, not to write history. The flow of events forms our external life, while within us a series of pictures is painted. The two correspond, but are not identical.

We do not make time for a proper look at this inner canvas. Now and then we catch glimpses of a fragment of it, but the bulk remains dark, invisible to us. Why the painter ceaselessly paints, when he will complete his work, and what gallery is destined to hang his paintings, who can say?

Some years ago, someone questioned me on the events of my past and I had occasion to explore this picture-chamber. I had imagined I would stop after selecting a few items from my life-story. But as I opened the door I discovered that memories are not history but original creations by the unseen artist. The diverse colours scattered about are not reflections of the outside world but belong to the painter himself, and come passion-tinged from his heart – thereby making the record on the canvas unfit for use as evidence in a court of law.

But though the attempt to gather a precise and logical story from memory's storehouse may be fruitless, it is fascinating to shuffle the pictures. This enchantment took hold of me.

As long as we are journeying, stopping only to rest at various shelters by the wayside, we do not see these pictures – things seem merely useful, too concrete for remembrance. It is when the traveller no longer needs them and has reached his destination that pictures start to come. All the cities, meadows, rivers and hills that he passed through in the morning of his life, float into his mind as he relaxes at the close of day. Thus did I look leisurely backwards, and was engrossed by what I saw.

Was this interest aroused solely by natural affection for my past? Some personal attachment there must have been, of course, but the pictures had a value independent of this. There is no event in my reminiscences worthy of being preserved for all time. Literary value does not depend on the importance of a subject, however. Whatever one has truly felt, if it can be made sensible to others, will always be respected. If pictures which have taken shape in memory can be expressed in words, they will be worthy of a place in literature.

So it is as literary material that I offer my memory pictures. To regard them as an attempt at autobiography would be a mistake. In such a light they would appear both redundant and incomplete.

## 2. *Teaching begins*

We three boys were brought up together. Both my companions were two years older than I. When they were placed under their tutor, my teaching also began, but of what I learnt I can remember nothing now.

What recurs to me constantly is this. 'The rain patters, the leaf quivers.' I first heard it when I had just come to anchor after crossing the stormy region of the *kara, khala* series; it struck me then as the first poem by the ancestor of all poets. Whenever the delight of that day comes back to me, even now, I realise why rhyme is so vital in poetry. Because of rhyme words come to an end, and yet end not; the utterance finishes, but not its ring; and the ear and the mind go on with their game of tossing the rhyme back and forth. Thus did the rain patter and the leaves quiver in my consciousness again and again.

Another episode from this period of my early boyhood sticks fast in my mind.

We had an old cashier, Kailash by name, who was like one of the family. He was a great wit, and would constantly crack jokes with everybody, old and young – recently married sons-in-law and other newcomers into the family circle being the special butt of his humour. Even after his death we came to suspect that his humour did not desert him. Once my elders were engaged in an attempt to start a message service to the other world with a planchette. At one of the sittings the pencil scrawled out the name of Kailash. He was asked what kind of life one led where he was. 'I had to find out the hard way, by dying,' came the reply. 'And now you survivors want a short cut. Nothing doing!'

Kailash used to rattle off for my special delectation a doggerel ballad composed by himself. The hero was myself, depicted awaiting in glowing anticipation the arrival of a heroine. She was so entrancing a bride that even fate was bewitched in her presence: her image burned brightly in my mind as I listened. The list of the jewellery which bedecked her from head to foot, and the unheard-of splendour of the preparations for the wedding, might have turned older and wiser heads; but what moved this boy, and set images of joy dancing before his eyes, was the jingle of the rhymes and the swing of the rhythm.

These two literary thrills still linger in my memory – and there is another, the nursery classic: 'The rain falls pit-a-pat, the tide comes up the river.'

The next thing I recall is the beginning of my school-life. One day I saw my elder brother, and my sister's son Satya, also a little older than myself, starting for school leaving me behind accounted unfit. I was yet to ride in a carriage or even go out of the house. So when Satya came back, full of unduly glowing accounts of his adventures on the way, I felt I simply could not stay at home. Our tutor tried to dispel my illusion with sound advice and a resounding slap: 'You're crying to go to school now, you'll have to cry a lot more later on to be let off.' I have no recollection of the name, face or character of this tutor, but the impression of his weighty advice and weightier hand has not yet faded. Never in my life have I heard a truer prophecy.

My crying drove me prematurely into the Oriental Seminary. What I learnt there I have no idea, but one of its methods of punishment I still bear in mind. A boy who was unable to repeat his lessons was made to stand on a bench with arms extended, and on his upturned palms were piled a number of slates. Let psychologists debate how far this method is likely to induce a better grasp of things.

I thus began my studies at an extremely tender age. My initiation into literature came around the same time, from the books that were in vogue in the servants' quarters. Chief among these were a Bengali translation of Chanakya's aphorisms, and the *Ramayana* of Krittivas. One particular day when I was reading this *Ramayana* comes back clearly.

The sky was cloudy. I was playing about in the long verandah overlooking the road. All of a sudden Satya, for some reason I do not remember, decided to frighten me by shouting, 'Policeman! Policeman!' My concept of the duties of a policeman was extremely vague. But of one thing I was certain: a person charged with a crime, once placed in a policeman's hands would, as sure as a wretch caught by a crocodile, go under and be seen no more. Not knowing how an innocent boy could escape such an unrelenting punishment, I bolted towards the inner apartments, shudders running down my back in blind fear of pursuing policemen. I broke the news of my impending doom to my mother, but it did not seem to disturb her much. Even so, I was not taking any chances; I sat down on the sill of my mother's door to read the dog-eared *Ramayana* with a marbled paper cover, which belonged to her old aunt. In front of me stretched the verandah running round the four sides of the inner courtyard, faintly aglow in the afternoon light of a cloudy sky. Coming upon me weeping over a sorrowful scene, my great-aunt took the book away from me.

## 3. *Within and without*

Luxury was a thing almost unknown in my early childhood. The standard of living was then much plainer than it is now, as a whole. But it meant at least that the children of our household were entirely free from the fuss of being too much looked after. The fact is that for guardians the looking after of children may be an occasional treat; but for children being looked after is always an unmitigated nuisance.

We lived under the rule of the servants. To save themselves trouble they virtually suppressed our right of free movement. This was hard to bear – but the neglect was also a kind of independence. It left our minds free, unpampered and unburdened by all the usual bother over food and dress.

What we ate had nothing to do with delicacies. Our clothing, were I to itemise it, would invite a modern boy's scorn. On no pretext might we wear socks or shoes until we had passed our tenth year. In the cold weather a second cotton shirt over our first one was deemed sufficient. It never entered our heads to consider ourselves ill clad. Only when old Niyamat, the tailor, forgot to put a pocket into a shirt would we complain – for the boy has yet to be born who is so poor that he cannot stuff his pockets; by a merciful dispensation of providence, there is not much difference in wealth between boys whose parents are rich and poor. We used to own a pair of slippers each, but not always where we put our feet. The slippers were generally several moves ahead of us, propelled there by the following feet, their *raison d'être* thrown into doubt with every step we took.

Our elders in every way kept a great distance from us, in their dress and eating, coming and going, work, conversation and amusement. We caught glimpses of all these activities, but they were beyond our reach. Elders have become cheap to modern children, too readily accessible; and so have all objects of desire. Nothing ever came so easily to us. Many trivial things were rarities, and we lived mostly in the hope of attaining, when we were old enough, the things that the distant future held in trust for us. The result was that what little we did get we enjoyed to the utmost; from skin to core nothing was thrown away. The modern child of a well-to-do family nibbles at only half the things he gets; the greater part of his world is wasted on him.

Our days were spent in the servants' quarters in the south-east corner of the outer apartments. One of our servants was Shyam, a dark chubby boy with curly locks, hailing from the district of Khulna. He would place me in a selected spot, trace a chalk line around me, and warn me with solemn face and uplifted finger of the perils of transgressing this circle. Whether the danger was physical or mental I never fully understood, but fear certainly possessed me. I had read in the *Ramayana* of the tribulations of Sita after she left the ring drawn by Lakshman, so I never for a minute doubted my ring's potency.

Just below the window of this room was a tank with a bathing ghat; on its west bank, along the garden wall, stood an immense banyan tree; and to the south was a fringe of coconut palms. Like a prisoner in a cell, I would spend the whole day peering through the closed Venetian shutters, gazing out at this scene as on a picture in a book. From early morning our neighbours would drop in one by one to take their baths. I knew the time of each one's arrival. I was familiar with the oddities of each one's toilet. One would stop his ears with his fingers while taking his regulation number of dips, and then depart. Another would not risk complete immersion but be content to squeeze a wet towel repeatedly over his head. A third would carefully flick the surface impurities away from him with rapid strokes of his arms, and then suddenly plunge in. Another would jump in from the top steps without any preliminaries at all. Yet another would lower himself slowly in, step by step, while muttering his morning prayers. Then there was one who was always in a hurry, hastening home as soon as his dip was over, and a second who was in no sort of hurry at all, following a leisurely bath with a good rub-down, changing from wet bathing clothes into clean dry ones with a careful adjustment of the folds of his waist-cloth, then ending with a turn or two in the outer garden and the gathering of flowers, after which he would finally saunter homewards, radiating cool comfort as he went. All this would go on till past noon. Then the bathing-place would become deserted and silent. Only the ducks would remain, paddling about and diving after water snails or frantically preening their feathers, for the rest of the day.

When solitude thus reigned over the water, my whole attention would focus on the shadows beneath the banyan tree. Some of its aerial roots, creeping down its trunk, had formed a dark complication of coils at its base. It was as if by some sorcery this obscure corner of the world had escaped the regime of natural laws, as if some improbable dreamworld, unobserved by the Creator, had lingered on into the light of modern times. Whom I saw there, and what those beings did, I am unable to express in intelligible language. It was of this banyan tree that I later wrote:

Day and night you stand like an ascetic with matted hair.
Do you ever think of the boy whose fancy played with your shadows?

That majestic banyan tree is no more, alas, and neither is the tank that served as her mirror. Many of those who once bathed in it have departed too, merging with the shade of the great tree. And the boy, grown older, has put down roots far and wide and now contemplates the pattern of shadow and sunlight, sorrow and cheer, cast by this tangled skein.

To leave the house was forbidden to us, in fact we did not even have the run of the interior. We had to get our glimpses of Nature from behind barriers. Beyond my reach stretched this limitless thing called the Outside, flashes, sounds and scents of which used momentarily to come and touch me through interstices. It seemed to want to beckon me through the shutters with a variety of gestures. But it was free and I was bound – there was no way of our meeting. So its attraction was all the stronger. Today the chalk line has been wiped away but the confining circle is still there. The horizon is just as far away; what lies beyond it is still out of reach, and I am reminded of the poem I wrote when I was older:

> The tame bird was in a cage, the free bird was in the forest,
> They met when the time came, it was a decree of fate.
> The free bird cries, 'O my love, let us fly to the wood.'
> The cage bird whispers, 'Come hither, let us both live in the cage.'
> Says the free bird, 'Among bars, where is there room to spread one's wings?'
> 'Alas,' cries the cage bird, 'I should not know where to sit perched in the sky.'

The parapets of our terraced roofs were higher than my head. When I had grown taller and when the tyranny of the servants had relaxed, when, with the coming of a newly married bride into the house, I had achieved some recognition as a companion of her leisure, I would sometimes climb to the terrace in the middle of the day. By that time everybody in the house would have finished their meal and there would be an interlude in the business of the household; over the inner apartments would settle the quiet of a siesta, with wet bathing clothes hanging over the parapets to dry, the crows picking at the leavings thrown on a refuse heap in the corner of the yard; and in the solitude, the cage bird and the free bird would commune with each other, beak to beak.

I loved to stand and look. My gaze fell first on the row of coconut trees at the far edge of our inner garden. Through these I could see the Singhi's Garden with its cluster of huts and its tank, and at the edge of the tank the dairy of our milkwoman, Tara; and beyond that, mixed up with the tree-tops, the various shapes and different levels of the terraced roofs of Calcutta flashing under the whiteness of the midday sun, stretching away and merging with the greyish blue of the eastern horizon. And some of these far distant dwellings, from which jutted out a covered stairway leading to the roof, seemed like upraised fingers signalling to me, with a wink, that there were mysteries below. The beggar at the palace door imagines impossible treasures in its strong-rooms. I can hardly describe the spirit of fun and freedom which these unknown dwellings seemed to me to suggest. In the farthest recesses of a sky full of burning sunshine I would just be able to detect the thin shrill cry of a kite; and from the lane adjoining the Singhi's Garden, past the houses dormant in noonday slumber, would float the sing-song of the bangle-seller – *chai churi chai* – at such times my whole being would float away too.

My father was constantly on the move, hardly ever at home. His rooms on the third storey remained shut up. I would pass my hands through the Venetian shutters, open the latch of the door and spend the afternoon lying motionless on his sofa at the south end. In the first place, a closed room is always fascinating; then there was the lure of stolen entry, with its savour of mystery; finally, there was the deserted terrace outside with the sun's rays beating upon it, which would set me dreaming.

And there was yet another attraction. The water-works had just started up in Calcutta, and in the first flush of triumphant entry it did not stint its supply even to the Indian quarters. In that golden age, piped water used to flow even to my father's third-storey rooms. Turning on his shower-tap I would take an untimely bath to my heart's content – not so much for the feel of the water, as to indulge my desire to do just as I fancied. The simultaneous joy of liberty and fear of being caught made that shower of municipal water seem like arrows of delight.

Perhaps because the possibility of contact with the outside was so remote, the excitement of it came to me much more readily. When things surround us at every hand, the mind becomes lazy, commissions others, and forgets that the joy of a feast depends more on nourishment by imagination than on external things. This is the chief lesson which infancy has to teach a human being. Then his possessions are few and trivial, yet he needs no more to be happy. For the unfortunate youngster who has an unlimited number of playthings, the world of play is spoilt.

To call our inner garden a garden is to go too far. It consisted of a citron tree, a couple of plum trees of different varieties, and a row of coconut trees. In the centre was a paved circle, cracked and invaded by grasses and weeds waving their victorious standards. Only those flowering plants which refused to die of gardener's neglect continued to perform their duties. In the northern corner was a rice-husking shed, where when need arose, the occupants of the inner apartments would congregate. This last vestige of rural life in Calcutta has since owned defeat and slunk silently away.

Nonetheless I have an idea that the Garden of Eden was no grander then this garden of ours, for Adam and his paradise were alike naked: they needed no embellishment with material things. Only since he tasted the fruit of the tree of knowledge, and until such time as he can fully digest it, has man's need for external trappings come to dominate him. Our inner garden was my paradise; it was enough for me. I clearly remember how in the early autumn dawn I would run there as soon as I was awake. A whiff of dewy grass and foliage would rush to meet me, and the morning, with cool fresh light, would peep at me over the top of the eastern garden wall from below the trembling tassels of the coconut palms.

Another piece of vacant land to the north of the house to this day we call the *golabari*. The name shows that in some remote past this must have been the barn where the year's store of grain was kept. In those days town and country visibly resembled each other, like brother and sister in childhood. Now the family likeness can hardly be traced. This *golabari* would be my holiday haunt when I got the chance. I did not really go there to play — it was the place itself that drew me. Why, is difficult to tell. Perhaps its being a deserted bit of waste land lying in an out-of-the-way corner gave it charm. Entirely outside the living quarters, it bore no stamp of functionality; what's more, it was as unadorned as it was useless, for no one had ever planted anything there. It was a desert spot. No doubt that is why it offered free rein to a boy's imagination. Whenever I saw a loophole in my warders' vigilance and could contrive to reach the *golabari*, I felt I had a real holiday.

Yet another region existed in our house and this I have still not succeeded in finding. A little girl playmate of the same age as I called it the 'King's palace.' 'I have just been there,' she would sometimes tell me. But somehow the right moment for her to take me never turned up. It was said to be a wonderful place, with playthings as fabulous as the games that were played there. It seemed to me it had to be somewhere very near – perhaps in the first or second storey – but I never seemed able to reach it. How often did I say to my friend, 'Just tell me, is it really inside the house or outside?' And she would always reply, 'No, no, it's right here in this house.' I would sit and wonder: 'Where? Where? Don't I know all the rooms in the house?' I never cared to enquire who the King was; his palace remains undiscovered to this day; only this much is clear – it lay within our house.

Looking back at my childhood I feel the thought that recurred most often was that I was surrounded by mystery. Something undreamt of was lurking everywhere, and every day the uppermost question was: when, oh! when, would we come across it? It was as if Nature held something cupped in her hands and was asking us with a smile: 'What d'you think I have?' We had no idea there might be any limit to the answer.

I vividly remember a custard apple seed which I planted and kept in a corner of the south verandah, and used to water every day. The idea that the seed might actually grow into a tree kept me in a state of fluttering anticipation. Custard apple seeds today still have the habit of sprouting, but no longer to the accompaniment of that feeling of wonder. The fault lies not in the custard apple but in my mind.

Once we stole some rocks from an elder cousin's rockery and started a little rockery of our own. The plants we sowed in its interstices we cared for so excessively that only the stoicism of vegetables can account for their survival. Words cannot express the excitement this miniature mountaintop held for us. We were never in any doubt that our creation would be

a wonderful thing to our elders too. The day that we
tried to put this to proof, however, our hillock, with all
its rocks and all its vegetation vanished from the corner
of our room. The knowledge that the schoolroom
floor was not a proper base for mountain-building
was imparted so rudely, and with such abruptness,
that it gave us quite a shock. A weight equivalent
to that of the stone lifted from the floor settled on
our minds as we realised the gulf between our fancies
and the will of our elders.

How intensely did life throb for us! Earth, water,
foliage and sky all spoke to us and would not be
disregarded. How often were we struck by poignant
regret that we could see only the upper storey of the
earth and knew nothing of its inner storey! All our
plans were aimed at prying beneath its dust-coloured
cover. If we could drive in bamboo after bamboo, one
over the other, we might somehow get in touch with
its inmost depths.

During the *Magh* festival a series of wooden pillars
used to be planted round the outer courtyard to support chandeliers. The digging of holes for these would
begin on the first of *Magh*. Preparations for a festival
interest children everywhere, but this digging had a
special attraction for me. Though I had watched it
done year after year – and seen a hole grow deeper
and deeper till the digger had completely disappeared
inside – nothing extraordinary, nothing worthy of the
quest of a prince or knight, had ever appeared; yet
every time I had the feeling that a lid was about to
be lifted off a treasure-chest. A little bit more digging
would surely do it. Year after year that little bit more
never got done. The mysterious veil was tweaked but
not drawn. Why did the elders, who could do whatever
they pleased, rest content with such shallow delving? If
we younger generation had been in charge, the inmost

enigma of the earth would not have been allowed to remain covered for very long.

The thought that behind every portion of the blue vault of the sky there reposed the secrets of the heavens also spurred our imaginations. When our pundit, wishing to illustrate some lesson in our Bengali science primer, told us that the sky was not a finite blue sphere, we were thunderstruck! 'Put ladder upon ladder,' he said, 'and go on mounting, but you will never bump your head.' He must be mean with his ladders, I thought, and aloud said in a tone of rising indignation, 'And what if we put more ladders, and more and more?' When I grasped that to multiply ladders was fruitless, I was dumbfounded. Surely, I concluded after much pondering, such an astounding fact must be part of the secret knowledge of schoolmasters, known to them and to no one else.

## 4. *Servocracy*

In the history of India the regime of the Slave Dynasty was not a happy one. In my own history I can find nothing glorious or cheerful to report about the reign of the servants. There were frequent changes of ruler, but never a variation in the code of restraints and punishments that afflicted us. At the time we had no opportunity to philosophise on the subject; we bore as best we could the blows that befell our backs, and accepted as one of the laws of the universe that it is the Big who hurt and the Small who get hurt. The opposite idea – that the Big suffer and the Small cause suffering – has taken me a long time to learn.

No hunter, whatever his intentions, looks at things from a bird's point of view. That is why the alert bird, which loudly warns the group before they are shot at, is shouted at severely. When we were beaten we howled, of which our chastisers strongly disapproved; in their eyes it was sedition against the servocracy. How well I recall their attempts to suppress our wailing by cramming our heads into nearby water-pitchers. Our outcry must have been most distasteful and inconvenient – that, no one can possibly deny.

Nowadays I sometimes wonder why such cruel treatment was meted out to us by the servants. I cannot admit that there was anything in our overall behaviour or demeanour to have put us beyond the pale of human kindness. The real reason must have been that the whole burden of us was thrown upon the servants, and that is something difficult to bear even by those who are nearest and dearest. If children are only allowed to be children, to run about and play and satisfy their curiosity, the burden becomes quite light. Insoluble problems are created only if one tries to confine children inside, keep them still or hamper their play. Then childishness becomes onerous and falls heavily on the guardian – like the horse, in the fable carried by bearers instead of being allowed to trot on its own legs: though money could procure bearers even for a horse, it could not prevent them from venting their anger on the unlucky beast at every step.

Of most of these tyrants of our childhood I remember only the cuffings and boxings, nothing more. Just one personality stands out. His name was Ishwar. Once he had been a village schoolmaster. He was a prim and prudent personage, sedately conscious of religious orthodoxy. The earth seemed too earthy for him, with too little water to keep it properly clean; he was engaged in constant warfare with its chronically soiled state. He would shoot his water-pot into the tank with a lightning movement so as to take his supply from an uncontaminated depth. It was he who, when bathing in the tank, continually thrust away the surface impurities until he took a sudden plunge, trying to catch the water unawares, as it were. When he walked, his right arm stood out at an angle from his body, as if, we liked to think, he could not trust the hygiene of even his own garments. Day and night he carried himself like someone on perpetual guard against the infinite kinds of pollution that might slip through his defences and infect his contact with earth, water and air. That his body had contact with the world at all seemed insufferable to him.

His gravity of manner was unfathomable. With head slightly cocked he minced his carefully selected words in a sonorous voice. His literary diction was food for merriment to our elders behind his back, some of his high-flown phrases acquiring currency in our family repertoire of witticisms. But I doubt whether the expressions he used would sound as odd today; the literary and spoken languages, which used to be as sky from earth asunder, are now nearer to each other.

This erstwhile schoolmaster had discovered a way of keeping us quiet in the evenings. He would gather us around the cracked castor-oil lamp and read aloud stories from the *Ramayana* and *Mahabharata*. Some of the other servants would join the audience. The lamp would throw huge shadows of us right up to the beams of the roof, and also pick out the little house lizards catching insects on the walls and the bats doing a dervish dance round and round the verandahs outside, while we sat listening in silent, open-mouthed wonder.

I still remember the evening we came to the story of Kusha and Laba, in which those heroic lads looked set to pulverise the renown of their father and uncles; the silence of that dimly lit room was tense with anticipation. But already the hour was late and

our prescribed period of wakefulness was almost up.
Yet the story still had far to go.

At this critical juncture my father's old follower
came to the rescue, and finished the episode for us at
express speed to the quickstep of Dashuraya's verses.
The soft slow chant of Krittivas' fourteen-syllabled
*payar* measure was cast clean aside, and we were bowled
over by the jingle of the alliteration and the jangle of
the rhyme.

On some occasions these ancient texts gave rise
to discussion and interpretation, which at length concluded with a profound pronouncement from Ishwar.
Though he was only one of the children's servants,
and therefore below many in domestic rank, like old
grandfather Bhishma in the *Mahabharata* his seniority
unfailingly asserted itself from his humble seat below
his juniors.

This high and principled guardian of ours had
one weakness to which I feel bound to allude for the
sake of historical accuracy. He used to take opium. It
created a craving for rich food. So when he brought us
our morning milk he was much attracted to it and,
unlike us, not in the least repelled. If we gave the
slightest hint of our natural repugnance, no sense
of responsibility for our health could prompt Ishwar
to press it on us a second time.

He also had severe doubts about our capacity
for solid nourishment. We would sit down to our
evening meal and a quantity of *luchis* heaped on a
thick round wooden tray would be placed before us.
He would gingerly drop a few on each platter – from
a sufficient height to safeguard himself from contamination – like boons wrested from the gods in reward for
human penance; there was never a hint of favouritism
or over-indulgence in hospitality. Next would come
an inquiry as to whether we should like any more.

I knew the reply which would most gratify him, and could not bring myself to deprive him by asking for another helping.

Then again Ishwar was entrusted with a daily allowance for procuring our afternoon light refreshment. Every morning he would ask us what item we should like to have. We knew that to mention the cheapest would be accounted best, so we sometimes requested a light snack of puffed rice, and at other times an indigestible one of boiled *gram* or roasted ground-nuts. It is obvious that Ishwar was not as painstakingly punctilious with our diet as with our spiritual sustenance.

## 5. *The Normal School*

While at the Oriental Seminary I had discovered a way out of the humiliation of being a pupil. I had started a class of my own in a corner of our verandah. The wooden bars of the railing were my pupils, and I would act the schoolmaster, cane in hand, seated on a chair in front of them. I had decided which were the good boys and which the bad – I could even distinguish clearly the quiet from the naughty, the clever from the stupid. The bad rails had suffered so much from my constant caning that they would have longed to give up the ghost had they been alive. And the more scarred they got with my strokes the worse they angered me, till I knew not how to punish them enough. None of that poor dumb class remains to bear witness how tremendously I tyrannised over them. My wooden pupils have been replaced by cast-iron railings, and the new generation has not taken up their education in the old manner; if they were to try, they could never achieve the same results.

I have since realised how much easier it is to acquire the style than the substance of teaching. Without effort I had assimilated all the impatience, short temper, partiality and injustice displayed by my teachers, to the exclusion of the rest of their teaching. My only consolation is that I had not the power of venting these barbarities on any sentient creature. Nevertheless, the difference between my wooden pupils and those of the Seminary does not stop my psychology from being identical with that of its schoolmasters.

I cannot have spent long at the Oriental Seminary, for I was still at a tender age when I joined the Normal School. The only one of its features which I remember is that before classes began all the boys had to sit in a row in the gallery and go through some kind of singing or chanting of verses – evidently an attempt to introduce an element of cheerfulness into the daily routine.

Unfortunately, the words were English and the tune quite as foreign, so that we did not have the faintest notion what sort of incantation we practised; neither did the meaningless monotony tend to make us cheerful. But this failed to disturb the serene self-satisfaction of the school authorities at having provided such a treat; they deemed it superfluous to ask the practical effect of their bounty; probably they would have called not being dutifully happy a crime. They were content to take the song as they found it, words and all, from the self-same English book that had furnished the theory.

The language into which this English resolved itself in our mouths is without doubt educative – to philologists at least. I can recall only one line: '*Kallokee pullokee singill mellaling mellaling mellaling.*'

After much thought I have been able to guess at

the original of a part of it. *Kallokee* still baffles me but the rest I think was: '. . . full of glee, singing merrily, merrily, merrily'.

As my memories of the Normal School emerge from haziness and become clearer they are not the least sweet in any particular. Had I been able to associate with the other boys, the business of learning might not have seemed so intolerable. But that turned out to be impossible – so nasty were most of their manners and habits. So, in the intervals between classes, I would go up to the second storey and while away the time sitting near a window overlooking the street. I would count: one year – two years – three years and wonder how many such I would have to get through.

I remember only one of the teachers, whose language was so foul that I steadily refused to answer any one of his questions, out of sheer contempt for him. Thus I sat silent throughout the year at the bottom of his class, and while the rest of the class was busy I would be left alone to attempt the solution of many an intricate problem.

One of these, I remember, on which I cogitated profoundly, was how to defeat an enemy without having arms. My preoccupation with this question, amidst the hum of the boys reciting their lessons, comes back to me even now. If I could properly train up a number of dogs, tigers and other ferocious beasts, and put a few lines of these on the field of battle, I reckoned they would make an arresting sight with which to begin the fight. After that it would be up to the prowess of my army to achieve success. As I vividly visualised this wonderfully simple strategy, the victory of my side became assured beyond doubt.

As long as work had not yet come into my life I found it easy to devise short cuts to achievement; since I have been working I find that which is hard is hard indeed, and what is difficult remains difficult. This is less comforting, of course, but nowhere near so bad as the discomfort of trying to take short cuts.

When at last a year had passed in that class, we were examined in Bengali by Pandit Madhushudan Vachaspati. I got the largest number of marks of all the boys. The teacher complained to the school authorities that there had been favouritism. So I was examined a second time, with the superintendent of the school seated beside the examiner. This time, also, I got top place.

# 6. *Versification*

I could not have been more than eight years old at the time. Jyoti, son of a niece of my father's, was considerably older. He had just gained access to English literature, and would recite Hamlet's soliloquy with great gusto. Why the idea entered his head that a mere child as I was should write poetry, I cannot tell but one afternoon he sent for me and asked me to try and make up a verse, after which he explained to me the construction of the *payar* metre of fourteen syllables.

Poems were things that up to then I had seen only in books – without mistakes inked out or visible sign of doubt or effort or human weakness. That any attempt of mine might produce a poem like these I could not even dare to imagine.

One day a thief had been caught in our house. Overpowered by curiosity yet trembling with fear, I had ventured to the spot to take a peep. He was just an ordinary man! When he was roughly handled by our door-keeper I felt real pity. My experience was similar with poetry.

After stringing together a few words at my own sweet will, I found them turned into *payar* verse and felt I had no illusions left about the glories of poetising. Now, when I see poor Poetry being mishandled, I feel pity. This has often moved me to restrain impatient hands, itching to assault her. Thieves have scarcely suffered as much as she, and from so many.

The first feeling of awe once overcome, there was no holding me back. I managed to get hold of a blue-paper manuscript book, courtesy of one of the officers of our estate. In my own hand I ruled it with pencil lines, at not very regular intervals, and began to write verses in a large scrawl.

Like a young deer which butts here, there and everywhere with its newly sprouted antlers, I and my budding poetry made a nuisance of themselves. More so my elder brother, whose pride in my performance impelled him to hunt about the house for an audience.

I recollect how, one day, as the pair of us were coming out of the estate offices on the ground floor after a conquering expedition against the officers, we came across the editor of the *National Paper*, Naba Gopal Mitra, who had just stepped into the house. My brother tackled him without further ado: 'Naba Gopal Babu! Rabi has written a poem. You must listen.' The reading followed forthwith.

My works were not yet voluminous. The poet could carry all his effusions about in his pockets. I was writer, printer and publisher all in one; my brother, as advertiser, was my only colleague. I had composed some verses on 'The Lotus' which I recited to Naba Gopal Babu then and there, at the foot of the stairs, in a voice pitched as high as my enthusiasm. 'Well done!' he said with a smile. 'But what is a *dwirepha*?'

The word had the same number of syllables as *moumachhi*, the ordinary word for 'bee'. How I had

got hold of *dwirepha* I do not remember. But it was the
one word in the whole poem on which I had pinned
my hopes. There was no doubt it had impressed our
officers. But curiously enough Naba Gopal Babu did
not succumb to it – on the contrary, he smiled! He
could not be an understanding man, I was sure. I
never read poetry to him again. I have added many
years to my age since then, but I have not been able
to improve upon my test of who is and who is not a
connoisseur. However much Naba Gopal Babu might
smile, the word *dwirepha*, like a bee drunk with honey,
remained stuck in position.

## 7. *Diverse lessons*

One of the teachers of the Normal School gave us
private lessons at home too. His body was lean and
dry, his voice sharp. He looked like a cane incarnate.
His hours were from six to half-past nine in the
morning. Our reading with him ranged from popular
literary and science readers in Bengali to the epic of
*Meghnadbadh*.

My third brother was very keen on imparting a
variety of knowledge to us, so at home we had to go
through much more than was required by the school
course. We had to get up before dawn and, clad in
loin-cloths, begin with a bout or two with a blind
wrestler. Then without a pause we donned shirts
over our dusty bodies, and started on our courses
of literature, mathematics, geography and history. On
our return from school our drawing and gymnastic
masters would be ready for us. In the evening Aghore
Babu came to give English lessons. It was nine o'clock
before we were free.

On Sunday morning we had singing lessons with

Vishnu. Then, almost every Sunday, came Sitanath Dutta to give us demonstrations in physical science. These last were of great interest to me. I remember distinctly the feeling of wonder which filled me when he put on the fire a glass vessel with some water and sawdust in it, and showed us how the lightened hot water rose up and the cold water went down, and how finally the water began to boil. I also felt a great elation the day I learnt that water is a separable part of milk, and that milk thickens when boiled because the water frees itself from the connexion as vapour. Sunday did not feel as if it were Sunday unless Sitanath Babu turned up.

There was also an hour when we would be told about human bones by a pupil of the Campbell Medical School, for which purpose a skeleton, with the bones fastened together by wires, was hung up in our schoolroom. And finally, time was also found for Pandit Heramba Tatwaratna to come and get us to learn rules of Sanskrit grammar by rote. I am not sure which of these, the names of the bones or the *sutras* of the grammarian, were the more jaw-breaking. The latter probably took the palm.

We began to learn English after we had made considerable progress in our education through Bengali. Aghore Babu, our English tutor, was attending the Medical College, so he taught us in the evening.

The discovery of fire was one of man's greatest discoveries so we are told. I do not dispute it. But I cannot help feeling how fortunate the little birds are that their parents cannot light lamps in the evening. They have their language lessons early in the morning – how gleefully everyone must have noticed. Of course we must not forget that it is not English they are learning!

This medical-student tutor of ours kept such good

health that even the fervent and united wishes of his three pupils were not enough to cause his absence even for a day. Only once was he laid up, when there was a fight between the Indian and Eurasian students of the Medical College and a chair was thrown at his head. This regrettable occurrence was undoubtedly a blow for our teacher, but it struck us somewhat differently; in fact we thought his recovery needlessly swift.

It is evening. The rain is pouring down in lance-like showers. Our lane is under knee-deep water. The tank has overflowed into the garden, and the shaggy tops of the bel trees are standing guard over the waters. Our whole being is radiating rapture like the fragrant stamens of the *kadamba* flower. Our tutor's arrival is already overdue by several minutes. But nothing is yet certain. We sit on the verandah overlooking the lane, waiting and watching with a pathetic gaze. All of a sudden our hearts seem to tumble to the ground with a great thump. The familiar black umbrella has turned the corner, undefeated even by such weather! Could it not be somebody else's? No, it could not! In the wide world there might be found another person, his equal in pertinacity, but never in this particular little lane.

Looking back on his period with us as a whole, I cannot say that Aghore Babu was a hard man. He did not rule us with a rod. Even his rebukes did not amount to scoldings. But whatever his personal merits, his time was *evening*, and his subject *English*! Even an angel, I am certain, would have seemed like a messenger of Yama, god of Death, to any Bengali boy if he had come to him at the end of a miserable day at school and lighted a dismally dim lamp to teach him English.

How plainly do I recall the day our tutor tried to impress on us the appeal of the English language. With great unction he recited to us some lines – prose or poetry we could not tell – from an English book. They had a most unlooked-for effect. We laughed so much that he had to dismiss us for the evening. He must have realised that he held no easy brief: that to get us to pronounce in his favour would entail a contest ranging over years.

Aghore Babu would sometimes try to bring the zephyr of outside knowledge to play on our arid schoolroom routine. One day he brought a paper parcel out of his pocket and said: 'Today I'll show you a wonderful piece of work by the Creator.' Then he untied the wrapping, produced a portion of the windpipe of a human being and proceeded to expound the marvels of its mechanism.

I still remember my shock. I had always thought the whole man spoke – had never even imagined that the act of speech could be viewed in this detached way. However wonderful the mechanism of a part may be, it is certainly less so than the whole person. Not that I put it to myself in so many words, but that was the cause of my dismay. Perhaps because the tutor had lost sight of this truth I could not respond to the enthusiasm with which he discoursed that day.

Another day he took us to the dissecting-room of the Medical College. The body of an old woman was stretched on the table. This did not disturb me over-much. But an amputated leg lying on the floor upset me altogether. To view man in this fragmentary way seemed to me so horrid, so absurd, that I could not rid myself of the impression of that dark, unmeaning leg for many days.

After getting through Peary Sarkar's first and second English readers we embarked on McCulloch's *Course of Reading*. Our bodies were weary at the end of the day, our minds yearned for the inner apartments, the book was black and thick with difficult words, and the subject-matter could hardly have been less inviting, for it contained none of Saraswati, goddess of learning's maternal tenderness. Children's books then were not full of pictures as they are now. Moreover, at the gateway to every lesson an array of words stood sentinel, with separated syllables and forbidding accent marks like fixed bayonets barring the way to the infant mind. I repeatedly attacked their serried ranks in vain.

Our tutor would try to shame us by recounting the exploits of some other brilliant pupil of his. We felt duly contrite and also not well disposed towards that other pupil, but this feeling did not help to dispel the darkness which clung to that black volume.

Providence, out of pity for mankind, has instilled a soporific charm into all tedious things. No sooner did our English lessons begin than our heads began to nod. Sprinkling water into our eyes or taking a run round the verandahs were palliatives with no lasting effect. If by any chance my eldest brother happened to pass that way and caught a glimpse of our sleep-tormented condition, we would be let off for the rest of the evening. It did not take another moment for our drowsiness to be completely cured.

## 8. *My first outing*

Once, when dengue fever was raging in Calcutta, a part of our extensive family had to take shelter in Chhatu Babu's riverside villa. We were among them.

This was my first outing. The bank of the Ganges welcomed me into its lap like a friend from a former birth. There, in front of the servants' quarters, was a grove of guava trees; my days would pass beneath their shade, sitting on the verandah gazing at the flowing current through the gaps between the trunks. Every morning, as I awoke, I felt the day somehow coming to me like a gilt-edged letter that would impart wonderful news upon my opening the envelope. So as not to miss any portion of it I would splash some water on my face and hurry to my chair outside. Every day there was the ebb and flow of the tide on the Ganges, the diverse movements of so many different boats, the shifting of the shadows of the trees from west to east, and, over the shady fringe of the woods on the opposite bank, the gush of golden life-blood through the pierced breast of the evening sky. Some days would be cloudy from early morning, the opposite woods black, black shadows moving over the river. Then with a rush would come vociferous rain, blotting out the horizon; the dim line of the other bank would take its leave in tears; the river would swell with suppressed heavings; and the moist wind would frolic among the foliage of the trees.

I felt that walls, beams, joists and rafters, had given me new birth into the world. As I made fresh acquaintance with things, their dingy covering, fashioned from habit, seemed to drop away. I am sure that the sugar-cane molasses, which I used to have with cold *luchis* for breakfast tasted no different from the ambrosia quaffed by Indra, lord of the gods, in his heaven; for immortality is in the taster not in the nectar and will be missed by those who seek it elsewhere.

Behind the house was a walled-in enclosure with a tank and a flight of steps leading into the water from a bathing ghat. On one side of this ghat was an immense *jambolan* tree, and all round were various fruit trees, growing in thick clusters, in the shade of which the tank nestled in privacy. The veiled beauty of this retiring little inner garden had a wonderful charm for me, so different from the broad expanse of riverbank in front. It was like the bride of the house, in the seclusion of her midday siesta, resting on a many-coloured quilt of her own embroidering, murmuring the secrets of her heart. I spent many midday hours under that *jambolan* tree alone dreaming of the fearsome kingdom of the *yakshas* within the depths of the tank.

I had a great curiosity to see a village in Bengal. Its dwellings and shrines, lanes and bathing ghats, games and gatherings, fields and markets, its whole world as I saw it in imagination, strongly attracted me. Just such a village was now on the other side of our garden wall, but it was off-bounds to us. We had come out, but not into freedom. Formerly caged, we were now on a perch – but the chain was still there.

One morning two of our elders went out for a stroll into the village. I could not restrain my urge any longer, and, slipping out unperceived, followed them for some distance. As I went along the deeply shaded lane, with its close thorny *sheora* hedges, by the side of a tank covered with green water weeds, I absorbed picture after rapturous picture. I still remember a bare-bodied fellow occupied in a belated bath at the edge of the tank, cleaning his teeth with the chewed end of a twig. Suddenly my elders became aware of me behind them. 'Get back, go back at once!' they scolded. They were scandalised. My feet were bare, I had no scarf or upper garment over my shirt, I was not fit to come out – as if this was my fault! I had never been burdened with socks or superfluous apparel, so I not only went back disappointed that morning, but had no chance any other day of repairing the omission and being allowed out.

I was cut off from behind, but out front the Ganges freed me from all bonds. My mind could hop aboard any boat I saw sailing by and journey away, without charge, to lands not named in any geography.

This was forty years ago. I have not set foot in

that *champak*-shaded villa garden since. The same old house and the same old trees must still be there, but I know the garden cannot be the same – for where am I now to recapture the freshness of wonder that made it what it was?

We returned to our Jorasanko house in town. And my days became like so many mouthfuls offered up and gulped down into the maw of the Normal School.

## 9. *Practising poetry*

That blue manuscript book was soon filled, like the hive of some insect, with a network of variously slanting lines and the thick and thin strokes of letters. The eager pressure of the boy writer soon crumpled its leaves; and then the edges got frayed, and twisted up like claws as if to hold fast the writing within, till at last, by what river Baitarani I know not, its pages were swept away into merciful oblivion. At any rate they escaped the pangs of passage through the printing-press and need not fear birth into this vale of woe.

I cannot claim to have been a passive witness to the spread of my reputation as a poet. Though Satkari Datta was not a teacher of our class he was very fond of me. He had written a book on natural history – a fact that will not, I hope, provoke any unkind comment regarding his interest in me. One day he sent for me and asked: 'So you write poetry, do you?' I did not attempt to hide it. From that time on he would now and then ask me to complete a quatrain by adding a couplet of my own to one given by him.

Gobinda Babu was very dark, short and fat. He was the school superintendent. He sat in his black suit with his account books in an office room on the second storey. We were all afraid of him, for he was the rod-bearing judge. Once I escaped into his room from some bullies, five or six older boys. I had no one to bear witness on my side – except my tears. I won my case, and after that Gobinda Babu kept a soft corner for me in his heart.

One day he called me into his room during the recess. I went in fear and trembling, but no sooner had I stepped before him than he accosted me with the same question as Satkari Babu: 'So you write poetry?' I did not hesitate to admit it. He commissioned me to write a poem on some high moral precept which I do not remember. The level of affable condescension involved in such a request can be appreciated only by those who were Gobinda Babu's pupils. When I handed him the verses next day, he took me to the highest class and made me stand before the boys. 'Recite,' he commanded. And I recited loudly.

The only thing praiseworthy about this poem was that it soon got lost. Its moral effect on that class was far from inspiring – and the sentiment it aroused was far from amicable. Most of them were certain that the poem was not my own composition. One said he could produce the book from which it was copied, but was not pressed to do so; to have to prove something is such a nuisance to those who want to believe. Finally, the number of seekers after poetic fame began to increase alarmingly; and the methods they chose were not among those which are recognised paths to moral improvement.

Nowadays there is nothing strange in a youth writing verses. The glamour of poesy is gone. I remember how the few women who wrote poetry in those days were looked upon as miraculous creations of the Deity. Today if one is told that some young lady does not write poems one feels sceptical. Poetry sprouts long

before the highest Bengali class is reached; a modern
Gobinda Babu would take no notice at all of the poetic
exploit I have recounted.

## 10. *Srikantha Babu*

At this time I was granted a listener the like of whom I
shall never have again. He had so inordinate a capacity
for being pleased as to have utterly disqualified him
for the post of critic on any of our monthly reviews.
The old man was like a perfectly ripe Alfonso mango
– not a trace of acid or coarse fibre in his composition.
His tender clean-shaven face was rounded off by an
all-pervading baldness; there was not the vestige of a
tooth to worry the inside of his mouth; and his big
smiling eyes gleamed with constant delight. When he
spoke in his soft deep voice, his mouth and eyes and
hands all spoke likewise. He was of the old school of
Persian culture, and knew not a word of English. His
inseparable companions were a hubble-bubble at his
left, and a sitar on his lap; and from his throat flowed
unceasing song.

Srikantha Babu had no need to wait for a formal
introduction, for none could resist the natural claims
of his genial heart. Once he took us to be photo-
graphed with him in some big English photographic
studio. There he so captivated the proprietor with his
artless story, in a jumble of Hindustani and Bengali,
of how he was a poor man, but badly wanted this
particular photograph taken, that the man smilingly
allowed him a reduced rate. Nor did the sound of
bargaining in that unbending English establishment
sound at all incongruous, so naïve was Srikantha
Babu, so unconscious of any possibility of giving
offence. He would sometimes take me along to a

European missionary's house. There also, with his playing and singing, his caresses of the missionary's little girl and his unabashed admiration of the little booted feet of the missionary's wife, he would enliven the gathering as no one else could. Another behaving so absurdly would have been deemed a bore, but his transparent simplicity pleased all and drew them in to join his gaiety.

Srikantha Babu was impervious to rudeness or insolence. There was at the time a singer of some repute retained in our establishment. When he was the worse for drink he would rail at poor Srikantha Babu's singing in no very choice terms. The latter would bear this unflinchingly, making no attempt to retort. When at last the man's incorrigible rudeness brought about his dismissal Srikantha Babu anxiously interceded for him. 'He was not the cause, it was the drink,' he insisted.

He could not bear to see anyone in sorrow or even to hear of it. So when any of the boys wanted to torment him they had only to read out passages from Vidyasagar's *Banishment of Sita* – and Srikantha Babu would become greatly exercised, thrusting out his hands in protest and begging and praying them to stop.

This old man was a friend of both my father, my elder brothers and us younger ones alike. He adjusted his age to suit each and every one of us. Just as any piece of stone is good enough for a freshet to dance and gambol around, so the least little stimulus would be enough to make Srikantha Babu beside himself with joy. I remember I once composed a hymn that did not stint the usual allusions to the trials and tribulations of this world. Srikantha Babu was convinced that my revered father would be overjoyed to hear such a gem. With his familiar unbounded enthusiasm he volunteered to acquaint him with it. Luckily I was not present at the time, but I heard later that my father was hugely amused that the sorrows of the world should have moved his youngest son so early to the point of versification. I am sure Gobinda Babu, the superintendent, would have shown more respect for my effort on so serious a subject.

In singing I was Srikantha Babu's favourite pupil. He had taught me a song: 'No more of Braja for me,' and would drag me about to everyone's rooms and get me to sing it to them. I would sing and he would thrum an accompaniment on his sitar and when we came to the chorus he would join in and repeat it over and over again, smiling and nodding his head at each one in turn, as if nudging them on to a more enthusiastic appreciation.

He was a devotee of my father. A hymn had been set to one of my father's tunes, 'For He is the heart of our hearts'. When he sang this to my father Srikantha Babu got so excited that he jumped up from his seat and twanged his sitar violently as he sang, 'For He is the heart of our hearts,' and then waved his hand about my father's face as he changed the words to 'For *you* are the heart of our hearts.'

When the old man paid his last visit to my father, the latter, by then bed-ridden, was at a riverside villa in Chunchura. Srikantha Babu, stricken with his last illness, could not rise unaided and had to push open his eyelids to see. In this state, tended by his daughter, he journeyed to Chunchura from his place in Birbhum. With a great effort he managed to take the dust of my father's feet and then return to his lodgings in Chunchura where he breathed his last a few days later. I heard afterwards from his daughter that he went to his eternal youth with the song 'How Sweet is Thy mercy, Lord!' on his lips.

## 11. *Our Bengali course ends*

At school we were then in the class below the highest one. At home we had advanced in Bengali much further than the subjects taught in the class. We had been through Akshay Datta's book on popular physics, and had finished the blank-verse epic *Meghnadbadh*. We read our physics without reference to physical objects, and so our knowledge of the subject was correspondingly bookish. In fact the time spent on it had been thoroughly wasted, much more so to my mind than if it had been wasted in doing nothing. The *Meghnadbadh*, also, was not a thing of joy to us. The tastiest titbit may not be relished when thrown at one's head. To employ an epic to teach language is like using a sword to shave – disrespectful to the sword, distressing to the cheek. A poem should be taught from the emotional standpoint; inveigling it into service as a grammar-cum-dictionary is not well-calculated to propitiate Saraswati, the goddess of learning.

All of a sudden our Normal School career came to an end, and thereby hangs a tale. One of our school teachers wanted to borrow a copy of my grandfather's life by Mittra from our library. My nephew and classmate Satya managed to screw up courage enough to mention this to my father. He had come to the conclusion that everyday Bengali would hardly do for the approach. So he concocted and delivered himself of an archaic phrase with such meticulous precision that my father must have felt our study of the Bengali language had gone a bit too far and was in danger of overreaching itself. The next morning, when our table had as usual been placed in the south verandah, the blackboard hung up on a nail in the wall, and everything was in readiness for our lessons with Nil Kamal Babu, we three were sent for by my father in his upstairs room.

'You need not do any more Bengali lessons,' he said. Our minds danced for joy.

Nil Kamal Babu was waiting downstairs, our books were lying open on the table, and the idea of getting us once more to go through the *Meghnadbadh* doubtless still occupied his mind. On one's death-bed the various routines of daily life are said to seem unreal: so, at that moment, everything, from the pandit down to the nail holding up the blackboard, became as empty as a mirage. Our sole difficulty was how to give this news to Nil Kamal Babu with due decorum. We did it at last with considerable restraint, while the geometrical figures on the blackboard stared at us in wonder and the *Meghnadbadh* looked blankly on.

The parting words of our pundit were: 'At the call of duty I may sometimes have been harsh with you – do not keep that in remembrance. You will learn the value of what I have taught you later on.'

I have appreciated that value. It was because we were taught in our own language that our minds quickened. Learning should as far as possible follow the process of eating. When the taste begins from the first bite, the stomach is awakened to its function before it is loaded, so that its digestive juices get full play. Nothing like this happens when the Bengali boy is taught in English, however. The first bite bids fair to wrench loose both rows of teeth – like an earthquake in the mouth! And by the time he discovers that the morsel is not of the genus stone, but a digestible bonbon, half his allotted span of life is over. While one is choking and spluttering over the spelling and grammar, the inside remains starved; and when at length the taste comes through, the appetite has vanished. If the whole mind is not functioning from the beginning its full powers remain undeveloped to the end. While all around was heard the cry for English teaching, my third brother

was brave enough to keep us to our Bengali course.
To him in heaven my reverential thanks.

## 12. *The Professor*

On leaving the Normal School we were sent to the
Bengal Academy, a Eurasian institution. We felt we
had gained an access of dignity, that we had reached
the first storey of freedom. In point of fact that was
the only progress we did make in that academy. What
we were taught there we never understood, neither did
we make any attempt to learn, and it did not seem to
make any difference to anybody. The boys there were
annoying but not disgusting – which was a great comfort. They wrote 'Ass' on their palms and slapped it on
to our backs with a jovial 'Hello!' They gave us a dig in
the ribs from behind and looked innocently in another
direction. They dabbed banana pulp on our heads and
made off unseen. Nevertheless it was like coming out
of slime on to rock – we were still harassed but we
were not soiled.

This school had one great advantage for me. No
one there cherished the forlorn hope that a boy of my
sort could make any advance in learning. In a petty
institution with an insufficient income, we had one
supreme merit in the eyes of its authorities – we paid
our fees regularly. This prevented even Latin grammar
from proving a stumbling-block: the most egregious of
blunders left our backs unscathed. Pity had nothing to
do with it – the school authorities had spoken to the
teachers!

Harmless the place might be, but it was still a
school. The rooms were cruelly dismal, their walls
on guard like policemen. The house was more like
a pigeon-holed box than a human habitation. No

decoration, no pictures, not a touch of colour, not an attempt to attract the boyish heart. The fact that likes and dislikes form a large part of the child mind was completely ignored. Naturally our whole being was depressed as we stepped through its doorway into the narrow quadrangle – and playing truant became chronic with us.

In this we found an accomplice. My elder brothers had a Persian tutor. We used to call him Munshi. He was of middle age and all skin and bone, as though dark parchment had been stretched over his skeleton without any filling of flesh and blood. He probably knew Persian well, his knowledge of English was fair, but his ambition lay in neither of these directions. His belief was that his skill in song was matched only by his proficiency in singlestick. He would stand in the sun in the middle of our courtyard and go through a wonderful series of antics with a staff – his own shadow being his antagonist. I need hardly add that his shadow never got the better of him, and when at the end he gave a great big shout and whacked it on the head with a victorious smile, it lay submissively at his feet. His singing, nasal and out of tune, sounded like a gruesome mixture of groaning and moaning coming from some ghost-world. Our singing master Vishnu would sometimes chaff him: 'Hold on, Munshi, you'll be taking the bread out of our mouths at this rate!' To which his only response would be a disdainful smile.

This shows that the Munshi was amenable to soft words; and whenever we wanted we could persuade him to write to the school authorities to excuse us from attendance. The school authorities took no pains to scrutinise these letters; they knew it would be all the same whether we attended or not, so far as educational results were concerned.

I have a school of my own now in which the

boys are up to all kinds of mischief; for boys will be mischievous – and schoolmasters unforgiving. When any of us becomes unduly agitated at their conduct and is stirred into a resolution to deal out condign punishment, the misdeeds of my own schooldays confront me in a row and grin at me.

I clearly see that the mistake is to judge boys by the standard of grown-ups, to forget that a child is quick and mobile like a running stream, and that any imperfection need cause no great alarm, for the speed of the flow is itself the best corrective. When stagnation sets in, then there is danger. Thus it is the teacher, more than the pupil, who should beware doing wrong.

There was a separate refreshment room for Bengali boys to meet their caste requirements. This was where we struck up friendships with some of the others. They were all older. One of them is worth a digression.

His speciality was the art of magic, so much so that he had actually written and published a little booklet on it, the front page of which bore his name with the title of Professor. I had never before come across a schoolboy whose work had appeared in print, so that my reverence for him – as a professor of magic, I mean – was profound. How could I permit myself to believe that anything questionable could possibly find its way into the straight and upright ranks of printed letters? To be able to record one's own words in indelible ink – was that a slight thing? To stand uncovered yet unabashed, self-confessed before the world – how could one withhold belief in the face of such supreme self-confidence? I remember once that I got the type for the letters of my name from some printing-press, and what a memorable thing it was when I inked and pressed them on paper and saw my name.

This schoolfellow and author-friend of ours used

to get a lift in our carriage. Soon we were on visiting terms. He was also great at theatricals. With his help we erected a stage on our wrestling ground, with painted paper stretched over a split bamboo framework. But a peremptory negative from upstairs prevented any play from being acted on it.

A comedy of errors was later played without any stage at all, however. Its author has already been introduced to the reader. He was none other than my nephew Satya. Those who see him now, calm and sedate, would be shocked to learn of the tricks he invented.

The event I am about to narrate happened a little later, when I was twelve or thirteen. Our magician friend had discoursed on things with such strange properties that I was consumed with curiosity to see them for myself. But the materials of which he spoke were invariably so rare or remote that one could hardly hope to get hold of them without the help of Sinbad the sailor. Once, though, the Professor forgot himself so far as to mention accessible things. Who could ever believe that a seed dipped and dried twenty-one times in the juice of a species of cactus would sprout and flower and fruit all in the space of an hour? I was determined to test this, without, of course, daring to doubt the assurance of a Professor whose name appeared in a printed book.

I persuaded our gardener to furnish me with a plentiful supply of the milky juice, and took myself one Sunday afternoon to our private mystery corner on the roof terrace, to experiment with the stone of a mango. I was quickly wrapped up in my task of dipping and drying – but the grown-up reader will probably not wait to ask me the result. In the meantime, I little knew that Satya, in another corner, had caused to root and sprout a mystical plant of his own creation all in the space of an hour. It was to bear curious fruit later on.

After my experiment the Professor rather avoided me, as I gradually came to perceive. He would not sit on the same side in the carriage, and seemed altogether to fight shy of me.

One day, all of a sudden, he proposed that each one should jump off the bench in our schoolroom in turn. He wanted to observe the differences in style, he said. Such scientific curiosity did not appear queer in a professor of magic. Every one jumped and so did I. He shook his head with a subdued 'Hmm.' No amount of cajoling could draw anything further from him.

Another day he informed us that some good friends of his wanted to make our acquaintance, and asked us to accompany him to their house. Our guardians had no objection, so off we went. The crowd in the room seemed full of curiosity. They expressed their eagerness to hear me sing. I sang a song or two. Mere child that I was, my voice was hardly likely to be a bull's bellow. 'Rather a sweet voice,' they all agreed.

When refreshments were put before us they sat round and watched us eat. I was shy by nature and not used to strange company; moreover the habits I had acquired while superintended by our servant Ishwar had left me a poor eater for good. They all seemed impressed with the delicacy of my appetite.

In the final act of this farce I received some curiously warm letters from our Professor that explained the whole situation. And here let the curtain fall.

I subsequently learned from Satya that while I had been practising magic on the mango seed, he had successfully convinced the Professor that I was dressed as a boy by our guardians merely to get me a better schooling, but that really this was only a disguise. To those who are inquisitive about imaginary science I should explain that a girl is supposed to jump with her left foot forward, and this is what I had done on the occasion of the Professor's trial. Little did I realise what a tremendously false step I had taken!

## 13. *My father*

Shortly after my birth my father took to constant travel. So it is no exaggeration to say that in my early childhood I hardly knew him. He would now and then come back home all of a sudden, and with him came outsiders as servants with whom I felt extremely eager to make friends. Once he brought a young Punjabi servant named Lenu. The cordiality of the reception we gave him would have been worthy of Maharaja Ranjit Singh himself. Not only was he a foreigner, but a Punjabi too – this really stole our hearts away. We had the same reverence for the whole Punjabi nation as we did for Bhima and Arjuna of the *Mahabharata*. They were warriors, and if they had sometimes lost the fight, that was clearly the enemy's fault. It was glorious to have Lenu of the Punjab in our very home.

My sister-in-law had a model warship under a glass case which, when wound up, rocked on blue-painted silken waves to the tinkling of a musical box. I would beg hard for the loan of this to display its marvels to the admiring Lenu.

Caged in the house as we were, anything savouring of foreign parts had a peculiar charm for me. It was one of the reasons why I made so much of Lenu. It was also why Gabriel, the Jew, with his embroidered gaberdine, who came to sell *attars* and scented oils, stirred me so; and why the huge Kabulis, with their dusty, baggy trousers and knapsacks and bundles, worked my young mind into a fearful fascination.

So, when my father came, we would be content with wandering among his entourage and keeping the company of his servants. We did not reach his actual presence.

Once, while my father was away in the Himalayas, that old bogy of the British government, a Russian invasion, became a subject of agitated conversation among the people. Some well-meaning lady friend had enlarged on the impending danger to my mother with all the fancy of a prolific imagination. How could anybody tell from which of the Tibetan passes the Russian host might suddenly flash forth like a baleful comet?

My mother was seriously alarmed. The other members of the family possibly did not share her misgivings so, despairing of grown-up sympathy, she sought my boyish support. 'Won't you write to your father about the Russians?' she asked.

My letter, bearing the tidings of my mother's anxieties, was the first I wrote to my father. I did not know how to begin or end a letter, or anything at all about it. I went to Mahananda, the estate *munshi*. My resulting form of address was doubtless correct enough, but the sentiments could not have escaped the musty flavour inseparable from correspondence emanating from an estate office.

I had a reply. My father asked me not to be afraid; if the Russians came he would drive them away himself. This confident assurance did not seem to have the effect of relieving my mother's fears, but it served to free me from all timidity as regards my father. After that I wanted to write to him every day, and pestered Mahananda accordingly. Unable to withstand my importunity he would make out drafts for me to copy. But I did not know that there was postage to be paid for. I had an idea that letters placed in Mahananda's hands got to their destination without any need for further worry. It is hardly necessary to add that Mahananda was old enough to ensure that these letters never reached the Himalayan hill-tops.

After his long absences, when my father came home even for a few days, the whole house seemed filled with the gravity of his presence. We would see our elders at certain hours, formally robed in their *chogas*, passing to his rooms with restrained gait and sober mien, casting away any *pan* they might have been chewing. Everyone seemed on the alert. To make sure that nothing went wrong, my mother would superintend the cooking herself. The old retainer Kinu, with his white livery and crested turban, on guard at my father's door, would warn us not to be boisterous in the verandah in front of his rooms during his midday siesta. We had to walk past quietly, talking in whispers, and dared not even take a peep inside.

On one occasion my father came home to invest the three of us with the sacred thread. With the help of Pandit Vedantavagish he had collected the old Vedic rites for the purpose. For days at a time we were taught to chant in correct accents the selections from the *Upanishads*, arranged under the name of *Brahma Dharma*, by my father seated in the prayer hall with Becharam Babu. Finally, with shaven heads and gold rings in our ears, we three budding Brahmins went into a three-days' retreat in a portion of the third storey.

It was great fun. The earrings gave us a good handle to pull each other's ears with. We found a little drum lying in one of the rooms; taking this we would stand out in the verandah, and when we caught sight of any servant passing along in the storey below, we rapped a tattoo on it. This would make the man look up, only to avert his eyes and beat a hasty retreat at the next moment. We certainly cannot claim that we passed these days of our retirement in ascetic meditation.

I am convinced that boys like us must have been common in the hermitages of old. If some ancient document has it that the ten- or twelve-year-old Saradwata or Sarngarava spent the whole of his boyhood offering oblations and chanting mantras, we are not compelled to put unquestioning faith in the statement; because the book of Boy Nature is even older and is also more authentic.

After we had attained full Brahminhood I became very keen on repeating the *gayatri*. I would meditate on it with great concentration. It is hardly a text of which the full meaning may be grasped at that age. I distinctly remember what efforts I made to extend the range of my consciousness with the help of the initial invocation of 'Earth, firmament and heaven'. How I felt or thought it is difficult to express clearly, but this much is certain: that to be clear about the meaning of words is not the most important part of the process of human understanding.

The main object of teaching is not to give explanations, but to knock at the doors of the mind. If any boy is asked to give an account of what is awakened in him by such knocking, he will probably say something silly. For what happens within is much bigger than what comes out in words. Those who pin their faith on university examinations as the test of education take no account of this.

I can recollect many things which I did not understand, but which stirred me deeply. Once, on the roof terrace of our riverside villa, at the sudden gathering of clouds my eldest brother repeated aloud some stanzas from *The Cloud Messenger* by Kalidas. I could not understand a word of the Sanskrit, neither did I need to. His ecstatic declamation and the sonorous rhythm were enough for me.

Then, again, before I could properly understand English, a profusely illustrated edition of *The Old Curiosity Shop* fell into my hands. I went through the whole of it, though at least nine-tenths of the words were unknown to me. Yet, with the vague ideas conjured up by the rest, I spun out a variously coloured thread on which to string the illustrations. Any university examiner would have given me zero, but for me the reading of the book had not proved quite so empty.

Another time I had accompanied my father for a trip on the Ganges in his houseboat. Among the books he had with him was an old Fort William edition of Jayadeva's *Gita Govinda*, printed in Bengali script. The verses were not in separate lines, but ran on like prose. I did not know any Sanskrit then, yet because of my knowledge of Bengali many of the words were familiar. How often I read that *Gita Govinda* I cannot say. I particularly remember this line:

The night extinguished in solitary forest exile.

It roused a feeling of beauty in my mind. That one Sanskrit word *nibhrita-nikunja-griham*, meaning 'solitary forest exile', was quite enough for me.

I had to work out for myself the intricate metre of Jayadeva's poetry, because its divisions were lost in the clumsy prose form of the book. And this discovery gave me very great delight. Of course I did not fully comprehend Jayadeva's meaning. One could not even truthfully say that I grasped it partly. But the sound of the words and the lilt of the metre filled my mind with pictures of such grace that I was impelled to copy out the whole book for my own use.

The same thing happened, when I was a little older, with a verse from Kalidas' *Birth of the War-God*. The verse really moved me, though the only words of which I gathered the sense, were 'the zephyr wafting the spray from the falling waters of the sacred Mandakini and trembling the deodar leaves.' They left me pining to taste the whole. When a pundit later explained to me that in the next two lines the breeze 'split the feathers of the peacock plume on the head of the eager deer-hunter', the thinness of the conceit disappointed me. I was much better off when I had relied only upon my imagination to complete the verse.

Whoever goes back to his early childhood will agree that his greatest gains were not in proportion to the completeness of his understanding. Our *kathakas* know this very well: when they give public recitals, their narratives always have a good proportion of ear-filling Sanskrit words and abstruse remarks calculated not to be fully understood by their simple hearers, but only to be suggestive.

The value of such suggestion is by no means to be despised by those who measure education in terms of material gains and losses. They insist on trying to tot up the account and find out exactly how much of a lesson can be rendered up. But children, and those who are not over-educated, dwell in that primal paradise where humans can obtain knowledge without wholly comprehending each step. Only when that paradise is lost comes the evil day when everything has to be understood. The road which leads to knowledge without going through the dreary process of understanding is the royal road. If that be barred, even though commerce may continue, the open sea and the mountain top cease to be possible of access.

So, as I was saying, though at that age I could

not realise the full meaning of the *gayatri*, something in me could do without a complete understanding. I am reminded of a day when, as I was seated on the cement floor in a corner of our schoolroom meditating on the text, my eyes overflowed with tears. Why they came I do not know; to a strict cross-questioner I would probably have given some explanation having nothing to do with the *gayatri*. The fact is that what goes on in the inner recesses of consciousness is not always known to the surface dweller.

## 14. *A journey with my father*

My shaven head after the sacred thread ceremony caused me one great anxiety. However partial Eurasian lads may be to the sacred Cow, their reverence for the Brahmin is definitely minimal. I expected that apart from other missiles, our shaven heads were sure to be pelted with jeers. While I kept worrying over this possibility I was summoned upstairs to my father. How would I like to go with him to the Himalayas? Away from the Bengal Academy and off to the Himalayas! How would I like it? Oh, I would have needed to rend the skies with a shout to give some idea of How!

The day we left home my father, as was his habit, assembled the whole family in the prayer hall for divine service. After I had taken the dust of my elders' feet I got into the carriage with my father. This was the first time in my life that I had a full suit of clothes made for me. My father had selected the pattern and colour himself. A gold embroidered velvet cap completed my costume. This I carried in my hand, assailed as I was with misgivings about its impact atop my hairless head. As I got into the carriage my father insisted on my wearing it, so I had to put it on. Every

time he looked away I took it off. Every time I caught
his eye it had to resume its proper place.

My father was very particular in all his arrangements. He disliked leaving things vague or undeter-
mined, and never allowed slovenliness or make-do. He
had a well-defined code to regulate his relations with
others and theirs with him. In this he was different
from the generality of his countrymen. Among the
rest of us a little laxity this way or that did not
signify; in our dealings with him we therefore had to
be anxiously careful. The size and significance of a task
did not concern him so much as failure to maintain its
required standard.

My father also had a way of picturing to himself
every detail of what he wanted done. On the occasion
of any ceremonial gathering at which he could not be
present, he would think out and assign a place for each
thing, a duty for each member of the family, a seat for
each guest; nothing would escape him. After everything was over he would ask each one for a separate
account and gain a complete impression of the whole
for himself. So while I was with him on his travels,
though nothing would induce him to interfere in how
I amused myself, no loophole was left in the strict rules
of conduct prescribed for me in other respects.

Our first halt was to be at Bolpur for a few days.
Satya had been there a short time before with his
parents. No self-respecting nineteenth-century boy
would have credited the account of his travels which
he gave us on his return. But I was different, and
had had no opportunity of learning to determine the
line between the possible and the impossible. Our
*Mahabharata* and *Ramayana* gave us no clue to it. Nor
had we then any illustrated books to guide us. All the
hard-and-fast rules that govern the world we learnt by
knocking ourselves against them.

Satya had told us that, unless one was exceedingly expert, getting into a railway carriage was a terribly dangerous affair – the least slip, and it was all up. Once aboard, a fellow had to hold on to his seat with all his might, otherwise the tremendous jolt on starting might throw him off – there was no telling where to.

When we got to the railway station I was all a-quiver. So easily did we enter our compartment that I felt sure the worst was yet to come. And when, at length, we made an absurdly smooth start without any hint of adventure, I felt woefully disappointed.

The train sped on; the broad fields bordered by blue-green trees and the villages nestling in their shade flew past in a stream of pictures that melted away like a flood of mirages. It was evening when we reached Bolpur. As I got into the palanquin I closed my eyes. I wanted to preserve the whole of the wonderful vision to be unfolded before my waking eyes in the morning light. The freshness of the experience would be spoilt, I feared, by incomplete glimpses caught in the vagueness of twilight.

When I woke at dawn I was tremulously excited as I stepped outside. My predecessor had told me that Bolpur had one feature which was to be found nowhere else in the world. This was a path leading from the main buildings to the servants' quarters, which, though not covered over in any way, did not allow a ray of sun or a drop of rain to touch anybody passing along it. I started to hunt for this wonderful path, but the reader will perhaps not wonder at my failure to find it to this day.

Town boy that I was, I had never seen a rice-field and had a charming portrait of the cowherd boy, of whom we had read, pictured on the canvas of my imagination. I had heard from Satya that the Bolpur house was surrounded by fields of ripening rice, and that playing in these with cowherd boys was an everyday affair, of which the plucking, cooking and eating of the rice was the crowning feature. I eagerly looked about me. Where was the rice-field on all that barren heath? Cowherd boys might have been somewhere about, but how to distinguish them from any other boys was the question!

What I could not see did not take me long to get over – what I did see was quite enough. There was no servant rule, and the only ring which encircled me was the blue of the horizon, drawn around these solitudes by their presiding goddess. Within this I was free to move about as I chose.

Though I was still a mere child my father did not place any restriction on my wanderings. In the hollows of the sandy soil the rain water had ploughed deep furrows, carving out miniature mountain ranges full of red gravel and pebbles of various shapes through which ran tiny streams, revealing the geography of Lilliput. From this region I would gather in the lap of my tunic many curious pieces of stone and take the collection to my father. He never made light of my labours. On the contrary he was enthusiastic.

'Splendid!' he exclaimed, 'Wherever did you get all these?'

'There are many many more, thousands and thousands!' I burst out. 'I could bring as many every day.'

'That *would* be nice!' he replied. 'Why not decorate my little hill with them?'

An attempt had been made to dig a tank in the garden but, the water-table proving too low, the digging had been abandoned with the excavated earth left piled up in a hillock. On top of this my father used to sit for his morning prayer, and as he did so the sun would rise at the edge of the undulating expanse which stretched away to the eastern horizon in front of him. It was this hill he asked me to decorate.

I was very troubled, on leaving Bolpur, that I could not carry away my store of stones. I had not yet understood the encumbrance entailed and that I had no absolute claim on a thing merely because I had collected it. If fate had granted me my prayer, as I had dearly desired, and determined that I should carry this load of stones about with me for ever, today this story would be no laughing matter.

In one of the ravines I came upon a hollow full of spring water which overflowed as a little rivulet, where tiny fish played and battled their way up the current.

'I've found such a lovely spring,' I told my father. 'Couldn't we get our bathing- and drinking-water from there?'

'Perfect,' he agreed, sharing my rapture, and gave orders for our water-supply to be drawn from that spring.

I was never tired of roaming these miniature valleys and plateaus in hopes of alighting on something never before discovered. I was the Livingstone of this land which looked as if seen through the wrong end of a telescope. Everything there, the dwarf date palms, the scrubby wild plums and the stunted *jambolans*, was in keeping with the miniature mountain ranges, the rivulet and the tiny fish.

Probably to teach me to be careful my father placed some small change in my charge and required me to keep an account of it. He also entrusted me with the winding of his valuable gold watch. He overlooked the risk of damage in his desire to train me to a sense of duty. When we went out together for our morning walk he asked me to give alms to any beggars we came across. I could never render him a proper account at the end. One day my balance was larger than the account warranted.

'I really must make you my cashier,' observed my father. 'Money seems to have a way of growing in your hands!'

His watch I wound with such indefatigable zeal that very soon it had to be sent to the watchmaker's in Calcutta.

I am reminded of the occasions in later life when I used to tender the estate accounts to my father, who was then living in Park Street. I would do this on the second or third of every month. He was by then unable to read them himself. I had first to read out the totals under each heading, and if he had any doubts on any point he would ask for the details. If I made any attempt to slur over or conceal any item I feared he would not like, it was sure to come out. These first few days of the month were very anxious ones for me.

As I have said, my father had the habit of keeping everything clearly before his mind – whether figures of accounts, or ceremonial arrangements, or additions or alterations to property. He had never seen the new prayer hall at Bolpur, and yet he was familiar with every detail of it from questioning those who came to see him after a visit there. He had an extraordinary memory, and when once he got hold of a fact it never escaped him.

My father had marked his favourite verses in his copy of the *Bhagavadgita*. He asked me to copy these out for him, with their translation. At home I had been a boy of no account, but here, when these important functions were entrusted to me, I felt the glory of the situation.

By this time I was rid of my blue manuscript book and had got hold of a bound volume, one of Letts' diaries. I saw to it now that my poetising should not be lacking in outward dignity. It was not just writing poems, but holding a picture of myself as a poet before my imagination. When I wrote poetry at Bolpur I loved to do it sprawling under a young coconut palm. This seemed to me the true manner. Thus resting on the hard unturfed gravel in the burning heat of the day, I composed a martial ballad on the 'Defeat of King Prithvi'. In spite of its superabundance of martial spirit, it could not escape early death. That bound volume of Letts' diary followed the way of its elder sister, the blue manuscript book, leaving no forwarding address.

We left Bolpur and, making short halts on the way at Sahibganj, Dinapur, Allahabad and Kanpur, we stopped at last at Amritsar.

An incident *en route* remains engraved on my memory. The train had stopped at some big station. The ticket collector came and punched our tickets. He looked at me curiously as if he had some doubt that he did not care to express. He went off and came back with a companion. Both of them fidgeted about for a time near the door of our compartment and then again retired. At last the station-master himself came. He looked at my half-ticket and then asked: 'Is not the boy over twelve?'

'No,' said my father.

I was then only eleven, but looked older than my age.

'You must pay the full fare for him,' said the station-master.

My father's eyes flashed as, without a word, he took out a currency note from his box and handed it to the station-master. When they brought the change my father flung it disdainfully back at them, while the station-master stood abashed at this exposure of the meanness of his doubt.

The Golden Temple of Amritsar comes back to me like a dream. On many a morning I accompanied my father to this *gurudarbar* of the Sikhs in the middle of the lake. There the sacred chanting continually resounds. My father, seated amidst the throng of worshippers, would sometimes add his voice to the hymn of praise and, finding a stranger joining in their devotions they would welcome him most cordially, and we would return loaded with the sanctified offerings of sugar crystals and other sweets.

One day my father invited one of the chanting choir to our place and had him sing us some of their sacred songs. The man went away probably more than satisfied with the reward he received. Soon we had to take stern measures in self-defence, such was the insistent army of singers that invaded us. When they found our house impregnable, the musicians began to waylay us in the streets. As we went out for our walk in the morning, from time to time would appear a *tanpura*, slung over a shoulder; it made us feel like game birds that had spotted the muzzle of a hunter's gun. So wary did we become that the twang of a *tanpura*, even in the distance, would scare us away and fail utterly to bag us.

When evening fell, my father would sit out on the verandah facing the garden. He would summon me to sing to him. I can see the moon risen; its beams, passing through the trees, falling on the verandah floor; and I am singing in raga Behag:

O Companion in the darkest passage of life . . .

My father with bowed head and clasped hands listens intently. I recall the evening scene quite clearly.

I have already told of my father's amusement on

hearing from Srikantha Babu of my maiden attempt at a devotional poem. I remember how, later, I had my recompense. On the occasion of one of our *Magh* festivals several of the hymns were of my composition. One of them was:

The eye sees thee not, who art the pupil of every eye.

My father was then bed-ridden at Chunchura. He sent for me and my brother Jyoti. He asked my brother to accompany me on the harmonium, and me to sing all my hymns one after the other, some of them twice over. When I had finished he said: 'If the king of the country had known the language and could appreciate its literature, he would doubtless have rewarded the poet. Since that is not so, I suppose I must do it.' With which he handed me a cheque.

My father had brought with him some volumes of the Peter Parley series from which to teach me. He selected *The Life of Benjamin Franklin* to begin with. He thought it would read like a story book and be both entertaining and instructive. But he found out his mistake soon after we began. Benjamin Franklin was much too business-like a person. The narrowness of his calculated morality disgusted my father. Sometimes he would become so impatient at Franklin's worldly prudence that he could not help using strong words of denunciation.

Until now I had had nothing to do with Sanskrit beyond learning some rules of grammar by rote. My father started me on the second Sanskrit reader at one bound, leaving me to learn the declensions as we went on. The advance I had made in Bengali stood me in good stead. My father also encouraged me to try Sanskrit composition from the very outset. With the vocabulary acquired from my Sanskrit reader I built up grandiose compound words with a profuse sprinkling of sonorous m's and n's, that made a most diabolical medley out of the language of the gods. But my father never scoffed at my temerity.

Then there were the readings from Proctor's *Popular Astronomy*, which my father explained to me in easy language and which I then rendered into Bengali.

Among the books which my father had brought for his own use, I often found myself gazing at a ten- or twelve-volume edition of Gibbon's *Rome*. They looked remarkably dry. I am only a helpless boy, I thought, I read many books because I have to. But why should a grown-up person, who doesn't have to read unless he pleases, give himself such bother?

## 15. *In the Himalayas*

We stayed about a month in Amritsar, and, towards the middle of April, started for the Dalhousie hills. The last few days in Amritsar seemed as if they would never pass, the Himalayas were calling me so strongly.

The terraced hillsides, as we went up in a *jhampan*, were aflame with flowering spring crops. Every morning we made a start after bread and milk, and before sunset took shelter in the next staging bungalow. My eyes had no rest the entire day, so much did I fear missing something. Wherever the great forest trees clustered together at a bend of the road into a gorge, a waterfall trickled out from beneath their shade, like a little daughter playing at the feet of hoary sages rapt in meditation and babbling over the black moss-covered rocks; there the *jhampan* bearers would put down their burden, and take a rest. Why had we ever to leave such spots, cried my thirsting heart. Why could we not stay on for good?

That is the great advantage of a first vision: the mind is not aware that there are many more to come. When this fact penetrates that calculating organ it promptly tries to make a saving in its expenditure of attention. Only when it believes something to be rare does the mind cease to be miserly. In the streets of Calcutta I sometimes imagine myself a foreigner, and only then do I discover how much is to be seen. The hunger to see properly is what drives people to travel in strange places.

My father left his little cash-box in my charge. He had no reason to imagine that I was the fittest custodian of the considerable sums he kept in it for use on the way. He would certainly have felt safer with it in the hands of Kishori, his attendant. So I can only suppose he wanted to instil in me the idea of responsibility. One day as we reached the staging bungalow, I forgot to make it over to him and left it lying on a table. This brought me a reprimand.

Every time we got down at the end of a stage, my father had chairs placed for us outside the bungalow and there we sat. As dusk came on the stars blazed wonderfully through the clear mountain atmosphere, and my father showed me the constellations or treated me to an astronomical discourse.

The house we had taken at Bakrota was on the highest hill-top. Though May had almost come it was still bitterly cold there, so much so that on the shady side of the hill the winter frosts had not yet melted.

My father was not at all nervous about my wandering freely even here. Some way below our house stretched a spur thickly wooded with deodars. I would go alone into this wilderness with my iron-tipped staff. What lordly trees, towering above me like giants! What vast shadows! What immense lives they had lived over the centuries! And yet this boy, born only the other day, crawled around between their trunks unchallenged. I seemed to feel a presence the moment I stepped into their shade like that of some ancient saurian whose cool, firm and scaly body was made of checkered light and shade on the leaf mould of the forest floor.

My room was at one end of the house. Lying on my bed I could see, through the uncurtained windows, the distant snow peaks shimmering dimly in the starlight. Sometimes, half-awake, at what hour I could not make out, I saw my father, wrapped in a red shawl, with a lighted lamp in his hand, softly passing by to the glazed verandah where he sat at his devotions. After dozing off, I would find him at my bedside, rousing me with a push before the darkness had yet passed from the night. This was the hour appointed for memorising Sanskrit declensions. What an excruciatingly wintry awakening from the caressing warmth of my blankets!

By the time the sun rose, my father, after finishing his prayers, joined me for our morning milk, and then stood with me, once more to hold communion with God by chanting the *Upanishads*.

Then we would go out for a walk. But how could I keep pace with him? Many adults could not! After a while, I would give up and scramble back home by some short cut over the mountainside.

Upon my father's return I had an hour of English lessons. At ten o'clock came a bath in ice-cold water. It was no use asking the servants to temper it with even a jugful of hot water without permission. To give me courage my father would tell of the unbearably freezing baths he had himself endured in his younger days.

Another penance was milk-drinking. My father was very fond of milk and could take quantities. But my appetite for it was grievously lacking, whether because I had failed to inherit it or because of my unfavourable early experiences with milk, I do not know. Unfortunately we used to have our milk together so I had to throw myself on the mercy of the servants, and to their human kindness (or frailty) I was indebted for my goblet being more than half full of foam.

After our midday meal lessons began again. This was more than flesh and blood could stand. My outraged morning sleep *would* have its revenge and I would be toppling over with uncontrollable drowsiness. But no sooner did my father take pity on my plight and let me off than my sleepiness was off likewise: the Lord of the mountains was calling!

Staff in hand I would often wander away from one peak to another, but my father did not object. To the end of his life, I have observed, he never stood in the way of our independence. Frequently I have said or done things repugnant to his taste and his judgement alike; with a word he could have stopped me but he preferred to wait until the prompting to refrain came from within. A passive acceptance of the correct and the proper did not satisfy him; he wanted us to love truth with our whole hearts; mere acquiescence without love he knew to be empty. He also knew that truth, if strayed from, can be found again, but a forced or blind adherence effectively bars access to it.

In my early youth I had conceived a fancy to travel the Grand Trunk Road, right up to Peshawar, in a bullock cart. No one else supported the scheme, and doubtless there was much to be urged against it as a practical proposition. But when I discoursed on it to my father he was sure it was a splendid idea – travelling by railway was not worth the name! And he forthwith proceeded to recount his own adventures on foot and horseback. Of any chance of discomfort or peril he had not a word to say.

Another time, when I had just been appointed

secretary of the Adi Brahmo Samaj, I went over to my father at his Park Street residence and informed him that I did not approve of the practice of having only Brahmins conducting divine service to the exclusion of other castes. He unhesitatingly gave me permission to correct this if I could. Armed with the authorisation I found I lacked the power. I was able to discover imperfections but could not create perfection! Where were the men? Where was the strength in me to attract the right man? Had I the means to build in place of what I might break? Until the right man arrives, any form is better than none – this, I felt, must have been my father's view. But not for a moment did he try to discourage me by pointing out these difficulties.

Just as he allowed me to wander the mountains at will, so he left me free to select my path in the quest for truth. He was not deterred by the risk of my making mistakes, neither alarmed at the prospect of my encountering sorrow. He held up a standard, not a disciplinary rod.

I would often talk to him of home. Whenever I got a letter from anyone there I immediately showed it to him. I believe I permitted him many a glimpse he could have had from no one else. My father also let me read letters to him from my elder brothers. It was his way of teaching me how I ought to write to him; for he by no means undervalued outward forms and ceremonial.

I remember how in one letter my second brother complained of being worked to death, tied by the neck to his post, expressing himself in somewhat Sanskritised language. My father asked me to explain briefly what was meant. I did so in my way, but he thought a different explanation better. In my overweening conceit I stuck to my guns and argued the point at length. Another person would have stopped me with a snub, but my father patiently heard me out and took pains to justify his view to me.

Sometimes he would tell me funny stories. He had many anecdotes of the gilded youth of his time. There were some exquisites for whose delicate skins the embroidered border of even Dacca muslins proved too coarse; among them, for a while, it was the tip-top thing to wear one's muslins with the borders torn off.

I was also highly amused to hear, first from my father, the story of the milkman suspected of watering his milk. The more men one of his customers detailed to supervise his milking the bluer the fluid became, until at last, when the customer himself interviewed the milkman and asked for an explanation, the man bluntly stated that if any more superintendents had to be satisfied the milk would be fit only to breed fish!

After I had spent a few months with him, my father sent me back home with his attendant Kishori.

## 16. *My return*

The chains of the rigorous regime which had bound me had snapped for good when I had set out from home. On my return I acquired some rights. My very proximity to others ruled me out of mind before; by going away and coming back I came into focus.

I had a foretaste of appreciation while on my way back. Travelling alone except for my attendant, brimming with health and spirits, and conspicuous in my gold-worked cap, I was made much of by all the English people I came across in the train.

My arrival was not merely a homecoming, but also a return from exile in the servants' quarters to my rightful place in the inner apartments. Whenever the inner household assembled in my mother's room I now occupied a seat of honour. And she, who was then the youngest bride of our house, lavished on me a wealth of affection and regard.

In infancy the loving care of woman is to be had without the asking, and, being as much a necessity as light and air, is simply taken for granted. In fact children often fidget to free themselves from the web of feminine solicitude. But any creature who is deprived of it at its proper time is beggared indeed. This had been my plight after being brought up in the servants' quarters. So, when I suddenly came in for a profusion of womanly affection, I could hardly remain unconscious of it.

In earlier days, when the inner apartments were far away from me, they were the Elysium of my imagination. The *zenana*, which looks from the outside a place of confinement, for me was the abode of all freedom. Neither school nor pundit was there; nor, it seemed to me, did anybody have to do what they did not want to do. Its secluded leisure had something mysterious about it; one played about, or did as one liked and did not have to render an account of one's doings. This seemed especially so of my youngest sister, who attended Nil Kamal Pandit's class with us but appeared to be unaffected whether she did her lessons well or ill. While we had to hurry through our breakfast by ten o'clock and be ready for school, she, her plait dangling behind, walked unconcernedly away withinwards, tantalising us to distraction.

And when the new bride, adorned with her necklace of gold, came into our house, the mystery of the inner apartments deepened. She, who came from outside and yet became one of us, who was unknown and yet our own, attracted me strangely: I burned to make friends. But if by much contriving I managed to draw near, my youngest sister would hustle me off with: 'What d'you boys want here? Keep away outside.' The insult, added to the disappointment, cut me to the quick. Through the glass doors of their cabinets one could catch glimpses of all manner of curious playthings, creations of porcelain and glass, gorgeous in colouring and ornamentation. We were not deemed worthy even to touch them, much less invited to play with them. These objects, rare and wonderful as they seemed to us, tinged the inner apartments with an additional allure.

Thus was I kept at arm's length by repeated rebuffs. The outside world was unavailable to me, and so, alas, was the inner. What little I saw of it impressed me like a series of paintings.

It is nine in the evening, for instance, and, my lessons with Aghore Babu over, I am retiring inside for the night. A murky flickering lantern hangs in the long Venetian-screened corridor leading from the outer to the inner apartments. At its end this passage becomes a flight of four or five steps, into which the light does not reach and down which I pass into the galleries running round the first inner courtyard. A shaft of moonlight slants from the eastern sky into the western section of these verandahs, leaving the rest in darkness. Within this patch of light the maids have gathered and sit on the floor close together, legs outstretched, rolling cotton waste on their thighs into lamp-wicks and chatting in undertones of their village homes.

Many such pictures are indelibly printed on my memory. Another is of the time after supper which begins with the washing of our hands and feet on the verandah before stretching ourselves on the ample expanse of our bed; whereupon one of the nurses, Tinkari or Shankari, comes and sits by our heads and softly croons to us the story of the prince travelling on and on over the lonely moor, and, as it reaches the end, silence falls on the room. With my face to the wall I stare at the black and white patches made by plaster that has fallen off here and there, faintly visible in the dim light; and I conjure many a fantastic image as I drop off to sleep. And sometimes, during the night, I hear in my half-broken sleep the calls of old Swarup, the watchman, going his rounds from verandah to verandah.

Then came the new order. From the inner dreamland known only in my fancies came all the recognition for which I had been pining, and more; when that which should have come naturally day by day was suddenly made good to me with accumulated arrears. I cannot say that my head was not turned.

The little traveller was full of his travels, and, with the strain of each repetition, the narrative got looser and looser until it utterly refused to fit the facts. Like everything else alas, a story also grows stale and the glory of the teller suffers likewise; that is why he has to add new colouring every time to maintain freshness.

After my return from the hills I was the principal speaker at my mother's open-air gatherings on the roof terrace in the evenings. The temptation to become famous in one's mother's eyes is as difficult to resist as such fame is easy to earn. While I was at the Normal School, when I first came across the information in some reader that the sun was hundreds and thousands of times bigger than the earth, I at once disclosed it to my mother. It served to prove that someone who looked small might yet have a certain grandeur. I used also to recite to her scraps of poetry used as illustrations in the chapter on prosody or rhetoric in our Bengali grammar. Now I retailed to her evening gatherings the astronomical tit-bits I had gleaned from Proctor.

My father's follower Kishori belonged at one time to a band of reciters of Dasharathi's jingling versions of the epics. While we were together in the hills he often said to me: 'Oh, my little brother, if I only had had you in our troupe we could have got up a splendid performance.' This would open up to me a tempting picture of wandering as a minstrel boy from place to place, reciting and singing. I learnt many of the songs in his repertoire, and these were in even greater demand than my talks about the photosphere of the sun or the many moons of Saturn.

But my greatest achievement in my mother's eyes was that while the rest of the inmates of the inner apartments had to be content with Krittivas' Bengali rendering of the *Ramayana*, I had been reading with my father the original of Maharshi Válmiki himself, Sanskrit metre and all. 'Read me some of that *Ramayana*, do!' she said, overjoyed when I mentioned this.

Alas, my reading of Valmiki had been limited to the short extract from his *Ramayana* given in my Sanskrit reader, and even that I had not fully mastered. Moreover, on looking over it again, I found that memory had played me false and much of what I thought I knew had become hazy. But I lacked the courage to plead 'I have forgotten' to my eager mother awaiting the display of her son's marvellous talents; so in the reading I gave, Valmiki's intention and my explanation widely diverged. That tender-hearted sage, from his seat in heaven, must have forgiven the temerity of a boy seeking the glory of his mother's approbation – but not so the god whose role is to puncture pride.

My mother, unable to contain her feelings at my extraordinary exploit, wanted all to share her admiration. 'You must read this to Dwijendra,' she said.

Now I've had it! I thought, as I offered all the excuses I could think of, but my mother would have none of them. She sent for my eldest brother and as soon as he arrived greeted him with: 'Just hear Rabi read Valmiki's *Ramayana*; how splendidly he does it.'

It had to be done! But the god of pride relented and let me off with just a whiff of his power. My brother had probably been called away from his literary work and was preoccupied. He showed no enthusiasm to hear me render the Sanskrit into Bengali; as soon as I had read out a few verses he remarked simply, 'Very good,' and walked off.

Following my promotion to the inner apartments I found it all the more difficult to resume my school life. I resorted to all kinds of subterfuge to escape the Bengal Academy. Then they tried putting me at St Xavier's. But the result was no better.

My elder brothers, after a few spasmodic efforts, gave up all hope of me – they even ceased to scold me. My eldest sister one day said: 'We had all hoped Rabi would grow up to be a man, but he has been our biggest disappointment.' I felt that my value in the social world was depreciating distinctly; nevertheless I could not commit my mind to the eternal grind of school which, divorced as it was from all life and beauty, seemed such a hideously cruel combination of hospital and gaol.

One memory of St Xavier's I still hold fresh and pure. It concerns the teachers. Not that they were all of the same excellence. Among those who taught our class I could discern no particular dedication or humility. As a group they were in no wise better than the teaching-machine brand of school master. On its own, the educational engine is remorselessly powerful, but when the outward forms of religion are coupled to it like a stone mill, the heart of youth is truly crushed dry. This is the type of grindstone we had at St Xavier's. Yet, as I say, I possess one memory that elevates my impression of the teachers there to an ideal plane.

Father DePeneranda had very little to do with us – if I remember right he was a temporary replacement for one of the masters of our class. He was a Spaniard who seemed to have an impediment in speaking English. Perhaps for this reason the boys paid little heed to what he said. I felt that his pupils' inattentiveness hurt him, but he bore it meekly day after day. I do not know why, but my heart went out to him. His features were not handsome, but his face had a strange appeal. Whenever I looked on him his spirit seemed to be in prayer, a deep peace to pervade him within and without.

We had half an hour for writing our copy-books, a time when, pen in hand, I became absent-minded and my thoughts wandered hither and thither. One day Father DePeneranda was in charge of this class. He was pacing up and down behind our benches. He must have noticed more than once that my pen was not moving. All of a sudden he stopped behind my seat. Bending over me he gently laid his hand on my shoulder and tenderly inquired: 'Are you not well, Tagore?' It was only a simple question, but one I have never been able to forget.

I cannot speak for the other boys, but I felt in him the presence of a great soul, and even today the recollection of it seems to transport me into the silent seclusion of the temple of God.

There was another old Father whom all the boys loved, Father Henry. He taught the higher classes, so I did not know him well. But I remember one thing about him: he knew Bengali. He once asked Nirada, a boy in his class, the derivation of his name. Poor Nirada! He had long been supremely

confident about himself – the derivation of his name
never giving him the least pause for thought; he was
utterly unprepared to answer this question. And yet,
with a whole dictionary full of abstruse and unknown
words to chose from, to be worsted by one's own name
would be as ridiculous as getting run over by one's
own carriage. So Nirada unblushingly replied: '*Ni* –
privative, *rode* – sun's rays; hence Nirode – that which
causes an absence of the sun's rays!'*

## 17. *Home studies*

Gyan Babu, son of Pandit Vedantavagish, was now our
tutor at home. When he found he could not secure my
attention for the school course, he gave up the attempt
as hopeless and tried a different tack. He took me
through Kalidas' *Birth of the War-God*, translating it to
me as he went along. He also read *Macbeth* to me, first
explaining the text in Bengali and then confining me
to the schoolroom till I had rendered the day's reading
into Bengali verse. In this way he had me translate
the whole play. I was fortunate enough to lose this
translation and so am relieved of the burden of my
karma to that extent.

It was Pandit Ramsarvaswa's duty to oversee our
progress in Sanskrit. He likewise gave up the fruitless
task of teaching grammar to his unwilling pupil, and
read *Sakuntala* with me instead. One day he took it into
his head to show my translation of *Macbeth* to Pandit
Vidyasagar and took me over to his house.

Raj Krishna Mukherji had called at the time and
was seated with him. My heart thumped as I entered the

---

*Nirada* is Sanskrit for cloud. It is a compound of *nira* = water and
*da* = giver. In Bengali it is pronounced 'nirode'

great pundit's study, packed full of books; nor did his austere visage help to revive my courage. Nevertheless, as this was the first time I had had such a distinguished audience, my desire to win renown was strong within me. I returned home, I believe, with some grounds for satisfaction. As for Raj Krishna Babu, he contented himself with admonishing me to be careful to keep the language and metre of the witches' parts different from that of the human characters.

During my boyhood Bengali literature was in meagre supply, and I think I must have finished all the readable and unreadable books then extant. Juvenile literature as such had not evolved – but I am sure that did me no harm. The watery stuff served up to the young is a kind of diluted literary nectar that takes full account of them as children, but none of them as potential adults. Children's books should be such as can partly be understood by them and partly not. In my childhood I read every available book from one end to the other, and both what I understood and what I did not went on working within me. That is how the world itself reacts on a child's consciousness. The child makes his own what he understands, while that which is beyond him takes him on a step.

When Dinabandhu Mitra's satires came out I was not of an age for which they were suitable. A kinswoman of ours was reading a copy, but no entreaties of mine could induce her to lend it to me. She used to keep it under lock and key. Its inaccessibility made me want it all the more, and I decided I must and would read the book.

One afternoon she was playing cards, and her keys, tied to a corner of her sari, hung over her shoulder. I had never paid any attention to cards, in fact I could not stand card games. But my behaviour that day would hardly have borne this out, so engrossed was

I in their play. At last, one side was about to make a
score and in the excitement I seized my opportunity
and hurriedly set about untying the knot which held
the keys. I was not skilful, and so I got caught. The
owner of the sari and of the keys took the fold off her
shoulder with a smile, and laid the keys on her lap as
she went on with the game.

Then I hit on a stratagem. My kinswoman was
fond of *pan*, and I hastened to place some before her.
In due course, she had to rise to get rid of the chewed
*pan*, and, as she did so, her keys fell off her lap and
were replaced over her shoulder. This time they were
stolen, the culprit got away, and the book was read!
Its owner tried to scold me, but the attempt was not
a success, we both laughed so.

Dr Rajendra Lal Mitra used to edit an illustrated
monthly miscellany. My third brother had a bound
annual volume of it in his bookcase. This I managed
to secure, and the delight of reading it through, over
and over again, still comes back to me. Many a holiday
siesta has passed with me stretched out on my bed, that
square volume resting on my chest, reading about the
narwhal or the curiosities of justice as administered
by the Kazis of old, or the romantic story of Krishna-
kumari.

Why do we not have such magazines nowadays?
We have philosophical and scientific articles on the
one hand, and insipid stories, poetry and travels on
the other, but no unpretentious miscellanies which
the ordinary person can read with comfort – such as
*Chambers'* or *Cassell's* or the *Strand* in England – offering
a simple but satisfying fare of the greatest use to the
greatest number.

I came across another little periodical in my young
days called *Abodhabandhu* (The Common Man's Friend).
I found a collection of its monthly numbers in my

eldest brother's library, and devoured them day after
day, seated on the door-sill of his study, facing a bit
of terrace to the south. It was in the pages of this
magazine that I made my first acquaintance with the
poetry of Bihari Lal Chakravarti. His poems appealed
to me the most of all that I read at the time. The artless
flute-strains of his lyrics awoke within me the music of
fields and forest glades.

Into these same pages I have wept many tears over
a pathetic translation of *Paul et Virginie*. That wonderful
sea, the breeze-stirred coconut forests on its shore, and
the slopes beyond lively with the gambols of mountain
goats – what a delightfully refreshing mirage the story
conjured up for me on that terraced roof in Calcutta.
And oh! the romance that blossomed along the forest
paths of that secluded island, between the Bengali
boy-reader and little Virginie with the many-coloured
kerchief round her head!

Then came Bankim's *Bangadarshan* (The Mirror of
Bengal), taking the Bengali heart by storm. It was
bad enough to have to wait till the next monthly
number was out, but to be kept waiting further
till my elders had done with it was simply intolerable! Nowadays anyone who wishes may swallow the
whole of *Chandrashekhar* or *Bishabriksha* at a mouthful.
But the process of longing and anticipating, month
after month, of spreading over wide intervals the
concentrated joy of each short reading, of revolving
every instalment over and over in the mind while
watching and waiting for the next; the combination
of craving with satisfaction, of burning curiosity with
its appeasement: those drawn-out delights, none will
ever taste again.

The compilations from the old poets by Sarada
Mitter and Akshay Sarkar were also of great interest to
me. Our elders were subscribers, but not very regular

readers of these series, so that it was not difficult for me
to get at them. Vidyapati's quaint and corrupt Maithili
language attracted me all the more because of its unin-
telligibility. I tried to make out his sense without the
help of the compiler's notes, jotting down in my own
notebook all the more obscure words with their context
as many times as they occurred. I also noted down whatever grammatical peculiarities I perceived.

## 18. *My home environment*

One great advantage which I enjoyed in my younger
days was the literary and artistic atmosphere which
pervaded our house. I remember how, when I was
quite small, I would lean against the verandah railings
which overlooked the detached building comprising
the reception rooms. These rooms would be lighted
up every evening. Splendid carriages would draw up
under the portico, and visitors would constantly come
and go. What was happening I could not really make
out, but I would keep staring at the rows of lighted
casements from my place in the darkness. My physical
distance from them was not great, but the mental gulf
between them and my childish world was immense.

My elder cousin Ganendra had just had written
a drama by Pandit Tarkaratna, and was having it
staged in the house. His enthusiasm for literature
and the fine arts knew no bounds. It was as if he and
his group were striving to bring about in every area
the renaissance which we see today. A pronounced
nationalism in dress, literature, music, art and drama
had been awakened in him and those around him. He
was a keen student of the history of different countries,
and had begun but could not complete a historical
work in Bengali. He had translated and published

the Sanskrit drama, *Vikramorvasi*, and composed many well-known hymns. He may be said to have given us the lead in writing patriotic poems and songs. This was in the days when the Hindu Mela was an annual institution, and there his song, 'Ashamed am I to sing of India's glories', used to be sung.

I was still a child when cousin Ganendra died in the prime of youth, but for those who once beheld him it is impossible to forget his handsome, tall and stately figure. He exerted an irresistible influence over others. He could draw men around him and keep them bound to him; and while they were in his physical presence, the bond was unbreakable. He was someone – a type peculiar to our country – who by their personal magnetism easily establishes himself in the centre of his family or village. In any other country, when important political, social or commercial groups are formed, such people naturally become national leaders. The capacity to organise a large number of men into a group involves a special kind of genius. In our country such genius runs to waste; a waste as extravagant, it seems to me, as that of plucking a star from the firmament instead of striking a match.

I remember still better his younger brother, my cousin Gunendra. He likewise kept the house filled with his personality. His large, gracious heart embraced relatives, friends, guests and dependants alike. Whether in his broad south verandah, or on the lawn by the fountain, or at the tank-edge on the fishing platform, people gathered around him graced by a presence like benevolence personified. His wide appreciation of art and talent kept him radiant with enthusiasm. New ideas for festivity or frolic, theatricals or other entertainments found a ready patron, and with his help flourished and found fruition.

We were too young then to take any part in

these doings, but the waves of merriment and life to
which they gave rise came and beat at the doors of
our curiosity. I remember how a burlesque composed
by my eldest brother was once being rehearsed in my
cousin's big drawing-room. From our place against the
verandah railings of our house we could hear, through
the open windows opposite, roars of laughter mixed
with the sounds of a comic song, and would also
occasionally catch glimpses of Akshay Mazumdar's
extraordinary antics. We could not gather exactly
what the song was about, but lived in hopes of being
able to find out some time.

I recall how a trifling circumstance earned me the
special regard of cousin Gunendra. I had never won
a prize at school except once for good conduct. Of
the three of us my nephew Satya was the best at his
lessons. Once he did well in some examination and
was awarded a prize. As we came home I jumped off
the carriage to give the great news to my cousin who
was in the garden. 'Satya has got a prize,' I shouted,
as I ran to him.

He drew me to his knees with a smile. 'And
have *you* not got a prize?' he asked.

'No,' said I, 'it's not mine, it's Satya's.' My pleasure
at Satya's success seemed to touch my cousin. He
turned to his friends and remarked on it as a very
creditable trait. I remember how mystified I felt, for
I had not thought of my feeling in that light. This
prize for not getting a prize did me no good. There is
no harm in making gifts to children, but they should
not be rewards. It is not healthy for youngsters to be
made self-conscious.

After the midday meal cousin Gunendra would
attend the estate offices in our part of the house.
The office room of our elders was a sort of club
where laughter and conversation were freely mixed

with matters of business. My cousin would recline on a couch, and I would seize some opportunity of edging up to him.

He usually told me stories from Indian history. I still recall my surprise on hearing how Clive, after establishing British rule in India, went back home and cut his throat: here was new history being made on the one hand and on the other a tragic chapter being hidden away in the darkness of a human heart. How could there be such brilliant success on the outside and such dismal failure within? This weighed heavily on my mind the whole day.

Some days cousin Gunendra would not be allowed to remain in any doubt as to the contents of my pocket. At the least encouragement out would come my manuscript book, unabashed. I need hardly state that my cousin was not a severe critic; in point of fact the opinions he expressed would have done splendidly as advertisements. Nonetheless, when my childishness became too obtrusive, he could not restrain his hearty 'Ha! Ha!'

One day it was a poem on 'Mother India', and as at the end of one line the only rhyme I could think of meant cart, I had to drag in a cart in spite of there not being a vestige of a road by which it could reasonably arrive, rhyme would not hear of any excuses from mere reason. A gale of laughter from cousin Gunendra greeted that cart and blew it back by the same impossible path it had come by, and it has not been heard of since.

My eldest brother was then busy with his master-piece *Swapnaprayan* (Dream Journey), his cushion seat placed in the south verandah, a low desk before him. Cousin Gunendra would come and sit there for a time every morning. His immense capacity for enjoyment helped poetry to bloom like the breezes of spring. My eldest brother would go on alternately writing and reading out what he had written, his boisterous laughter at his own conceits making the verandah tremble. He wrote a great deal more than he finally used in his finished work, so fertile was his inspiration. Like the flowerets that carpet the feet of the mango groves in spring, the rejected pages of his *Dream Journey* lay scattered all over the house. Had anyone preserved them they would have made a basketful of blossoms to adorn today's literature.

Eavesdropping at doors and peeping round corners, we used to get our full share of this feast. My eldest brother was then at the height of his powers and from his pen surged, in wave after untiring wave, a tidal flood of poetic fancy, rhyme and expression, filling and overflowing its banks in an exuberant paean. Did we really understand the *Dream Journey*? But then did we need to understand it absolutely in order to enjoy it? We might not have reached the wealth in the ocean depths – what could we have done with it if we had? – but we revelled in the surf on the shore; and how gaily, at its rise and fall, our life-blood coursed through every vein and artery!

The more I think of that period the more I realise that we no longer have the thing called a *majlis*. In our boyhood we beheld the dying rays of the intimate sociability characteristic of the last generation. Neighbourly feelings were then so strong that the *majlis* was a necessity, and those who could contribute to it were in much demand. Nowadays people call on each other on business, or as a matter of social duty, but not to foregather as a *majlis*. They have not the time, nor are there the same intimate relations! What comings and goings we used to see: how merry were the rooms and verandahs with the hum of conversation and the snatches of laughter! Our predecessors' faculty of becoming the centre of groups and gatherings, of starting and keeping up animated and amusing gossip, has vanished. Men still come and go, but those same rooms and verandahs seem empty and deserted.

In those days everything from furniture to festivity was designed to be enjoyed by the many; whatever pomp or magnificence there might have been did not savour of hauteur. Since then everything has become much grander, but hosts have become unfeeling, and have lost the art of indiscriminate invitation. The indigently clad, or even bare-bodied, no longer have the right to appear without a permit on the strength of their smiling faces alone. Those whom we nowadays seek to imitate in our house-building and furnishing have their own society, with its own wide hospitality. Our predicament, as I see it, is that we have lost what we had, but lack the means of building up afresh on the European standard, with the result that our home life has become joyless. We still meet for business or for politics but never for the pleasure of simply being together, with no purpose in mind than good fellowship – that has vanished. I can imagine few things more ugly than this social miserliness; and, when I look back on those whose ringing laughter coming straight from their hearts used to lighten the burden of our worldly cares, they seem like visitors from some other land.

## 19. *Literary companions*

There came to me in my boyhood a friend whose literary help was invaluable. Akshay Chaudhuri was a school-fellow of my fifth brother. He was an MA in English literature, for which his love was as great as his aptitude. On the other hand, he had an equal fondness for the older Bengali authors and the Vaishnava poets. He knew hundreds of Bengali songs of unknown authorship, on which he would launch, with voice uplifted, regardless of tune, consequence, or the express disapproval of his hearers. Nor could anything, within him or without, prevent his loudly beating time to his own music, rapping the nearest table or book with his nimble fingers in a vigorous tattoo to help to enliven the audience.

He was also someone with an inordinate capacity for extracting enjoyment from all and sundry. He was as ready to absorb every bit of goodness in a thing as he was lavish in singing its praises. As a lightning composer of lyrics and songs of no mean merit he had an extraordinary gift, in which he took no personal pride. He had no concern for the future of the heaps of scattered paper on which his pencil had scrawled. He was as indifferent to his powers as his powers were prolific.

One of his longer poetic pieces was much appreciated when it appeared in the *Bangadarshan*, and I have heard his songs sung by many who knew nothing at all of their composer.

A genuine delight in literature is much rarer than erudition, and it was this unusual faculty in Akshay Babu which awakened my own literary appreciation. He was as liberal in friendship as in literary criticism. Among strangers he was like a fish out of water, but among friends discrepancies in wisdom or age made no difference to him: with us boys he was a boy. When he took his leave from the *majlis* of our elders late in the evening, I would buttonhole him and drag him to our schoolroom. There, seated on our study table, with undiminished geniality he would make himself the life and soul of our little gathering. Many times I have listened to him in rapturous dissertation on some English poem, engaged him in some appreciative discussion, critical enquiry, or heated dispute, or read to him some of my own writings and be rewarded in return with unsparing praise.

My fifth brother Jyotirindra was one of the chief helpers in my literary and emotional training. An enthusiast himself, he loved to evoke enthusiasm in others. He did not allow our difference in age to be any bar. This great boon of freedom which he allowed me, no one else would have dared to give; many even criticised him for it. His companionship made it possible for me to shake off my shrinking sensitiveness. It was as necessary to my soul after its rigorous repression as the monsoon after a fiery summer.

But for such snapping of my shackles I might have become crippled for life. Those in authority are never tired of holding forth the possibility of freedom's abuse as a reason for withholding freedom, but without that risk freedom would not really be free. The only way of learning how to use a thing properly is by misuse. For myself, at least, I can truly say that what little mischief resulted from my freedom always led on to the means of its cure. I have never been able to make my own anything which others tried to compel me to swallow by getting hold of me, physically or mentally, by the ears. Nothing but sorrow has resulted except when I have been left freely to myself.

My brother Jyotirindra unhesitatingly let me loose in the fields of knowledge for better or worse, enabling me to put forth flowers or thorns, as my powers dictated. This experience has made me dread not so much evil itself, as tyrannical attempts to create goodness. Of punitive police, political or moral, I have a wholesome horror. The state of slavery which they induce is the worst form of cancer to which humanity is subject.

My brother would at one time spend days at his piano engrossed in the creation of new tunes. Showers of melody would stream from his fingers, while Akshay Babu and I, seated on either side, would busily fit words to the tunes as they grew in shape to help hold them in our memories. This is how I served my apprenticeship in song composition.

We cultivated music in our family from our early childhood. This had the advantage of allowing me to imbibe it into my whole being without effort. It also had the disadvantage of not giving me that technical mastery which learning step by step alone can produce. Of what may be called musical proficiency, I therefore acquired none.

Ever since my return from the Himalayas I had been getting more and more freedom. The rule of the servants came to an end; the bonds of my school life I deliberately loosened; neither did I give much scope to my home tutors. After taking me through *The Birth of the War-God* and one or two other books in a desultory fashion, Gyan Babu went off to take up a legal career. Then came Braja Babu. The first day he set me *The Vicar of Wakefield* to translate. I found that I did not dislike the book, but when this encouraged him to make more elaborate arrangements for my learning, I made myself scarce.

As I have said, my elders gave me up. Neither I nor they were troubled with any more hopes of my future so I felt free to devote myself to filling my manuscript book. And the writings which appeared in it were no better than might have been expected. My mind contained nothing but hot vapour; and vapour-filled bubbles frothed and eddied around a vortex of lazy fancy, aimless and unmeaning. No forms were evolved, there was only agitated movement: a bubbling up, followed by a bursting back into froth. What little substance was there was not mine, but borrowed from other poets. What belonged to me was the restlessness, the seething tension. When motion has been born, but a balance of forces has yet to be achieved, there is blind chaos indeed.

My sister-in-law was a great lover of literature. She read not to kill time like others, but to fill her whole mind. I was her partner in literary enterprise. She was a devoted admirer of the *Dream Journey*. So was I, the more particularly because, having been brought up in the atmosphere of its creation, its beauties had become intertwined with every fibre of my heart. Fortunately it lay entirely beyond my power of imitation, so the idea never occurred to me.

The *Dream Journey* may be likened to a superb palace of allegory, with innumerable halls, chambers, passages, corners and niches full of statuary and pictures of wonderful design and workmanship; and, in the grounds around, gardens, bowers, fountains and shady nooks in profusion. Not only do poetic thought and fancy abound, but the richness and variety of language and expression are also marvellous. It is not a small thing, this creative power which can bring into being so magnificent a structure complete in all its artistic detail, and that is perhaps why the notion of imitation never occurred to me.

At this time Bihari Lal Chakravarti's series of songs called 'Sarada Mangal' were coming out in the *Arya Darshan*. My sister-in-law was greatly taken with the sweetness of these lyrics. Most of them she knew by heart. She used often to invite the poet to our house, and had embroidered a cushion-seat for him with her own hands. This gave me the opportunity of making friends with him. He developed great affection for me, and I took to dropping in on his house at all times of the day, morning, noon or evening. His heart was as large as his body, and a halo of fancy seemed to surround him like a poetic astral body – which was perhaps his true incarnation. He was full of artistic joy, and whenever I have been with him I have absorbed my share of it. Often I have come upon him in his little room on the third storey, in the heat of noon, sprawling on the cool polished cement floor, writing his poems. Mere boy though I was, his welcome was always so genuine and hearty that I never felt the least awkwardness in approaching him. Then, rapt in his inspiration and forgetful of all surroundings, he would read out his poems or sing his songs to me. Not that he had much of the gift of song in his voice, but he was not altogether tuneless, and one could get a fair idea of the intended melody. When with eyes closed he raised his rich deep voice, his expression made up for what he lacked in execution. I still seem to hear some of his songs as he sang them. I would also sometimes set his words to music and sing them to him.

He was a great admirer of Valmiki and Kalidas. I remember how once after reciting a description of the Himalayas from Kalidas with all the strength in his voice, he said: 'The succession of long "a" sounds here is not an accident. The poet has deliberately repeated this sound all the way from *Devatatma* down to *Nagādhirāja* as an aid to realising the glorious expanse of the Himalayas.'

The height of my ambition at the time was to become a poet like Bihari Babu. I might even have succeeded in working myself up into a belief that I was actually writing like him, but for my sister-in-law, his zealous devotee, who stood in the way. She would keep reminding me of a Sanskrit saying that the unworthy aspirant after poetic fame departs in jeers! Very possibly she knew that if my vanity was once

allowed to get the upper hand it would be difficult
afterwards to bring it under control. So neither my
poetic abilities nor my powers of song readily received
any praise from her; rather she would never let slip an
opportunity of praising somebody else's singing at my
expense, with the result that I gradually became quite
convinced of the defects of my voice. Misgivings about
my poetic powers also assailed me, but, as this was the
only field of activity left in which I had any chance of
retaining my self-respect, I could not allow the judgement of another to deprive me of all hope; moreover,
so insistent was the spur within me that to stop my
poetic adventure was a matter of sheer impossibility.

## 20. *Publication*

My writings so far had been confined to the family
circle. Then the monthly *Gyanankur* (Seeds of Knowledge), started up and, as befitted its name, secured
an embryo poet as one of its contributors. It began
indiscriminately to publish all my ravings, and to this
day a corner in my mind harbours the fear that when
the day of judgement comes, some zealous literary
detective will begin a search in the inmost *zenana*
of lost literature, ignoring the claims of privacy, and
expose these poems to the pitiless public gaze.

My first prose writing also saw the light in the
pages of *Gyanankur*. It was a critical essay, and had a
bit of a history.

A book of poems had been published entitled
*Bhubanmohini Pratibha* (The Genius of Bhubanmohini).
Akshay Babu in *Sadharani* and Bhudeb Babu in the
*Education Gazette* hailed this new poet effusively. A
friend of mine, older than me, whose friendship dates
from this time, would come and show me letters he had

received signed Bhubanmohini. He was one of those captivated by the book, and used frequently to send reverential offerings of books or cloth to the address of the reputed authoress.

Some of these poems were so wanting in restraint, both of thought and language, that I could not bear the idea of their having being written by a woman. The letters made it still less possible to believe that the writer was female. But my doubts did not shake my friend's devotion, and he went on with the worship of his idol.

Then I launched into a critique of the work of this writer. I let myself go, and held forth eruditely on the distinctive features of lyric and other short poems, my great advantage being that printed matter is unblushing; it does not betray the writer's real attainments. My friend turned up in a great passion and hurled at me the threat that a BA was writing a reply. A BA! I was struck dumb – like the time when I was younger and my nephew Satya had shouted for a policeman. I could see my triumphal pillar of argument, erected upon layers of nice distinction, crumbling before my eyes at the merciless assault of authoritative quotations, and the door effectually barred against my ever showing my face to the reading public again. Alas for my critique – under what evil star was it born! I spent day after day in the direst suspense. But, like Satya's policeman, the BA failed to appear.

# 21. *Bhanu Singh*

As I have said I was a keen student of the series of old Vaishnava poems being collected and published by Babus Akshay Sarkar and Sarada Mitter. Their language, well mixed with Maithili, I found difficult to understand, but for that very reason I took all the more pains to get at their meaning. My feeling towards them was the same eager inquisitiveness I felt towards an ungerminated sprout in a seed or the mysteries lying beneath the earth's surface. My enthusiasm was sustained by the hope of bringing to light some unknown poetical gems as I went deeper and deeper into the unexplored darkness of this treasure house.

While I was engaged in this, Akshay Chaudhuri happened to tell me the story of the English boy-poet Chatterton. What his poetry was like I had no idea; neither perhaps had Akshay Babu. Had we known, the story might have lost its charm. But the melodramatic element in it fired my imagination: the idea of Chatterton deceiving so many with his imitation of some ancient poet, followed by the unfortunate youth's taking his own life. Leaving aside suicide, I girded my loins to emulate young Chatterton.

One noon the clouds had gathered thickly. In the depths of this shady siesta I lay prone on the bed in my inner room and on a slate wrote *Gahana kusuma kunja majhe* . . . I was highly pleased with my imitation Maithili poem, and lost no time in reading it out to the first person I encountered. There was not the slightest danger of his understanding a word of it; consequently he could not but gravely nod and say, 'Good, very good indeed!'

Later, I showed the poems to a friend and said: 'A tattered old manuscript has been discovered while rummaging in the Adi Brahmo Samaj library. I've copied some poems from it by an old Vaishnava poet named Bhanu Singh.' Then I read some of my imitation poetry to him. He was profoundly stirred. 'These could not have been written even by Vidyapati or Chandidas!' he rapturously exclaimed. 'I really must have that manuscript so Akshay Babu can publish it.'

After that I showed him my manuscript book and proved conclusively that the poems could not have been written by either Vidyapati or Chandidas because the author happened to be myself. My friend's face fell as he muttered, 'Yes, yes, they're not half bad.'

When these poems of Bhanu Singh later appeared in *Bharati*, Dr Nishikanta Chatterji was in Germany. He wrote a thesis on the lyric poetry of our country comparing it with that of Europe. Bhanu Singh was given a place of honour as one of the old poets, such as no modern writer could have aspired to. This was the thesis on which Nishikanta Chatterji got his PhD!

Whoever Bhanu Singh might have been, had his writings fallen into my hands I swear I would not have been deceived. The language might have passed muster, for the old poets always wrote in an artificial language variously handled by different poets, not in their mother tongue. But there was nothing artificial about their sentiments. Any attempt to test Bhanu Singh's verse by its ring would have revealed base metal. It had none of the ravishing melody of our ancient pipes – only the cheap tinkle of a modern-day English barrel organ.

## 22. *Patriotism*

Looked at from the outside, our family appears to have accepted many foreign customs, but at its heart flames a national pride that has never flickered. The genuine regard my father had for his country he never forsook through all the vicissitudes of his life, and in his descendants it took shape as a strong patriotic feeling. Such, however, was by no means characteristic of the times of which I am writing. Our educated men were then keeping at arms' length both the language and thought of their native land. My elder brothers had, nevertheless, always cultivated Bengali literature. On one occasion when some new connection by marriage wrote my father a letter in English it was promptly returned to the writer.

The Hindu Mela was an annual fair, which had been instituted with the assistance of our family. Babu Naba Gopal Mitra was appointed its manager. It was perhaps the first occasion dedicated to serving all India as our country. My second brother's popular national anthem, 'Bharater Jaya,' was composed for the Mela. The singing of songs glorifying the motherland, the recitation of poems about love of country, the exhibition of indigenous arts and crafts and the encouragement of national talent and skill were the features of this Mela.

On the occasion of Lord Curzon's Delhi *durbar* I wrote an essay, but at the time of Lord Lytton's it was a poem. The British government of those days feared the Russians, it is true, but not the pen of a fifteen-year-old poet. So, although my poem lacked none of the fire appropriate to my age, there were no signs of consternation in the ranks of the authorities from commander-in-chief down to commissioner of police. Nor did any letter to *The Times* allude to apathy among the men on the spot in dealing with such impudence and go on in tones of sorrow more than anger to predict the downfall of the British Empire. I recited the poem under a tree at the Hindu Mela, and one of my hearers was Nabin Sen, the poet. He reminded me of this after I had grown up.

My fifth brother, Jyotirindra, was responsible for a political association of which old Raj Narain Bose was the president. It held its sittings in a tumble-down building in an obscure Calcutta lane. The proceedings were shrouded in mystery. This was its only claim to inspire awe, for there was nothing in our deliberations or doings of which government or people need have been afraid. The rest of our family had no idea where we spent our afternoons. Our front door would be locked, the meeting room in darkness, the watchword a Vedic mantra, our talk in whispers. These alone provided us with enough of a thrill, and we wanted nothing more. Though a mere child, I was also a member. We surrounded ourselves with such an atmosphere of hot air that we seemed constantly to be floating aloft on bubbles of speculation. We showed no bashfulness, diffidence or fear; our main object was to bask in the heat of our own ardour.

Heroism may have its drawbacks, but it has always maintained a deep hold on mankind. The literature of every country keeps alive this reverence. No matter where a man may find himself, he cannot escape the impact of this tradition. We in our association had to be content with responding to it as best we could, by letting our imaginations roam, talking tall and singing fervently.

There can be no doubt that to block all outlets to an urge so deep-seated in man and so prized by him, creates an unnatural condition favourable to degenerate activity. To leave open only avenues to clerical employment in any comprehensive scheme of imperial government is not enough; if no path is left for adventure men will pine for one, and secret passages will be sought, with tortuous pathways and ends unthinkable. I firmly believe that if the government had been suspicious and come down hard on us, then the comedy in the activities of our association's youthful members would have turned into grim tragedy. The play concluded, however; not a brick of Fort William is any the worse and we are now smiling at the memory.

My brother Jyotirindra began to busy himself with a costume for all India, and submitted various designs to the association. The dhoti was not deemed business-like; trousers were too foreign; so he hit upon a compromise which detracted considerably from the dhoti while failing to uplift the trousers. That is to say, the trousers were decorated with the addition of a false dhoti-fold in front and behind. The even more fearsome thing that resulted from the combination of turban and Sola topee even our most enthusiastic member would not have had the temerity to call an ornament. No person of ordinary courage could have dared to wear it, but my brother unflinchingly wore the complete outfit in broad daylight, passing through the house of an afternoon to the carriage waiting outside, indifferent alike to the stare of relation or friend, door-keeper or coachman. There may be many a brave Indian ready to die for his country, but there are few, I am certain, who even for the good of the nation will walk the streets in such pan-Indian garb.

Every Sunday my brother would get up a shikar party. Many of those who joined it, uninvited, we did not even know. There was a carpenter, a smith and others from all ranks of society. Bloodshed was the only thing lacking – at least I cannot recall any. Its other perquisites were so abundant and satisfying that we felt the absence of dead or wounded game to be a trifling omission. As we were out from early morning, my sister-in-law furnished us with a plentiful supply of *luchis* with appropriate accompaniments. Since our bag did not depend upon the fortunes of the chase we never had to return empty-bellied.

The neighbourhood of Maniktola has no lack of villa-gardens. We would turn into the bottom of any one of these, settle ourselves on the bathing platform of a tank and fling ourselves on the *luchis* in earnest. All that was left were the vessels used to carry them.

Braja Babu was one of the most enthusiastic of these blood-thirstless shikaris. He was the superintendent of the Metropolitan Institution and had also been our private tutor for a time. One day he had the happy idea of accosting the *mali* in charge of the garden into which we had trespassed with 'Hallo, has uncle been here lately?'

The *mali* lost no time in saluting respectfully before replying: 'No, sir, the master hasn't been lately.'

'All right, get us some green coconuts off the trees.' We had a fine drink after our *luchis* that day.

A small-time zamindar was among our party. He owned a villa by the riverside. One day we had a picnic there together, in defiance of caste rules. In the afternoon there was a tremendous storm. We stood on the steps leading into the water and shouted out songs. I cannot truthfully claim that all seven notes of the scale could be distinguished in Raj Narain Babu's singing, but he certainly sang as lustily as he could; and, as in the old Sanskrit works where the text is drowned by the notes, so the vigour of his limbs and features made up for his vocal performance. His head swung from side to side while marking time and the storm played havoc with his beard. It was late when we turned our hackney carriage homewards. The storm clouds had dispersed and the stars were twinkling. The darkness had become intense, the atmosphere silent, the village roads deserted, and the thickets on either side filled with fireflies like a carnival of sparks scattered by some ghostly revellers.

One of the objects of our association was to encourage the manufacture of lucifer matches and similar small industries. Each member had to contribute a tenth of his income for this purpose. Matches were wanted, but matchwood was hard to get; for though everyone knows about *Kangra* sticks and how fiercely a bundle is supposed to be wielded by an irate housewife, they inflame only bare backs and not lamp wicks. After many experiments we succeeded in making a boxful of matches. The patriotic fire that went into them was not their only value: the money we spent on them might have kept the family hearth burning for a year. Another little defect was that our matches would not burn unless there was a light handy to encourage them. If they could only have absorbed some of the patriotic spirit which conceived them, they might have been marketable even today.

News reached us of some young student who was trying to make a power-loom. Off we went to see it. None of us had any knowledge by which to judge the loom's practicality; but our capacity for believing and hoping was inferior to none. The poor fellow had got into debt over the cost of his machine, which we repaid for him. One day we found Braja Babu coming over to our house with a flimsy *gamcha* tied round his head. 'Made on our loom!' he shouted as he threw up his hands and executed a war-dance. Even then Braja Babu had grey hairs!

At last some worldly-wise people came and joined our society, made us bite the fruit of knowledge, and broke up our little paradise.

When I first knew Raj Narain Babu, I was not old enough to appreciate his many-sidedness. He combined many opposites. In spite of his hoary hair and beard he was as young as the youngest of us, his venerable exterior being simply a white mantle that kept his youth perpetually fresh. Even his extensive learning had been unable to do him any harm. He was absolutely transparent. To the end of his life his hearty laughter suffered no check, whether from the gravitas of age, ill-health, domestic affliction, profound introspection, or diversity of knowledge, all of which were his in ample measure. He had been a favourite pupil of Richardson, brought up in an atmosphere of English learning; but he had flung aside all obstacles created by his early habit and given himself up lovingly and devotedly to Bengali literature. The meekest of men, his inner fire flamed at its fiercest in his patriotism, as though to burn the shortcomings and destitution of his country to ashes. The memory of this saintly person – sweetly smiling, ever-youthful and unwearied by sickness or grief – is something worth cherishing by our countrymen.

## 23. Bharati

The period of which I am writing was one of ecstatic excitement for me as a whole. Many nights did I spend sleeplessly, not for any reason but from mere caprice, a desire to do the reverse of the obvious. I would stay up reading all alone in the dim light of our schoolroom; the distant church clock would chime the quarters as if each passing hour was being put up to auction; and now and then the bearers of the dead, passing along the Chitpur Road on their way to the Nimtollah cremation ground, would utter loud cries of '*Haribol!*' Throughout moonlit nights in summer I would sometimes wander like an unquiet spirit among the patches of light and shadow made by the tubs and pots on the garden of the roof-terrace.

Those who are inclined to dismiss this as sheer poetising are wrong. The earth itself, in spite of its age, occasionally surprises us still by shifting from sober stability. In the days of its youth, when it had

not become congealed and crusty, it was ebulliently
volcanic and indulged in many wild escapades. The
same is true of a young man. So long as the materials
which go to make him have yet to acquire their final
shape they are apt to be turbulent.

This was the time when my brother Jyotirindra
decided to start *Bharati* with my eldest brother as
editor, giving fresh food for our enthusiasm. I was then
just sixteen, but I was not left off the editorial staff.
A short time before, with all the insolence of youthful
vanity, had I written a criticism of *Meghnadbadh*. As
acidity is characteristic of the unripe mango so abuse
is of the immature critic. When other powers are
lacking, the power to prick seems to become sharpest.
Thus had I sought to achieve immortality by leaving
my scratches on that immortal epic. This impudent
criticism was my first contribution to *Bharati*.

I also published a long poem called 'Kabikahini'
(The Poet's Story) in the first volume. It was a product
of that age at which a writer has seen practically
nothing of the world except an inflated image of his
own nebulous self. Its hero was naturally a poet, but
not the writer as he really was, rather as he thought
he ought to be seen. Not that he desired to *be* what
he appeared, just that he wanted the world to nod
admiringly and say: 'Yes, here indeed is a poet – just
the thing to be.' The story made a great parade of universal love, pet subject of budding poets, which sounds
as important as it is easy to talk about. While truth is
yet to dawn upon one's mind, and others' words are
one's only stock-in-trade, simplicity and restraint in
expression are not possible. Instead, in the endeavour
to magnify that which is already big, a grotesque and
ridiculous exhibition becomes inevitable.

As I blush to read these effusions of my boyhood I
am struck with the fear that in my later writings too

the same distortion, wrought by straining after effect, may likely lurk in a less obvious form. The loudness of my voice often drowns the thing I would say, I cannot doubt; and some day or other Time will find me out.

The 'Kabikahini' was the first work of mine to appear in book form. When I went with my second brother to Ahmedabad, an enthusiastic friend took me by surprise by printing and publishing it and sending me a copy. I cannot imagine this was a good idea, but the feeling it aroused in me at the time was not that of indignation. He got his come-uppance not from the author but from the public who hold the purse-strings. I have heard that a dead weight of these books lay heavy for many a day on the shelves of booksellers and the mind of the luckless publisher.

Writings done at the age I began to contribute to *Bharati* cannot possibly be fit for publication. There is no better way of ensuring repentance in maturity than to rush into print in youth. But it has one redeeming feature: the irresistible impulse to see one's writings in print exhausts itself early. Who are one's readers, what do they say, what printer's errors have remained uncorrected? These and like worries run their course as infantile maladies and leave one leisure in later life to attend to one's literary work in a healthier frame of mind.

Bengali literature is not old enough to have developed the internal checks which can serve to control its votaries. As he gains in experience, the Bengali writer has to evolve a restraining force from within himself. It is impossible for him to avoid creating a great deal of rubbish over a considerable length of time. His ambition to work wonders with the modest gifts at his disposal is bound to obsess him in the beginning, and spur him to transcend his natural powers at every step, and the bounds of truth and beauty therewith; this is always visible in early writings. To recover one's normal self, to learn to respect one's powers as they are, takes time.

That said, I have left much youthful folly to be ashamed of, besmirching the pages of *Bharati*; and this shames me not for its literary defects alone but for its atrocious cheek, its extravagance and its high-sounding artificiality. At the same time I recognise in the writings of that period a pervasive enthusiasm which I cannot discount. If error was natural, so was boyish hope, faith and joy. And if error was necessary for fuelling the flame, it has now been reduced to ashes leaving the good work done by the flame, which did not burn in vain.

## 24. *Ahmedabad*

When *Bharati* entered its second year, my second brother proposed to take me to England. My father gave his consent, and so, rather to my surprise, this further unasked favour of providence became a reality.

As a first step I accompanied my brother to Ahmedabad where he was posted as judge. My sister-in-law with her children was then in England, so the house was practically empty.

The judge's house is known as Shahibagh and was a palace of the Badshahs of old. At the foot of the wall supporting a broad terrace flowed the thin summer stream of the Sabarmati river along one edge of its ample bed of sand. When my brother used to go off to his court, I would be left all alone in the vast expanse of the palace, with only the cooing of the pigeons to break the midday lull. An unaccountable curiosity would keep me wandering about the empty rooms.

Into niches in the wall of a large chamber my brother had put his books. One of these was a gorgeous edition of Tennyson's works, with big print and numerous pictures. That book, for me, was as silent as the palace, and, in much the same way I wandered among its coloured plates. I could make nothing of the text, but it nevertheless spoke to me in inarticulate cooings rather than words. In my brother's library I also found a book of collected Sanskrit poems edited by Dr Haberlin and printed at the old Serampore press. This too was beyond my understanding, but the sonorous Sanskrit words, and the march of the metre, kept me tramping among the 'Amaru Shataka' poems to the deep beat of their drum.

The upper room of the palace tower was my hermit cell, a nest of wasps my only companions. In unrelieved darkness I slept there alone. Sometimes a wasp or two dropped off the nest on to my bed; if I happened to roll on one, the encounter was displeasing to the wasp and distressing to me.

To pace back and forth across the extensive terrace overlooking the river on a moonlit night was one of my whims. It was while doing so that I first composed tunes for my songs. The song addressed to the rose-maiden was one of these, and it still finds a place in my published works.

Realising how imperfect was my knowledge of English I set to work reading English books with the help of a dictionary. From my earliest years my habit has been not to let any lack of complete comprehension obstruct the flow of reading, but to feel quite satisfied with the structure my imagination rears upon the bits that I do understand. I am reaping both the good and bad effects of this habit even today.

## 25. *England*

After six months in Ahmedabad we started for England. In an unlucky moment I began to write letters about my journey to my relatives and to *Bharati*. Now it is beyond my power to call them back. They were nothing but the outcome of youthful bravado. At that age the mind refuses to admit that its greatest cause for pride is in its power to understand, to accept, to respect; and that modesty is the best means of enlarging its domain. To admire and praise becomes a sign of weakness or surrender, and the desire to cry down and hurt and demolish with argument gives rise to a kind of intellectual fireworks. These attempts of mine to establish my superiority by revilement might have amused me today, had not their want of straightforwardness and common courtesy been too painful.

From my earliest years I had had practically no commerce with the outside world. To be plunged in this state, aged seventeen, into the midst of the social sea of England must have justified considerable doubt as to whether I would stay afloat. But as my sister-in-law happened to be in Brighton with her children I was able to weather the first shock under her shelter.

Winter was approaching. One evening as we chatted round the fireside, the children came running with the exciting news that it was snowing. We went out at once. The air was bitingly cold, the sky was bright with moonlight, the earth white with snow. This was not the face of Nature familiar to me, but something quite other – like a dream. Everything near seemed to have receded far off, leaving behind a still white ascetic in deep meditation. Such a sudden revelation of immense beauty on merely stepping through a door had never before happened to me.

My days passed merrily under the affectionate care of my sister-in-law and in boisterous romping with the children. They were greatly tickled by my curious English pronunciation; I failed to see the fun of this, though I joined wholeheartedly in the rest of their games. How could I explain to them that there was no logical means of distinguishing between the sound of 'a' in warm and 'o' in worm? I was forced to bear the brunt of ridicule more properly the due of the vagaries of English spelling.

I became quite adept at inventing new ways to keep the children occupied and amused. This art has stood me in good stead ever since, but I no longer feel in myself the same unlimited profusion of spontaneous invention. This was the first opportunity I had to give my heart to children, and it had all the freshness and overflowing exuberance of such a first gift.

However, I had not made this journey in order to exchange a home beyond the seas for the one on this side. The idea was that I should study law and come back a barrister. So one day I was put into a school in Brighton. The first thing the headmaster said after scanning my features was: 'What a splendid head you have!' This detail lingers in my memory because of the way that she in Bengal had enthusiastically taken it upon herself to keep my vanity in check, and impressed on me that, generally speaking, my cranium and features, compared with those of many another, were barely of average standard. I hope the reader will not fail to give me credit for implicitly believing her and inwardly deploring the parsimony of my Creator. On many other occasions, finding myself differently estimated by my English acquaintances from what she had accustomed me to, I began seriously to worry about the divergence in standards of taste between the two countries!

One thing in the Brighton school seemed truly

wonderful: the other boys were not at all rude to me. On the contrary they would often thrust oranges and apples into my pockets and run away. I can only ascribe this uncommon behaviour to my being a foreigner.

I was not long in the school – but that was not its fault. Mr Tarak Palit was then in England. He could see that this was not the way for me to get on, and prevailed upon my brother to let him take me to London, and leave me there in a lodging-house. The lodgings he selected faced Regent's Park – in the depths of winter. Not a leaf was to be seen on the row of trees out front whose scraggy snow-covered branches stood staring at the sky: the sight chilled my very bones.

For the newly arrived stranger there can hardly be a more cruel place than London in winter. I knew no one nearby, nor could I find my way about. Days in which I sat alone at a window, gazing at the outside world, returned to my life. But the new view was not attractive. There was a frown on its countenance; the sky was turbid, lacking lustre like a dead man's eye; everything seemed turned in upon itself, shunned by the rest of the world. The room was scantily furnished, but there happened to be a harmonium which I used to play according to my fancy after the daylight came to its untimely end. Sometimes Indians would come to see me and, though my acquaintance with them was but slight, when they rose to leave I wanted to hold them back by their coat-tails.

While I lived in these rooms a man came to teach me Latin. His gaunt figure with worn-out clothing seemed no better able to withstand the winter's grip than the naked trees. I do not know what his age was, but he clearly looked older than his years. Some days, in the course of our lessons, he would suddenly be at a loss for a word, and look vacant and ashamed. His family thought him a crank. He had become possessed of a theory. He believed that in each age one dominant idea is manifested in every human society in all parts of the world; and though it may take different shapes under different degrees of civilisation, it is at bottom one and the same; nor does such an idea pass from one society to another by contact, for it holds even where no intercourse exists. This man's great preoccupation was the gathering and recording of facts to prove his theory. And while so engaged his home lacked food, his body clothes. His daughters had little respect for his theory, and were probably upbraiding him constantly for his infatuation. On occasion one could see from his face that he had lighted upon some new proof, and that his thesis had advanced correspondingly. Then I would broach the subject, and become enthusiastic for his enthusiasm. Other days he would be immersed in gloom, as if his burden was too heavy to bear. Then our lessons would stop at every step, his eyes would wander away into empty space, and his mind refuse to be dragged into the pages of the *First Latin Grammar*. I felt keenly for his poor starved body and theory-burdened soul, and though I was under no delusion as to his capacity to assist me in learning Latin, I could not make up my mind to get rid of him. Our pretence of learning Latin lasted as long as I was at these lodgings. On the eve of my departure, when I offered to settle his dues he said piteously: 'I have done nothing, and only wasted your time. I cannot accept any payment from you.' With great difficulty I at last got him to take his fees.

Though my Latin tutor never ventured to trouble me with proofs of his theory, I still do not disbelieve it. I am convinced that men's minds are connected through some deep-lying continuous medium, and that a disturbance in one part is secretly communicated by it to other parts.

Mr Palit next placed me in the house of a coach named Barker. He lodged and prepared students for examinations. His mild little wife apart, not a thing about this household had beauty. One can understand how such tutors manage to attract pupils, for these unfortunate creatures do not often get the chance to make a choice. But it is painful to think of the conditions under which such men get wives. Mrs Barker had attempted to console herself with a pet dog, and so when Barker wanted to punish his wife he tortured the dog. Her dependence on this animal therefore made only for an extension of her own vulnerability.

From these surroundings I was only too glad to escape when my sister-in-law sent for me from Torquay in Devonshire. I cannot express how happy I was among the hills there, by the sea, in the flower-covered meadows, under the shade of the pine woods, and with my two restlessly playful little companions. Nevertheless I was sometimes tormented with doubts as to why, when my eyes were so surfeited with beauty, my mind so saturated with joy, and my leisurely days stretched to a limitless horizon of unalloyed happiness, poetry should refuse to call me. So one day I went forth along the rocky shore, armed with manuscript book and umbrella, to fulfil my poet's destiny. The spot I selected was of undoubted beauty, independent of my rhyme or fancy. A slab of rock hung over the waters as if perpetually eager to reach them; the sun slept smiling in the liquid blue below, rocked by the lullaby of the foam-flecked waves; behind, a fringe of pines spread its shadow like a garment slipped off by some languorous wood-nymph. Enthroned on my stony seat I wrote a poem, 'Magnatari' (The Sunken Boat). I might have believed it was good today, had I taken the precaution of drowning it then. But such consolation is not open to me, for the poem happens to exist and, though banished from my published works, a writ might yet cause it to be produced.

The call of duty was insistent, however. I returned to London. This time I found a refuge in the house of a Dr Scott. On a fine evening I invaded his home with bag and baggage. Only the white-haired doctor, his wife and their eldest daughter were there. The two younger girls, alarmed at the incursion of a strange Indian, had gone off to stay with a relative. I think they came back only after they received word that I was harmless.

In a very short time I became like one of the family. Mrs Scott treated me as a son, and the heartfelt kindness of her daughters was something rare even from one's own relations.

One thing struck me when living in this family: human nature is everywhere the same. We are fond of saying, and I also then believed, that the devotion of an Indian wife to her husband is something unique, not to be found in Europe. But I at least was unable to discern any difference between Mrs Scott and an ideal Indian wife. She was entirely wrapped up in her husband. With their modest means there was no fussing about by too many servants; Mrs Scott herself attended to every detail of her husband's wants. Before he came home from work in the evening, she would arrange his armchair and woollen slippers before the fire. She never allowed herself for a moment to forget the things he liked, or the behaviour which pleased him. She would go over the house every morning with their only maid from attic to kitchen, and the brass rods on the stairs and the door knobs and fittings would be scrubbed and polished till they shone again. Over and above this domestic routine there were the many calls of social duty. After getting through her daily tasks she would join in our evening readings and music with zest; to add gaiety to the leisure hour being part of the duties of a good housewife.

Some evenings I and the girls took part in a table-turning seance. We would place our fingers on a small tea-table, and it would go capering about the room. Things reached the point where whatever we touched began to quake and quiver. Mrs Scott did not quite like all this. Sometimes she would gravely shake her head and say she had her doubts about its rightness. But she bore it bravely, not liking to put a damper on youthful spirits: until one day we put our hands on Dr Scott's chimney-pot hat to make it turn, and that was too much for her. She rushed up in a great state and forbade us to touch it. She could not bear the idea of Satan even momentarily having anything to do with her husband's headgear.

In all her actions her reverence for her husband was the one thing that stood out. The memory of her sweet self-abnegation makes it clear to me that the ultimate expression of all womanly love is to be found in reverence; that where no extraneous cause hampers its true development woman's love grows naturally into worship. Where the trappings of luxury are plentiful, and frivolity tarnishes both day and night, this love is degraded, and woman's nature does not get a chance of perfect expression.

I spent some months in this house. Then it was time for my brother to return home, and my father wrote to me to accompany him. The prospect delighted me. The light of my country, and its sky, had been silently calling me. When I said goodbye Mrs Scott took me by the hand and wept. 'Why did you come to us,' she said, 'if you must go so soon?'

That household in London no longer exists. Some of the doctor's family have departed to the other world, others have scattered to places unknown. But it lives still inside my head.

One winter's day, as I passed down a street in Tunbridge Wells, I saw a man standing by the roadside. His bare toes showed through his gaping boots, his chest was partly bare. He said nothing to me, perhaps because begging was forbidden, but he looked up at my face just for a moment. The coin I gave him was perhaps more valuable than he expected, for after I had gone on a bit, he came after me, said, 'Sir, you have given me a gold piece by mistake,' and offered to return it. I might not have particularly remembered this, but for a similar thing which happened another time. When I first reached Torquay railway station a porter took my luggage to the cab outside. After searching my purse for small change in vain, I gave him half-a-crown as the cab started. Soon he came running after us, shouting at the cabman to stop. I imagined that finding me to be such an innocent he had hit upon an excuse to demand more. As the cab stopped he said: 'You must have mistaken half-a-crown for a penny, sir!'

I do not say I have never been cheated in England, but not in any way which it would be fair to hold in remembrance. What grew chiefly upon me, rather, was the conviction that only those who are trustworthy know how to trust. I was an unknown foreigner, and could easily have evaded payment with impunity – yet no London shopkeeper ever mistrusted me.

During the whole of my English stay I was mixed up in a farce I had to play out from start to finish. I happened to get acquainted with the widow of some high Anglo-Indian official. She was good enough to call me by the pet name Ruby. An Indian friend of hers had composed in English a doleful poem in memory of her husband. I need say nothing of its merit as poetry

or of its felicity of diction. The composer, as ill-luck
would have it, had indicated that the dirge was to
be chanted in the raga Behag. One day the widow
entreated me to sing it to her thus. Silly innocent
that I was, I weakly acceded. Unfortunately no one
present but I could realise the atrocious combination
made by those absurd verses and the raga Behag. The
widow seemed intensely touched to hear the Indian's
lament for her husband sung to its native melody. I
thought the matter would end there, but this was not
to be.

I met the widowed lady frequently at different
social gatherings, and after dinner when we joined
the ladies in the drawing-room, she would ask me
to sing that Behag. Everyone clearly anticipated some
extraordinary specimen of native music and added
their entreaties to hers. From her pocket would
emerge printed copies of the fateful composition,
and my ears would begin to redden and tingle. At
last, with head bowed and quavering voice I would
have to make a stab at it – while only too keenly
conscious that no one but me in the room would
find the performance heartrending. Afterwards, amidst
much suppressed tittering, would come a chorus of
'Thank you very much!' 'How interesting!' And in spite
of its being winter I would perspire all over. Who
would have predicted at my birth or at his death
what a severe blow the demise of this estimable Anglo-
Indian would be to me!

Then, for a time, while I was living with Dr
Scott and attending lectures at University College,
I lost touch with the widow. She was in the suburbs
some way out of town, though I frequently got letters
from her inviting me there. But my dread of the
dirge kept me from accepting. At length I received
a pressing telegram. It reached me when I was on

my way to college. My stay in England was about to come to a close. I thought: I ought to see the widow once more before I leave, and so I yielded to her importunity.

Instead of coming home from college I went straight to the railway station. It was a horrible day, bitterly cold, snowing and foggy. My destination was the terminus of the line. So I felt quite easy in my mind and did not think it worthwhile to enquire about the time of arrival.

The station platforms were all coming on the right-hand side. I had ensconced myself in a right-hand corner seat reading a book. Outside it was already so dark that nothing was visible. One by one the other passengers got off. We reached and then left the station just before the last one. Then the train stopped again, but there was nobody to be seen, neither lights nor platform. A mere passenger has no means of divining why trains sometimes stop at the wrong times and places, so I decided to go on with my reading. The train began to move backwards. There seems to be no accounting for the eccentricity of railways, I thought, as I returned to my book. But when we came right back to the previous station, I could remain indifferent no longer. 'When are we getting to ―― ?' I enquired.

'You are just coming from there,' was the reply.

'Where are we going now, then?' I asked, thoroughly flustered.

'To London.' And then it dawned on me that this was a shuttle. On enquiring about the next train to ―― I was told there were no more trains that night. And in reply to my next question I gathered there was no inn for five miles.

I had left home after breakfast at ten in the morning, and had eaten nothing since. When abstinence is the only choice, an ascetic frame of mind comes easily. I buttoned my thick overcoat up to the neck and, seating myself under a platform lamp, went on reading. The book I had with me was Spencer's *Data of Ethics*, then recently published. I consoled myself with the thought that I might never again get such an opportunity to concentrate so single-mindedly on such a subject.

After a short time a porter came and informed me that a special was running and would be ready in half an hour. I felt so cheered by the news that I closed the *Data of Ethics*. Where I had been due at seven I at length arrived at nine. 'What is this, Ruby?' asked my hostess. 'Whatever have you been doing with yourself?' I was unable to take much pride in the account I gave her of my adventures. Dinner was over; nevertheless, as my misfortune was hardly my fault, I did not expect condign punishment, especially from a woman. But all that the widow of the high Anglo-Indian official said was: 'Come along, Ruby, have a cup of tea.'

I was never a tea-drinker, but in the hope that it might partially allay my aching hunger I managed to swallow a cup of strong decoction with a couple of dry biscuits. When I finally reached the drawing-room I· found a gathering of elderly ladies, and among them one pretty young American who was engaged to a nephew of my hostess and seemed busy going through the usual premarital love rites.

'Let us have some dancing,' said my hostess. I was in neither the mood nor condition for it. But it is the meek who achieve the seemingly impossible on this earth, and soon, although the dance was primarily for the benefit of the engaged couple, I found myself dancing with ladies of advanced years, with only tea and biscuits between myself and starvation.

But my sorrows did not end there. 'Where are you putting up for the night?' asked my hostess.

This was a question for which I was not prepared. I stared at her, speechless, while she explained that since the local inn closed at midnight I had better betake myself thither without further ado. Hospitality was not entirely wanting, however, for a servant showed me the way to the inn with a lantern. At first I thought it might prove a blessing in disguise, and at once made enquiries for food: flesh, fish or vegetable, hot or cold, anything! I was told I could have drinks aplenty, but nothing to eat. When I then looked to slumber to forget my cares, there seemed to be no solace even in her world-embracing lap. My bedroom had a sandstone floor and was icy cold; an old bedstead and worn-out washstand were its only furniture.

In the morning the widow sent for me to breakfast. I found a cold repast spread out, evidently the remnants of last night's dinner. A small portion of this, lukewarm or cold, offered to me the previous night could not have hurt anyone, and might have made my dancing less like the agonised wrigglings of a landed carp.

After breakfast my hostess informed me that the lady for whose delectation I had been invited to sing was ill in bed, and that I must serenade her from the bedroom door. I was made to stand on the landing of the staircase. Pointing to a closed door, the widow said: 'That's where she is.' And I gave voice to that Behag dirge while facing the mysterious unknown on the other side. Of the consequent fate of the invalid I have heard nothing.

When I reached London I had to expiate in bed the results of my fatuous complaisance. Dr Scott's girls implored me, on my conscience, not to take this as a sample of English hospitality: it was surely the effect of India's salt.

## 26. *Loken Palit*

While I was attending lectures on English literature at University College, Loken Palit was my class-fellow. He was about four years younger than I. At the age I am writing these reminiscences a difference of four years is insignificant. But the gulf between seventeen and thirteen is difficult for friendship to bridge. Lacking weight in years, the older boy is always anxious to maintain the dignity of seniority. But this did not create any barrier in my mind in the case of Loken, for I could not regard him in any way as my junior.

Boy and girl students sat together in the college library for study. This was the place for our *tête-à-tête*. Had we been fairly quiet about it none need have complained, but my young friend was surcharged with high spirits that would burst forth as laughter at the least provocation. In all countries girls have a perverse degree of application to their studies, and I feel repentant as I recall the multitude of reproachful blue eyes which vainly showered disapproval on our merriment. I had not the slightest sympathy then with the distress of disturbed studiousness. By the grace of providence I have never had a headache in my life nor a moment of compunction on account of interrupted school studies.

With our laughter as an almost unbroken accompaniment we managed also to have some literary discussion, and though Loken's reading of Bengali literature was less extensive than mine, he made up with keenness of intellect. Among the subjects we discussed was Bengali orthography.

The way it arose was this. One of the Scott girls wanted me to teach her Bengali. As I took her through the alphabet I expressed my pride that Bengali spelling has a conscience, and does not delight in overstepping rules at every turn. I made clear to her how laughable the waywardness of English spelling would have been but for the tragic compulsion to cram it for examinations. But my pride took a fall. It became apparent that Bengali spelling was quite as impatient of bondage; force of habit had blinded me to its transgressions. I began to search for laws that regulated its lawlessness. I was quite surprised at the wonderful assistance Loken was able to offer.

After he had entered the Indian Civil Service and returned home, the work which had begun in University College library in rippling merriment flowed on in a widening stream. Loken's boisterous delight in literature was like the wind in the sails of my literary adventure. In the peak of youth I was driving my prose and poetry like a tandem at a furious rate, and Loken's unstinted appreciation kept my energies from flagging for a moment. Many an extraordinary flight of imagination began in his bungalow in the remote *mofussil*. On many occasions our literary and musical gatherings assembled under the evening star's auspices, finally to disperse beneath the morning star like lamps in the breezes of dawn.

Of the many kinds of lotus flowers that decorate the goddess Saraswati's feet the lotus of friendship must be her favourite. I have not been so lucky as to enjoy much of its golden pollen, but I cannot complain of any dearth of the aroma of good-fellowship.

## 27. *'The Broken Heart'*

While in England I began another poem, which I went on with during my journey home and finished after my return. This was published under the name of 'Bhagna Hriday' (The Broken Heart). At the time

I thought it very good. Nothing strange in that, you may think, but it did not fail to attract appreciation from readers too. I remember how, after it came out, the chief minister of the late Raja of Tripura called on me solely to deliver the message that the Raja admired the poem and entertained high hopes of the writer's future literary career.

Let me set down here what I wrote about this poem of my eighteenth year in a letter when I was thirty:

> When I began to write 'Bhagna Hriday' I was eighteen – neither in my childhood nor in my youth. This border-land age is not illumined by the direct rays of Truth; they are scattered here and there, and the rest is in shadow. And its imaginings are drawn-out and vague like twilight shades, making the real world seem like a world of fantasy. The curious part of all this is not that I was eighteen, but that everyone around me seemed to be eighteen also; we all flitted about in the same baseless, substanceless world of dream, where even the most intense joys and sorrows seemed insubstantial. There being nothing real against which to weigh them, the trivial did duty for the great.

This period of my life, from fifteen or sixteen to twenty-two or twenty-three, was one of utter disarray.

In the early life of the earth, before land and water had distinctly separated, giant malformed amphibians moved about the treeless jungles that flourished in the primeval ooze. The swirling passions of the immature mind are similar; twilit, misshapen and overblown, they haunt the trackless, nameless wilderness of the mind. They do not know what they are, nor why they wander, and, because they do not, they are inclined towards grotesque mimicry. For me it was an age of unmeaning activity when my undeveloped powers, unaware of and unequal to their real goals, jostled each other for an outlet, each seeking to assert superiority through hyperbole.

When milk-teeth try to push their way through, they work an infant into a fever. The agitation has no apparent justification until the teeth are out and have begun assisting the ingestion of food. Our early passions torment the mind in the same way, like maladies, until they realise their true relationship with the world.

The lessons I learned from my experiences at this time are to be found in every moral textbook, but are not therefore to be despised. Whatever confines our urges inside us, and checks their free access to the outside, poisons our life. Selfishness, for instance, refuses to give free play to our desires and so prevents them from working themselves through; that is why its close associate is always festering untruth. When our desires have a chance to be released in the form of worthwhile work the aberration is dispelled and a more natural condition asserts itself. That is the true state of human nature, and the joy of being human.

The immature condition of my mind that I have just described was fostered by the example and precept of the time, and I am not sure that the effects of these are not still lingering. Glancing back at that earlier period, I feel that English literature offered more stimulant than nourishment. Our literary gods were Shakespeare, Milton and Byron and the quality in their work which stirred us most was strength of passion. In English social life passionate outbursts are kept severely in check; for which very reason, perhaps, they so dominate English literature. Its characteristic is the suppression of vehement feelings to a point of inevitable explosion. At least this was what we in Bengal came to regard as the quintessence of English literature.

In the impetuous declamation of English poetry by Akshay Chaudhuri, who initiated us into English literature, there was the wildness of intoxication. The frenzy of Romeo's and Juliet's love, the fury of King Lear's impotent lamentation, the all-consuming fire of Othello's jealousy – these roused our admiration. Our restricted social life with its narrow field of activity was hedged in by such monotony that tempestuous feelings found no entrance; all was as calm and as quiet as could be. So our hearts naturally craved the life-bringing shock of emotion in English literature. This was not an aesthetic pleasure, but the jubilant welcome of a turbulent wave, even though it might bring to the surface the slime of the stagnant bottom.

In Europe, at the time when the repression of the human heart finally provoked the reaction known as the Renaissance, Shakespeare's plays were the equivalent of war-dances. The consideration of good and evil, beauty and ugliness was not their main concern. Man was consumed instead with an anxiety to break through all barriers to the inmost sanctuary of his being, there to discover an ultimate image of his own most violent desire. That is why we find such harshness, exuberance and wantonness in Shakespeare.

This spirit of bacchanalian revelry found a way into our demurely well-behaved social world, woke us up, and made us lively. Our hearts, smothered by ritual, pined for a chance to live, and we were dazzled by the unfettered vista revealed to us.

Something comparable happened in English literature when the slow measure of Pope's common time gave place to the dance rhythm of the French Revolution. Byron was its poet. His impetuosity pierced the veil that kept our hearts in virginal seclusion.

Thus did the pursuit of English literature sway the youth of our time, including me; a surf of excitement kept beating at me from every side. This first awakening was a time of quickening, not repression.

And yet our case was so different from that of Europe. There, excitability and impatience with shackles was a reflection of history in literature. It was an authentic exposure of feeling. The roaring of the storm was heard because a real storm was raging. But by the time it reached our world, it was little more than a gentle breeze. It failed to satisfy our minds, and our attempts to make it imitate the blast of a hurricane led us easily into sentimentality, a tendency that still persists and may not prove easy to cure.

The trouble is, English literature is a literature in which the reticence of true art is yet to appear. Passion is only one of the ingredients of literature and not its sum – which lies finally in simplicity and restraint. English literature does not fully admit this proposition.

Our minds are being moulded from infancy to old age by English literature alone. But other literatures of Europe, both classical and modern, which show the development of systematic self-control, are not subjects of our study and so, it seems to me, we are still unable to arrive at a correct perception of the true aim and method of literary work.

Akshay Babu, who made the passion in English literature came alive for us, was himself a votary of the emotional life. To comprehend truth seemed less significant to him than to feel it in his heart. He had no intellectual respect for religion, but songs of Shyama (the dark Mother) would bring tears to his eyes. He felt no call to search for ultimate reality; whatever moved his heart served him for the time being as the truth – even obvious coarseness not proving a deterrent.

Atheism was the dominant note of the English prose writings then in vogue – Bentham, Mill and Comte being favourite authors. Theirs was the reasoning in terms of which our youths argued. The age of Mill constitutes a natural epoch in English history. It represents a healthy reaction of the body politic: these destructive forces having been brought in, temporarily, to get rid of accumulated thought-rubbish. Our country adopted their letter, but not their spirit; we never sought to make practical use of them, employing them instead only as a stimulant to incite ourselves to moral revolt. For us atheism was mere intoxication.

For these reasons educated men fell mainly into two classes. One class would always thrust itself forward with unprovoked argument to cut all belief in God to pieces. Like the hunter whose hands itch to kill a living creature as soon as he spies it on a tree, these people, whenever they learn of a harmless belief lurking in fancied security, feel stirred to sally forth and demolish it. We had a tutor for a short time for whom this was a pet diversion. I was only a boy, but I could not escape his onslaughts. His attainments were not of any account, neither were his opinions the result of any enthusiastic search for truth, being gathered mostly from others' lips. But though I fought him with all my strength, I was no match and I suffered many a bitter defeat. Sometimes I felt so mortified I wanted almost to cry.

The second class consisted not of believers but religious epicureans, who found comfort and solace in gathering together and steeping themselves in pleasing sights, sounds and scents galore, under the garb of religious ceremonial; they luxuriated in the paraphernalia of worship. In neither of these classes were doubt or denial the outcome of the travail of their quest.

Though such religious aberrations pained me, I do not say I was entirely uninfluenced by them. With the intellectual impudence of youth I revolted. The religious services held in our family I would have nothing to do with, because I did not accept them. I busied myself in fanning a flame with the bellows of my emotions. This was only fire worship, the giving of oblations to increase the flame – with no other aim. And because my efforts had no purpose in mind they had no limit, always reaching beyond any prescription.

In religion and in my emotional life I felt no need for any underlying truth; excitement was everything. It brings to mind some lines by a poet of that time:

> My heart is mine
> I have sold it to none,
> Be it tattered and torn and worn away,
> My heart is mine.

In truth the heart need not worry itself so, for nothing compels it to wear itself to tatters. Sorrow is not truly to be coveted, but taken in isolation from life sorrow's poignancy may appear pleasurable. Our poets have often made much of this, forgetting the god they intended to worship. This is a childishness our country has not yet rid itself of. So today we often fail to see the truth of religion and indulge instead in aesthetic gratification. Equally, much of our patriotism is not genuine service of the motherland, but simply emotional gratification.

## 28. *European music*

When I was in Brighton I once went to hear some *prima donna*. I forget her name. It may have been Madame Nilsson or Madame Albani. Never before had I heard such extraordinary command over the voice. Even our best singers cannot hide their sense of effort; nor are they ashamed to bring out, as best they can, top notes or bass notes beyond their proper register. The receptive portion of our audience have nothing against keeping the performance up to standard by dint of their own imagination. For the same reason they do not mind any harshness of voice or uncouthness of gesture in the exponent of a perfectly formed melody; on the contrary, they seem sometimes to believe that such minor external defects serve better to set off the internal perfection of the raga – like the outward poverty of the great ascetic Mahadeva, whose divinity shines forth naked.

This feeling seems entirely lacking in Europe. There, outward embellishment must be perfect in every detail, and the least defect stands shamed and unable to face the public gaze. In our musical gatherings no one minds if half an hour is spent in tuning up the *tanpuras*, or hammering into tone the drums, small and big. In Europe such duties are performed in advance, behind the scenes, for what appears out front must be faultless. There is no allowance for any weak spot in the singer's voice. In our country a correct and artistic exposition of the melody is the main object, all effort is concentrated upon it. In Europe the voice is the object of culture, and with it they perform impossibilities. Our connoisseurs are content if they hear the song; in Europe, they go to hear the singer.

That is what I saw in Brighton. It was as good as a circus. I admired the performance, but I could not appreciate the song. I could hardly keep from laughing when some of the *cadenzas* imitated the warbling of birds. I felt all the time that it was a misapplication of the human voice. When the turn came of a male singer I was considerably relieved. I especially liked the tenor voices, which had more flesh and blood in them, and seemed less like the disembodied laments of forlorn spirits.

After this, as I went on hearing and learning more and more of European music, I began to get into the spirit of it; but still I am convinced that our music and theirs abide in altogether different apartments, and do not gain access to the heart by the same door.

European music seems to be intertwined with the material life of Europe, so that the text of its songs may be as various as life itself. If we attempt to put our tunes to the same variety of uses they tend to lose their significance, and become ludicrous; for our melodies are meant to transcend everyday life and carry us deep into Pity, high into Aloofness: to reveal the core of our being, impenetrable and ineffable, where the devotee may find his ashram, or even the epicurean his paradise, but where there is no room for the busy man of the world.

I cannot claim that I felt the soul of European music but what little of it I came to understand from the outside attracted me greatly in one way. It seemed so romantic. To analyse what I mean by that word is somewhat difficult. What I have in mind is the diversity, the superfluity of waves on the sea of life, of the ceaseless play of light and shade over their undulations. There is the opposite aspect – of infinite extension, of the unwinking blue of the sky, of the silent hint of immeasurability in the distant circle of the horizon. Notwithstanding, let me repeat, lest I am not perfectly clear, that whenever I have been moved by European music I have said to myself: it is romantic, it translates into melody the evanescence of life.

Not that we wholly lack the same aim in some forms of our music, but it is less pronounced, less accomplished. Our melodies give voice to the stars that spangle the night, to the reddening sky of early dawn. They speak of the pervasive sorrow which lowers in the blackness of storm-clouds; the dumb intoxication of the forest-roaming spring.

## 29. Valmiki Pratibha

We had a profusely decorated volume of Moore's *Irish Melodies*. I often listened to their enraptured recitation by Akshay Babu. The poems combined with the pictorial designs conjured up a dream of Old Ireland. I had not then heard the original tunes, but had sung these Irish melodies to myself to the accompaniment of the harps in the pictures. I longed to hear the real tunes, to learn them, and sing them to Akshay Babu. Some such longings are unfortunately fulfilled, and die in the process. When I went to England I heard some of the Irish melodies and learnt them too, and that put an end to my keenness to learn more. They were simple, mournful and sweet, but they somehow did not fit the silent melody of the harp which filled the halls of the Ireland of my dreams.

When I came back home I sang the Irish melodies I had learnt to my family. 'What is the matter with Rabi's voice?' they exclaimed. 'How funny and foreign it sounds!' They even felt I spoke differently.

From this mixed cultivation of foreign and native melody was born *Valmiki Pratibha* (The Genius of Valmiki). The tunes in this musical drama are mostly

Indian, but they have been dragged out of their classic
dignity; that which soared in the sky has been taught
to run on the earth. Those who have seen and heard it
performed will, I trust, bear witness that the harness-
ing of Indian melodic modes in the service of the drama
has proved neither demeaning nor futile. This conjunction is the only special feature of *Valmiki Pratibha*.
The pleasing task of loosening the chains on melodic
forms and making them adaptable to a variety of treatment completely engrossed me.

Several of the songs of *Valmiki Pratibha* were set to
tunes originally severely classical in mode; some of
the tunes were composed by my brother Jyotirindra;
a few were adapted from European sources. The *telena*
style of Indian modes specially lends itself to dramatic
purposes, and has been frequently utilised in this work.
Two English tunes served for the drinking-songs of the
robber band, and an Irish melody for the lament of the
wood-nymphs.

*Valmiki Pratibha* is not a composition which will
bear being read. Its significance is lost if it is not
sung and acted. It is not what Europeans call an
opera, but a small drama set to music. That is
to say, it is not primarily a musical composition.
Very few of the songs are important or attractive in
themselves; they serve merely as the musical text of
the play.

Before I went to England we occasionally had
gatherings of literary men in our house, at which
music, recitations and light refreshments were served
up. After my return one more such gathering was
held, which happened to be the last. It was for this
that *Valmiki Pratibha* was composed. I played Valmiki
and my niece, Pratibha, took the part of Saraswati
– a bit of history that is recorded in the drama's
name.

I had read in some work by Herbert Spencer that speech takes on tuneful inflexions whenever emotion comes into play. It is a fact that the tone or tune is as important to us as the spoken word for the expression of anger, sorrow, joy and wonder. Spencer's idea that, through a development of these emotional modulations of voice, man found music, appealed to me. Why should I not try to act a drama in a kind of recitative based on this idea? The *kathakas* of our country attempt this to some extent, for they frequently break into a chant which, however, stops short of full melodic form. As blank verse is more elastic than rhymed, so such chanting, though not devoid of rhythm, can more freely adapt itself to the emotional interpretation of the text because it does not attempt to conform to the more rigorous canons of tune and time required by a regular melodic composition. The expression of feeling being the object, these deficiencies in form do not jar on the hearer.

Encouraged by the success of this new line in *Valmiki Pratibha*, I composed another musical play of the same class. It was called *Kal Mrigaya* (The Fateful Hunt). The plot was based on the story in the *Ramayana* of the accidental killing of a blind hermit's only son by King Dasharatha. It was played on a stage erected on our roof-terrace, and the audience seemed profoundly moved by its pathos. Afterwards, with slight changes, much of it was incorporated in *Valmiki Pratibha*, and the play ceased to be separately published in my works.

Much later, I composed a third musical play, *Mayar Khela* (The Play of *Maya*), an operetta of a different type. In this the songs were important, not the drama. In the other two a series of dramatic situations were threaded with a melody; here a garland of songs was threaded on the slimmest of plots. The play of feeling, and not action, was its main feature. While composing it I was indeed saturated with the mood of song.

The vigour which went into the making of *Valmiki Pratibha* and *Kal Mrigaya* I have never felt for any other work of mine. In these two works the musical ferment of the time found expression.

My brother Jyotirindra was engaged the livelong day at his piano, refashioning the classic melodic forms at his pleasure. And, at every turn of his instrument, the old modes took on unthought-of shapes and expressed new shades of feeling. The melodic forms which had become habituated to their pristine stately gait, when compelled to march to more lively unconventional measures, displayed an unexpected agility and power, and moved us correspondingly. We could plainly hear the tunes speak to us, while Akshay Babu and I sat on either side fitting words to them as they grew out of my brother's nimble fingers. I do not claim that our libretto was good poetry, but it served as a vehicle for the tunes.

In riotous revolutionary joy were these two musical plays composed. They danced merrily to every measure, whether or not technically correct, indifferent as to whether the tunes were indigenous or foreign.

The Bengali reading public has on many an occasion been grievously exercised over some opinion or literary form of mine, but it is curious to find that the daring with which I played havoc among accepted musical notions did not arouse any resentment; on the contrary, those who came to listen departed pleased. A few of Akshay Babu's compositions found place in *Valmiki Pratibha*, along with adaptations of Bihari Chakravarti's 'Sarada Mangal' series of songs.

I used to take the leading part in the performance

of these musical dramas. From my early years I had a
taste for acting, and firmly believed that I had a special
aptitude for it. I think I proved that my belief was not
ill-founded. My earliest role was the part of Alik Babu
in a farce written by my brother Jyotirindra. I was then
very young, and nothing seemed to fatigue or trouble
my voice.

In our house, at that time, a cascade of musical
emotion was gushing forth day after day, hour after
hour, its spray scattering into our being the whole
gamut of colours. With the freshness of youth and
energy, impelled by new-born curiosity, we struck
out on paths in every direction. We felt we would
try to test everything, and no achievement seemed
impossible. We wrote, we sang, we acted, we poured
ourselves out on every side. This was how I stepped
into my twentieth year.

Of the forces which pushed our lives along so
triumphantly, my brother Jyotirindra was the charioteer. He was absolutely fearless. Once, when I was
a mere lad and had never ridden a horse before, he
made me mount one and gallop by his side. At the
same age when we were at Shelidah (the headquarters
of our estate) and news was brought of a tiger, he took
me with him on a hunting expedition. I had no gun
– if I had it would have been more dangerous to me
than to the tiger. We left our shoes at the edge of
the jungle and crept in on bare feet. At last we
scrambled up into a bamboo thicket, partly stripped
of its thorn-like twigs, where I somehow managed to
crouch behind my brother till the deed was done, with
no means of administering even a shoe-beating to the
unmannerly brute had he dared to lay an offending
paw on me!

Thus my brother gave me full freedom, inside
and out, in the face of all dangers. No custom or

convention restrained him, and so he was able to rid
me of my shrinking diffidence.

## 30.  Evening Songs

In the state of self-absorption of which I have been
telling, I wrote a number of poems which have been
grouped together, under the title of *Hriday Aranya* (The
Heart-Wilderness) in Mohit Babu's edition of my
works. In one of the poems subsequently published
in a volume called *Prabhat Sangit* (Morning Songs), the
following lines occur:

There is a vast wilderness whose name is Heart;
Whose interlacing forest branches dandle and rock darkness
   like an infant.
I lost my way in its depths.

From which came the name for this group of poems.

   Much of what I wrote, when my life had no
commerce with the outside, when I was engrossed
in the contemplation of my own heart, when my
imaginings wandered in many a disguise amidst
causeless emotions and aimless longings, has been
left out of that edition; only a few of the poems
originally published in the volume entitled *Sandhya
Sangit* (Evening Songs) are republished there, in the
section entitled 'The Heart-Wilderness'.

   My brother Jyotirindra and his wife had left home
travelling on a long journey, and their rooms on the
third storey, facing the terraced roof, were empty. I
took possession of these and the terrace, and spent my
days in solitude. While left in communion with myself
I do not know how I slipped out of the poetical groove
into which I had fallen. Perhaps because I was cut off

from those whom I sought to please and whose taste in
poetry moulded the form I tried to give my thoughts,
I freed myself naturally.

I began to use a slate for my writing. That helped
in my emancipation. The manuscript books in which
I had been indulging now bothered me. To make an
entry in them seemed to demand a supply of poetic
fancy commensurate with that of poets of renown.
But to write on slate was clearly a matter of the
mood of the moment. 'Fear not,' it seemed to say.
'Write just what you please, one rub will wipe all
away!'

I wrote a poem or two, thus unfettered, and
felt a real joy well up within me. 'At last,' said
my heart, 'what I write is my own!' No one should
mistake this feeling for pride. It was pride I had felt
in my former productions, that being all the tribute I
had to pay them. I refuse to call the sudden onset of
self-confidence the same as the gratification of vanity.
The joy of parents in their first-born is not due to
pride in its appearance, but because it is their very
own. If the child happens to be extraordinary they
may also take pride in that – but that is another
thing.

In the first flood-tide of that joy I paid no heed
to the bounds of metrical form; just as a stream does
not flow straight but winds as it lists, so did my verse.
Before, I would have held this to be a crime, but now
I felt no compunction. Freedom first breaks laws; then
it makes laws that bring it under true self-rule.

The only listener to these erratic productions of
mine was Akshay Babu. When he heard them for the
first time he was as surprised as he was pleased, and
with his approbation my path to freedom broadened.

The poems of Bihari Chakravarti were in a three-
beat metre. Unlike the square-cut multiple of two

this produces a globular effect. It rolls on easily, gliding as it dances to the tinkling of its anklets. I was once very fond of this metre. It felt more like riding a bicycle than walking. And to its stride I became accustomed. In the *Evening Songs*, without thinking of it, I somehow broke this habit. Neither did I fall under any other spell. I felt entirely free and unconcerned. I had no thought or fear of being taken to task.

The strength I gained by working freed from the trammels of tradition led me to discover that I had been searching in impossible places for something which was actually within myself. Nothing but want of self-confidence had stood in the way of my coming into my own. I felt as if I had risen from a nightmare to find myself unshackled. I cut extraordinary capers just to make sure I was free to move.

To me this is the most memorable period of my poetic career. *Evening Songs* may not have been worth much as poems, in fact they are fairly crude. Neither their metre, nor their language, nor their thought had taken definite shape. But for the first time I had written what I really meant, exactly as I felt. Even if the compositions have no lasting value, that pleasure certainly had.

## 31. *An essay on music*

I had been proposing to study for the bar when my father had recalled me home from England. Some friends, concerned at this curtailment of my career, pressed him to send me off again. This led to my starting on a second voyage towards England, this time with a relative as my companion. My fate, however, had so strongly vetoed my being called to the bar that this time I was not even to reach England.

We disembarked at Madras and returned home to Calcutta. The reason was by no means as grave as the decision, but as the laugh was not against *me*, I refrain from setting it down here. Thus both my attempted pilgrimages to the shrine of Lakshmi, goddess of wealth, were scotched. I hope that the law-god, at least, will look on me with a favourable eye for not adding to the encumbrances on the bar-library premises.

My father was then in the Mussoorie hills. I went to him in fear and trembling. He showed no sign of irritation, but rather seemed pleased. He must have seen in my return the blessing of divine providence.

The evening before I started on this voyage I read a paper at the Medical College Hall on the invitation of the Bethune Society. This was my first public reading. The Reverend K. M. Banerji was the president. The subject was music. Leaving aside instrumental music, I tried to argue that the chief aim of vocal music was to bring out better what the words sought to express. The text of my paper was meagre; instead I sang and acted songs throughout, illustrating my theme. The only reason for the flattering eulogy which the president bestowed on me at the end must have been the moving effect of my young voice, together with the earnestness and variety of its efforts. Today I must confess that the opinion I once voiced with such enthusiasm is wrong.

Vocal music has its own special features. When it happens to involve words the latter must not presume too much on the melody of which they are but the vehicle or seek to supersede it. If a song is great in itself, why should it wait upon words? It begins where mere words fail. Its power lies in the region of the ineffable; it tells us what the words cannot.

So the less a song is burdened with words the better. In the classic style of Hindustan the words are of no account, and leave the melody to make its appeal in its own way. Vocal music achieves perfection when the melodic form is allowed to develop freely, and carry our consciousness with it to its own wonderful plane. In Bengal, the words have always asserted themselves so much that our songs have failed to develop their full musical capabilities and have remained content to be handmaidens of poetry. From the old Vaishnava songs down to the songs of Nidhu Babu, the Bengali song has displayed her charms only in the background. She should follow the example of wives in our country who formally obey their husbands but actually rule them; music, while professedly in attendance on words, should in fact dominate them.

I have often felt this while composing my songs. As I hummed to myself and wrote the lines:

> Do not keep your secret to yourself, my love,
> But whisper it gently to me, only to me.

I found that the words by themselves had no means of reaching the region into which they were borne away by the tune. The tune told me that the secret, which I was so importunate to hear, had mingled with the green mystery of the forest glades, was steeped in the silent whiteness of moonlight nights, was peeping out from behind the veil of illimitable blue at the horizon – and is the most intimate of all the secrets of earth, sky and waters.

In my early boyhood I heard a snatch of a song:

> Who dressed you, love, as a foreigner?

This one line painted such wonderful pictures in my mind that it haunts me still. One day I sat down to set to words a composition of my own while full of this fragment of song. Humming my tune I wrote to its accompaniment:

> I know you, O Woman from the strange land!
> Your dwelling is across the Sea.

Had the melody not been there I do not know what shape the rest of the poem might have taken, but as it was it revealed to me the stranger in all her loveliness. It is she, said my soul, who comes and goes, a messenger to this world from the other shore of the ocean of mystery. It is she, of whom we now and then catch glimpses in the dewy autumn mornings, in the scented nights of spring, in the inmost recesses of our hearts – and whose song we sometimes strain skywards to hear. To the door of this charming stranger the melody wafted me, and to her were the rest of my words addressed.

Long after this, in a street in Bolpur, a mendicant Baul was singing as he walked along:

> How does the unknown bird flit in and out of the cage!
> Ah, could I but catch it, I'd ring its feet with my love!

I found this Baul to be saying the very same thing as my song. The unknown bird sometimes settles within the cage and whispers tidings of the infinite world beyond the bars. The heart eagerly desires to hold on to the bird for ever, but cannot. What else but melody can capture for us the comings and goings of the unknown bird?

That is why I am always reluctant to publish

the words of my songs, for the soul will inevitably
be lacking.

## 32. *The riverside*

When I returned home from the outset of my second
voyage to England, my brother Jyotirindra and sister-
in-law were living in a riverside villa at Chandannagar
and there I went to stay with them.

The Ganges again! Again those indescribable days
and nights, languid with joy, piquant with yearning,
attuned to the babbling of the river beneath the shade
of its wooded banks. This Bengal sky full of light, this
south breeze, this flow of the river, this right royal
laziness stretching from horizon to horizon and from
the green earth to the blue sky were all as food and
drink to the hungry and thirsty. Indeed the place was
like home, and these natural ministrations like that of
a mother.

I am not speaking of very long ago, and yet time
has wrought many changes. Our little riverside nests,
sheltering in greenery, have been replaced by dragon-
like mills which everywhere rear their hissing heads,
belching forth black smoke. In the midday glare of
modern life even our hours of mental siesta have been
narrowed down to the lowest limit, and hydra-headed
unrest has invaded every department of life. Maybe
this is for the better, but I, for one, cannot account
it wholly to the good.

These riverside days of mine passed by like con-
secrated lotus blossoms floating in the sacred stream.
Some rainy afternoons I spent in a veritable frenzy,
singing old Vaishnava songs to my own tunes, accompanying myself on a harmonium. Other afternoons we
would drift along in a boat, my brother Jyotirindra

accompanying my singing on his violin. Beginning with raga Puravi, we went on varying our ragas with the declining day, and saw, on reaching raga Behag, that the western sky had pulled down the shutters on its storehouse of golden playthings, and the moon had risen in the east.

Then we would row back to the landing-steps of the villa and seat ourselves on a quilt spread on the terrace facing the river. A silvery peace by then rested on both land and water: hardly any boats were about, the fringe of trees on the bank was in deep shadow, and moonlight glimmered over the smooth flowing current.

The villa we lived in was known as Moran's Garden. A flight of stone-flagged steps led up from the water to a long, broad verandah which formed part of the house. The rooms were not regularly arranged, nor all on the same level, and some had to be reached by short flights of stairs. The big sitting-room overlooking the landing-steps had stained-glass windows with coloured pictures.

One of the pictures was of a swing hanging from a branch half hidden in dense foliage, and in the check- ered light and shade of this bower two persons were swinging; and there was another of a broad flight of steps leading into some castle-like palace, up and down which men and women in festive garb were coming and going. When light fell on the windows, these pictures shone wonderfully, putting me in a carefree mood. Some far-away, long-gone revelry seemed to coruscate silently in the light, and to animate the surrounding woods with some of the thrill of the couple swinging alone in the shadows of that unknown story.

The topmost room of the house was in a round tower with windows opening on every side. This was my poetry-writing room. Nothing could be seen from it save the tops of the trees, and the open sky. I was then busy with the *Evening Songs*, and of this room I wrote:

> Here, wherein the lap of limitless space clouds lie down
>    to sleep,
> I have built my house for thee, O Poesy!

## 33. *More about* Evening Songs

My reputation amongst literary critics at this time was that of a poet of broken cadence and lisping utterance. Everything about my work was dubbed misty, shadowy. However little I might have relished the charge, it was not wholly unfounded. My poetry did lack the backbone of worldly reality. How, amid the ringed-around seclusion of my early years, was I to get the necessary material?

But one thing I refuse to admit. Behind this charge of vagueness was the insinuation that it was a deliberate affectation. The fortunate possessor of good eyesight is apt to sneer at the youth with glasses, as if he wears them for ornament. While it may be permissible to reflect upon the poor fellow's infirmity, it is too bad to charge him with pretending not to see.

The nebula is a phase in creation, not something wholly outside the universe. To reject all poetry which has not attained definition would not bring us any closer to truth in literature. Any phase of man's nature that has found true expression is worth preserving – it may be cast aside only if it is not expressed truly. There is a period in a man's life when his feelings have the pathos of the inexpressible, the anguish of vagueness. His poetry cannot be called baseless – at worst it may be worthless, but it is not necessarily even that. Sin lies not in expressing a thing, but in failing to express it.

There is a duality in man. Of the inner person, beneath the outward flow of thoughts, feelings and events, little is known or heed taken; for all that, he cannot be ignored in living one's life. When the inner life fails to harmonise with the outer, this inner dweller is hurt, and his pain manifests itself outwardly in a manner to which it is difficult to give a name, or even describe; it is a cry more akin to an inarticulate wail than to words of precise meaning.

The pathos which sought expression in *Evening Songs* had its roots in my depths. Just as one's consciousness smothered in sleep wrestles with a nightmare in its efforts to awake, so the submerged inner self struggles to free itself from complexities and emerge into the open. These *Songs* are the story of that struggle. In poetry, as in all creation, there is opposition of forces. If the divergence is too wide, or the unison too close, there is no opportunity for poetry. Where discord strives to attain and resolve itself into harmony, then words pour forth as poetry, like breath through a flute.

When *Evening Songs* first saw the light they were not announced by any flourish of trumpets, but nonetheless they did not lack admirers. I have told elsewhere the story of how when Bankim Babu arrived at the wedding of Mr Ramesh Chandra Dutt's eldest daughter, the host welcomed him with the customary garland of flowers. As I came up Bankim Babu eagerly took the garland, placed it round my neck and said: 'The wreath to him, Ramesh; have you not read *Evening Songs*?' And when Mr Dutt avowed he had not yet done so, the manner in which Bankim Babu spoke of some of them was ample reward.

*Evening Songs* gained me a friend whose approval, like the rays of the sun, stimulated and trained the shoots of my newly sprouted efforts. This was Babu Priyanath Sen. Just before this 'The Broken Heart' had led him to give up all hopes for me. I won him back with these *Evening Songs*. Those who are acquainted with him know him as an expert navigator of all seven seas of literature, whose highways and byways he is constantly traversing in almost all languages, Indian and foreign. To converse with him is to gain glimpses of the most out-of-the-way scenery in the world of ideas. This experience proved of the greatest value to me.

He was able to give his literary opinions with full confidence, for he did not rely on his unaided taste to guide his likes and dislikes. His authoritative criticism assisted me more than I can tell. I used to read him everything I wrote, and, but for his timely showers of discriminating appreciation my early ploughings and sowings might not have yielded what they did.

## 34. Morning Songs

At the riverside I also did a little prose writing, not on any definite subject or plan, but in the way that boys catch butterflies. When spring comes within the mind, many-coloured short-lived fancies are born and flit about. Ordinarily they are unnoticed: it was probably mere whim of mine to collect those which came to me then. Or perhaps my emancipated self threw out its chest and decided to write just as it pleased. What I wrote was unimportant; the fact of writing was what mattered. These prose pieces were later published under the name *Bibidha Prabandha* (Divers Essays), but they received no further lease of life in a second edition.

At this time, I think, I began my first novel, *Bouthakuranir Hat* (The Young Queen's Market).

After we had stayed for a time by the river my brother Jyotirindra took a house in Calcutta, on Sudder Street near the Museum. I remained with him. While I was writing the novel and *Evening Songs* here, a momentous revolution took place within me.

I was pacing the terrace of our Jorasanko house late in the afternoon. The afterglow of sunset combined with the wanness of twilight lent the approaching evening an unearthly wonder. Even the walls of the adjoining house grew beautiful. Could this lifting of the cover of triviality from the everyday world be some trick of the light? Never!

I could see at once that the evening had entered me; its shades had obliterated my *self*. While the self was rampant during the glare of day, everything was mingled with and hidden by it. Now that the self was in the background, I could see the world in its true aspect. That aspect has nothing trivial in it, but is full of beauty and joy.

Since this experience I have repeatedly tried the effect of suppressing my self deliberately and viewing the world as a mere spectator, and have invariably been rewarded with a sense of special pleasure. I remember I tried too to explain to a relative how to see the world in its true colours, and the lightening of one's sense of burden that follows such vision, without success I think.

Then I gained a further insight – one which has lasted all my life.

The end of Sudder Street, and the trees on the Free School grounds opposite, were visible from our Sudder Street house. One morning I happened to be standing on the verandah looking that way. The sun was just rising through the leafy tops of the trees. As

I gazed, all of a sudden a lid seemed to fall from my eyes, and I found the world bathed in a wonderful radiance, with waves of beauty and joy swelling on every side. The radiance pierced the folds of sadness and despondency which had accumulated over my heart, and flooded it with universal light.

That very day the poem 'Nirjharer Swapnabhanga' (The Awakening of the Waterfall), gushed forth and coursed on like a cascade. The poem ended, but the curtain did not fall upon my joy. No person or thing in the world seemed trivial or unpleasing to me – not even, to my astonishment, the person who dropped in the next day or the day after.

He was a curious fellow who came to me now and then and asked all manner of silly questions. One day it was: 'Sir, have you seen God with your own eyes?' And on my having to admit that I had not, he averred that he had.

'What was it you saw?' I asked.

'He seethed and throbbed before my eyes!' was the reply.

Ordinarily one would not relish being drawn into the discussions of such a person. Moreover, at the time I was entirely absorbed in my writing. Still, as he was a harmless sort of fellow, I did not like to hurt his susceptibilities and so tolerated him as best I could.

This time when he came I actually felt glad to see him, and welcomed him cordially. His mantle of oddity and foolishness had slipped off, and the person I hailed was the real man whom I felt to be in no wise inferior to myself and, furthermore, in close relationship with me. Finding in myself no trace of annoyance at the sight of him, nor any sense of my time being wasted, I was filled with an immense gladness and felt rid of some enveloping tissue of untruth which had been causing me needless discomfort and pain.

As I stood on the balcony, the movements, figures and features of each one of the passers-by, whoever they were, seemed extraordinarily wonderful as they flowed past – ripples on the ocean of the universe. From infancy I had been seeing only with my eyes, now I began to see with the whole of my consciousness. I caught sight of two smiling youths, walking nonchalantly, the arm of one on the other's shoulder, and I could not see it as of small moment; for in it I sensed the fathomless depths of the eternal well of joy, from which numberless sprays of laughter fly and scatter throughout the world.

I had never before marked the play of limbs and lineaments which accompanies even the least of man's actions; now I was spellbound by their variety on all sides, at every moment. Yet I saw them not as independent, separate, but as parts of the amazingly beautiful dance that always underlies the world of men, permeating every home and every multifarious human want and activity.

Friend laughs with friend, mother fondles child, cow sidles up to cow and licks its body – the immeasurability of these acts struck me with a shock that savoured almost of pain.

When I wrote of this period:

I know not how my heart flung open its doors of a sudden,
And let the crowd of worlds rush in, greeting each other –

it was no poetic exaggeration. Rather, I lacked the power to express all I felt.

For some time I remained in this state of self-forgetful bliss. Then my brother thought of going to the Darjeeling hills. So much the better, I thought. On the vast Himalayan tops I shall be able to look more deeply into what has been revealed to me in Sudder Street; at any rate I shall see how the Himalayas display themselves to my new gift of vision.

But victory lay in that little house in Sudder Street. After ascending the mountains, when I looked around, I was at once aware I had lost my new vision. My mistake must have been to imagine that still more truth could come from the outside. However sky-piercing the king of mountains may be, there was nothing for me in his gift; while He who is the Giver can vouchsafe a vision of the eternal in the dingiest of lanes, and in an instant of time.

I wandered about amongst the firs, I sat near the falls and bathed in their waters, I gazed at Kanchenjunga's grandeur against a cloudless sky, but there in what had seemed to me the likeliest of places I found *it* not. I had come to know it, but could no longer see it. While I was admiring the gem the lid had suddenly closed, leaving me staring at the casket. But, for all the high quality of its workmanship, there was now no danger of my mistaking it merely for an empty box.

*Morning Songs* came to an end, their last notes dying out with 'Pratidhani' (The Echo) which I wrote at Darjeeling. This proved such an abstruse affair apparently that two friends laid a wager as to its real meaning. My only consolation was that, as I was equally unable to explain the enigma to them when they came to me for a solution, neither had to lose any money over it. Alas, the days when I wrote thoroughly direct poems about 'The Lotus' or 'A Lake' had gone for ever.

But does one write poetry to explain something? It is a feeling within the heart that tries to find outside shape in a poem. When, after listening to a

poem, someone says he has not understood it, I am
nonplussed. If he were to smell a flower and say the
same thing, the reply would be, 'There is nothing to
understand, it is only a scent.' If he persisted, saying,
'*That* I know, but what does it all *mean*?' then one either
has to change the subject, or make it more abstruse by
telling him that the scent is the form taken by universal
joy in this particular flower.

That words have meanings is just the difficulty.
That is why poets have to turn and twist them in metre
and rhyme, so that meaning may be held somewhat in
check and feeling allowed to express itself.

The utterance of feeling does not involve the
statement of some fundamental truth or a scientific
fact or a useful moral precept. Like a tear or a smile,
a poem is only a picture of what is taking place within.
If science or philosophy gain anything from it they are
welcome, but that is not why it was written. If you catch
a fish from a ferry-boat you are a lucky man, but it does
not make the ferry-boat a fishing-boat; neither should
you abuse the ferryman if he does not make fishing his
business.

'The Echo' is a poem I wrote so long ago that I
am now no longer called upon to render an account
of its meaning. Nevertheless, whatever its other merits
or defects, I shall assure my readers it was not my
intention in it to propound a riddle, or cleverly to
impart some esoteric message. The fact of the matter
was that a longing had been born within my heart, and
I, unable to find any other name, had called the thing
I desired an Echo.

When from the *fons et origo* of the universe streams
of melody issue forth, their echo is reflected from
the faces of those we love and the other lovely
things around us into our hearts. What we love
must be this echo, as I say, and not the things

from which it happens to be reflected, for what we one day hardly deign to glance at may, on another day, be the very thing that claims our whole devotion.

I had viewed the world with external vision for so long I had been unable to see its universal aspect, its joy. When a ray of light suddenly found its way out from some innermost depth of my being, it spread everywhere and illuminated all things, which no longer appeared as discrete objects and events but were disclosed to my vision as a whole.

The stream which flows from the infinite towards the finite is Truth and Good; and it is subject to laws and definite in form. Its echo is Beauty and Joy, the very intangibility of which makes us beside ourselves. This is what I tried to say in 'The Echo' by way of a parable or song. That the result was not clear is not to be wondered at, for neither was the attempt clear to the attempter.

Let me set down here part of what I wrote in a letter at a more advanced age, about *Morning Songs*:

Nothing in the world truly exists, except my heart is a state of mind typical of a certain age. When the heart is first awakened it puts out its arms and tries to grasp the whole world, like a baby with new teeth which thinks everything is meant for its mouth. Gradually it comes to understand what it really desires and what it does not. Then its nebulous urges narrow, acquire form, and may be kindled or themselves kindle.

If one begins by wanting the whole world one gets nothing. When desire is concentrated with the whole strength of one's being upon any one object whatsoever it may be, then the gateway to the infinite becomes accessible. *Morning Songs* were the first projection of my inner self, and they consequently lack any sign of such concentration.

This first all-pervading outburst of joy has the effect of leading us in a more distinct direction – just as a lake eventually seeks an outlet as a river. In Mohit Babu's edition of my works, *Morning Songs* has been placed in the group of poems entitled 'Nishkraman' (The Emergence). In these poems was to be found the first news of my escape from the heart-wilderness into the open world. Since then, this pilgrim heart has made contact with that world, bit by bit, aspect by aspect, its woes as much as its joys, its shadows as much as its sunshine. And in the end, after gliding past a multitude of landing-ghats of ever-changing contour, it will reach the infinite – not a vague diffuseness, but the consummate perfection of Truth.

In my earliest years I enjoyed a simple and intimate communion with Nature. Each one of the coconut trees in our garden had a distinct personality. On coming home from the Normal School, when I saw behind the sky-line of our roof-terrace blue-grey water-laden clouds thickly banked up, the immense depth of gladness which filled me, all in a moment, I can recall clearly even now. When my eyes opened every morning, the blithely awakening world used to call me to join it like a playmate; the perfervid noon-day sky, during the silent watches of the siesta hours, would spirit me away from workaday existence into the recesses of its hermit cell, and the darkness of night would open the door to phantom paths and bear me over the seven seas and across the thirteen rivers, past all possibilities and impossibilities, into its wonderland.

Then one day, with the dawn of youth, my hungry

heart began to cry out for sustenance and a barrier
to the interplay of inside and outside was set up. My
whole being eddied round and round my troubled
heart, creating a vortex in which my consciousness
was confined. This loss of harmony as a result of the
overriding claims of the heart, and the consequent
constriction of the communion which had been mine,
I mourned in my *Evening Songs*.

After that, in *Morning Songs*, I celebrated the sudden
opening of a gate in the barrier as a result of some
unknown shock – through which I regained my lost
contact, not only as I knew it before but more deeply
and fully by virtue of the intervening estrangement.

Thus the first book of my life came to an end
with these chapters of union, separation and reunion.
Actually, it is not true that it has come to an end.
The same theme will continue, underpinning worse
complexities and more elaborate solutions and leading
towards a grander conclusion. Each of us comes along
and completes one chapter only of a larger book, which
is like a spoke on a wheel. At the circumference each
spoke appears independent to a cursory glance but,
in fact, it and every other spoke leads back to the
self-same centre.

The prose writings of the *Evening Songs* period
were published, as I have said, under the name
*Bibidha Prabandha*. Others, which correspond to the
time of my writing *Morning Songs*, came out under
the title *Alochana* (Discussions). The different charac-
teristics of these two collections are a good index
of the change that had taken place within me mean-
while.

## 35. *Rajendra Lal Mitra*

It was about this time that my brother Jyotirindra had the idea of founding a literary academy by bringing together all the men of letters with a reputation. To compile authoritative technical terms for the Bengali language and in other ways to assist in its growth was to be its object – an idea very similar to that of the modern Sahitya Parishad (Academy of Literature).

Dr Rajendra Lal Mitra took up the notion with enthusiasm, and was in due time its president for the short interval it lasted. When I went to invite Pandit Vidyasagar to join it, he gave a hearing to my explanation of its aims and the names of the proposed members, then said: 'My advice to you is to leave us out – you will never accomplish anything with bigwigs; they can never be got to agree with one another.' Saying which he refused to come in. Bankim Babu became a member, but I cannot say that he took much interest in the work.

To be plain, so long as this academy lived Rajendra Lal Mitra did everything single-handed. He began with geographical terms. The draft list was compiled by Dr Rajendra Lal himself, and was printed and circulated for the suggestions of the members. We had an idea also of transliterating in Bengali the name of each foreign country as pronounced by itself.

Pandit Vidyasagar's prophecy was fulfilled. It proved impossible to get the bigwigs to do anything, and the academy withered away shortly after sprouting. But Rajendra Lal Mitra was an all-round expert, an academy in himself. My labours in this cause were more than repaid by the privilege of his acquaintance. I have met many Bengali men of letters in my time, but none who left an impression of such brilliance.

I used to go and see him in the office of the Court of Wards in Maniktola. I would go in the mornings, always find him busy with his studies and, with the inconsiderateness of youth, feel no hesitation in disturbing him. But I have never seen him the least bit put out on that account. As soon as he saw me he would put aside his work and begin to talk to me. It is a matter of common knowledge that he was somewhat hard of hearing, so he hardly ever gave me the occasion to ask a question. He would take up some broad subject and talk away upon it, and that was the attraction which drew me there. The conversation of no other person has given me such a wealth of ideas on so many different subjects. I listened enraptured.

I think he was a member of the textbook committee, and every book he received for approval he read through and annotated in pencil. Sometimes he would select one of these books as a text for discourses on the construction of Bengali or philology in general, that were of the greatest benefit to me. There were few subjects he had not studied, and anything he had studied he could clearly expound.

If we had relied not on the other members of the fledgling academy but left everything to Dr Rajendra Lal, the present Sahitya Parishad would doubtless have inherited the matters that now occupy it in a much more developed state.

Dr Rajendra Lal Mitra was a profound scholar, but he was also a striking personality, which shone through his features. Full of fire in public life, he could also unbend graciously and talk on the most difficult subjects to a stripling like me without being in the least patronising. I even took advantage of this to the extent of getting a contribution from him, 'Yama's Dog', for *Bharati*. I would not have ventured to take such a liberty with other great contemporaries of his; neither would I have met with such response if I had.

And yet when he was on the war-path his opponents on the Municipal Corporation or the Senate of the University were mortally afraid of him. In those days it was Krishna Das Pal who was the diplomat in politics, and Rajendra Lal Mitra who was the doughty fighter.

For the purposes of Asiatic Society publications and researches, he had to employ a number of Sanskrit pundits to do the mechanical work. I remember this gave certain envious and mean-minded detractors the opportunity to say that really everything was done by these pundits, while Rajendra Lal fraudulently appropriated all the credit. Today, too, we often find tools arrogating to themselves the lion's share of an achievement, regarding their wielder as a mere figurehead. If pens had minds they would certainly bemoan the unfairness of their getting all the stain and the writer all the glory!

Curiously this extraordinary man has been accorded no recognition from his countrymen even posthumously. One of the reasons may be that the national mourning for Vidyasagar, whose death followed shortly after, left no room for recognition of other bereavements. Another reason may be that since his main contributions lay beyond the pale of literature, he was unable to reach the heart of the people.

## 36. *Karwar*

Our Sudder Street party transferred itself next to Karwar on the western sea-coast. Karwar is the headquarters of the Kanara district in the southern portion of the Bombay Presidency. It is the tract of the Malaya hills of Sanskrit literature, where grow the cardamum creeper and the sandal tree. My second brother was then a judge there.

The little harbour, ringed by hills, is so secluded that there is nothing of a port about it. Its crescent-shaped beach flings out its arms around the open sea exactly as if eagerly striving to embrace the infinite. The edge of the broad sandy beach is fringed with a forest of casuarinas, broken at one end by the Kalanadi river, which flows into the sea after passing through a gorge flanked by rows of hills.

I remember how, one moonlit evening, we went up-river in a little boat. We stopped at one of Shivaji's old hill-forts, and stepping ashore found ourselves in the clean-swept little yard of a peasant's home. We sat in a spot lit by moonbeams glancing over the top of the outer wall, and there we dined off food we had brought with us. On our way back we let the boat glide. The night brooded over the motionless hills and forests and the silent flow of the Kalanadi, throwing its spell over all of them. We took a good long time to reach the mouth of the river, so, instead of returning by sea, we left the boat and walked home over the sands. The night was by then far advanced, the sea without a ripple, and even the murmur of the ever-troubled casuarinas had ceased. Their shadow hung motionless along the edge of the vast expanse of sand, and the ring of blue-grey hills around the horizon slept calmly beneath the heavens.

In this still and limitless whiteness we walked along with our shadows without a word. When we reached home my urge to sleep was lost in something deeper. The poem I wrote is mingled inextricably with the night on that distant seashore. I do not know how it will strike a reader without those memories. This doubt led to its omission from Mohit Babu's edition of my works. I trust that my reminiscences may be deemed its fit home:

Let me sink down, losing myself in the depths of midnight.
Let the earth leave hold of me, let her free me from the
    obstacle of dust.
Keep your watch from afar, O stars, drunk though you
    be with moonlight,
    and let the horizon hold its wings still around me.
Let there be no song, no word, no sound, no touch; nor
    sleep, nor awakening,
    but only the moonlight like a swoon of ecstasy over
    the sky and my being.
To me the world seems like a ship with countless pilgrims,
    vanishing in the remote blue of the sky,
    its sailors' song becoming fainter and fainter on the air,
While I sink in the folds of the endless night, fading away
    from myself, dwindling to a point.

One needs to add here that just because feeling is brimming over when something is being written, does not ensure it is good. Rather, the utterance is likely to be thick with emotion. Just as a writer should not be entirely removed from the feeling to which he is giving expression, so also if he is too close to it the truest poetry does not result. Memory is the brush which best lays on authentic colour. Proximity may be too compelling, leaving the imagination insufficiently free. In all art, not only in poetry, the mind of the artist must attain a degree of aloofness – the *creator* within man must be allowed sole control. If the material at hand gets the better of the creation, the outcome is a mere replica of the event, not a reflection of it from the artist's mind.

## 37. *'Nature's Revenge'*

In Karwar I wrote the 'Prakritir Pratishodh' (Nature's Revenge), a dramatic poem. The hero was a sanyasi who was striving for a victory over Nature by cutting the bonds of desire and affection to arrive at a true knowledge of himself. A little girl brings him back to the world from communion with the infinite and into the bondage of human affection. Then the sanyasi realises that the great is to be found in the small, the infinite within the bounds of form, and the eternal freedom of the soul in love. Only in the aura of love does every limit merge with the limitless.

The sea beach at Karwar is certainly the ideal place to appreciate that the beauty of Nature is not a mirage of the imagination, but a reflection of the joy in the infinite which entices us to lose ourselves. It is not surprising if we miss this infinitude in the abstract expression of this universal joy. But when we see beauty in the meanest of things and the heart is put into immediate touch with immensity, is any room left for argument?

Nature transported the sanyasi to the presence of the infinite enthroned in the finite, by way of the heart. In 'Nature's Revenge' on one side were shown the wayfarers and the villagers, content with domestic routine and unconscious of anything beyond it; and on the other the sanyasi busy casting away his all, along with himself, into self-imagined infinitude. When love bridged the gulf between the two, and householder and hermit met, the apparent triviality of the finite and the apparent nullity of the infinite alike disappeared. This, in a slightly different form, was the story of my own experience of the entrancing ray of light which found its way into the depths of the cave in which I had retired away from all touch with the outer world, and brought me more fully in touch with Nature again. 'Nature's Revenge' may be seen as an introduction to the whole of my future literary work or, rather, to the subject on which all my writings have dwelt: the delight of attaining the infinite within the finite.

On our way back from Karwar I wrote some songs for 'Nature's Revenge' on board ship. The first one filled me with great gladness as I sang and wrote it sitting on deck:

> Mother, leave your darling boy to us,
> And let us take him to the field where the cattle graze.

The sun has risen, the buds have opened, the cowherds are going to pasture; and they cannot allow the sunlight, the flowers, and their play in the grazing grounds to be empty. They want their Shyama (Krishna) to be with them there, in the midst of all these. They want to see the infinite in all its carefully adorned loveliness; they have turned out early because they want to join in frolics amid ghat and field and forest and mountain – not to admire from a distance, neither to be spellbound by majesty. Their requirements are of the slightest. A simple yellow garment and a garland of wild-flowers are all the raiment they need. For where joy reigns on every side, to search for it earnestly, or with pomp and ceremony, is to miss it.

Shortly after my return from Karwar, I was married. I was then twenty-two years old.

# 38.  Pictures and Songs

*Chhabi o Gan* (Pictures and Songs) is the title of a book of poems, most of which were written at this time.

We were then living in a house with a garden on Lower Circular Road. Adjoining it on the south side was a large *busti*. I would often sit near a window and watch the goings-on in this populous settlement. I loved to see the inhabitants work, play and rest, and come and go multifariously. To me it was like a story come alive.

A faculty of many-sightedness possessed me at this time. Each separate picture I ringed with light from my imagination and joy from my heart and infused with a pathos of its own. The pleasure of demarcating each picture was much the same as that of painting it; both were the outcome of a desire to apprehend with the mind what the eye sees, and to see with the eye what the mind imagines.

Had I been a painter I should doubtless have tried to keep a record of the visions and creations of that period when I was so alert and responsive. But that instrument was not available to me. What I had was words and rhymes, and even with these I had not yet learnt to draw firm strokes or to colour without overflowing. Still, like a boy with his first paint-box, I passed an entire day creating pictures out of the many-coloured fancies of youth. If these pictures are viewed today, with the fact that I was twenty-two when I made them kept in mind, some worthwhile features may be discerned even through the crude execution and blurred colouring.

I have remarked that the first book of my literary life came to an end with *Morning Songs*. The same subject was then continued under a different title. Many pages at the start of this book are of no value, I know. New beginnings inevitably require much in the way of superfluous preliminaries. Had these been leaves on a tree they would have duly dropped off. Unfortunately, leaves of a book cling on even when they are no longer wanted. The feature of these poems was the close attention they paid even to trifling things. *Pictures and Songs* seized every opportunity of giving value to trivia by saturating them with colours straight from the heart.

That does not really do justice to the process of composition. When the mind is properly tuned, all parts of the universal song awaken its sympathetic vibrations. This music, roused within me, was the reason why nothing felt trivial to me as I wrote. Whatever my eyes fell upon prompted a response inside. Like children who play with sand or stones or shells or whatever they can find (for the spirit of play is within them), so we, when filled with youth, become aware that the universe is a harp of many thousand tunes, any one of which may serve for our accompaniment; there is no need to seek afar.

## 39. *An intervening period*

Between *Pictures and Songs* and *Kari o Komal* (Sharps and Flats) a child's magazine called *Balak* sprang up, flourished and died like an annual plant. My second sister-in-law felt the want of an illustrated magazine for children. Her idea was that the young people of the family would contribute to it, but as she felt that alone would not be enough, she took up the editorship herself and asked me to help by contributing.

After one or two numbers of *Balak* had come out I happened to go on a visit to Raj Narain Babu at

Deoghar. On the return journey the train was crowded, and as there was an unshaded light just above the only berth I could get, I could not sleep. I thought I might as well take this opportunity of thinking out a story for *Balak*. In spite of my efforts a story eluded me, but sleep came to my rescue. In a dream I saw the stone steps of a temple stained with the blood of victims of sacrifice – and a little girl standing there with her father, asking him in piteous accents: 'Father, what is this, why all this blood?' and the father, inwardly moved, trying to quiet her questioning with a show of gruffness. When I awoke I felt I had got my story. Many of my stories have been given in dreams – and other writings too. This dream episode I made part of the annals of King Gobinda Manikya of Tripura and created out of it a short serial story, *Rajarshi* (The Royal Sage) for *Balak*.

Those were days of utter freedom from care. Nothing seemed to be anxious to express itself through my life or writings. I had not yet joined the throng of travellers on the path of life, but was a mere spectator at the window. Many wayfarers passed me by on various errands as I gazed out, and the seasons entered unasked and stayed with me like visitors in a foreign land.

Not only the seasons either. Men of all kinds, curious types floating about like boats adrift from their anchors, periodically invaded my little room. They sought to further their own ends at the cost of my inexperience with many an extraordinary device. They need not have taken such pains to get the better of me. I was entirely unsophisticated, my own wants were few, and I was not at all clever at distinguishing between good and bad faith. I have often imagined that I was assisting persons with their school fees to whom such fees were as irrelevant as books.

Once a long-haired youth brought me a letter from his 'sister' in which she asked me to take under my protection this brother of hers who was suffering from the tyranny of a stepmother (as imaginary as herself). That the brother was not imaginary was enough for me; his sister's letter was as unnecessary as expert marksmanship to bring down a bird that cannot fly.

Another young fellow came to inform me he was studying for the BA, but could not take the examination as he was afflicted with brain trouble. I was concerned, but since I was far from proficient in medical science, or in any other science, I was at a loss for advice. He, however, went on to explain that he had seen in a dream that my wife had been his mother in a former birth, and that if he could but drink some water which had touched her feet he would be cured. 'Perhaps you don't believe in such things,' he concluded with a smile. My belief did not matter, I said, but if he thought he could be cured, he was welcome; and so I procured him a phial of water supposed to have touched my wife's feet. He felt immensely better, he said. Beginning with water, in the natural course of evolution he came to solid food. Then he took up his quarters in a corner of my room and began to hold smoking parties with his friends, till I had to take refuge in flight from the smoke-laden air. He gradually proved beyond doubt that though his brain might have been diseased, it certainly was not weak.

After this experience I needed no end of proof before I could bring myself to put trust in children of previous births. My reputation must have spread though, for I received a letter now from a distressed daughter. Here, I gently but firmly drew the line.

Throughout this time my friendship with Babu Shrish Chandra Majumdar ripened apace. Every evening he and Priya Babu would come to my little room and we would discuss literature and music far into the

night. Sometimes a whole day would be spent in this
way. The fact is my *self* had not yet been moulded and
nourished into a strong and definite personality, and so
my life drifted along as lightly and easily as an autumn
cloud.

## 40. *Bankim Chandra*

This was the time when my acquaintance with Bankim
Babu began. My first sight of him was a matter of long
before. The alumni of Calcutta University had started
an annual reunion, of which Babu Chandranath Basu
was the leading spirit. Perhaps he entertained a hope
that in the future I might become one of them; anyhow
I was asked to read a poem. Chandranath Babu was
then quite a young man. I remember he had translated some martial German poem into English which
he proposed to recite himself on the day, and came to
us to rehearse it, full of energy. That a warrior poet's
ode to his beloved sword was once his favourite poem
will convince the reader that even Chandranath Babu
once was young; and what's more, that those times
were indeed peculiar.

While wandering about in the crush at the students' reunion, I suddenly came across a figure which
struck me as distinguished beyond that of any other
and who could not possibly have been lost in any
crowd. The features of this tall fair personage shone
with radiance and I could not contain my curiosity
about him: he was the only person whose name I
felt concerned to know that day. When I learnt he
was Bankim Babu I marvelled all the more because
it seemed a wonderful match of creator and creation.
His aquiline nose, compressed lips, and keen glance
betokened immense intellect. With his arms folded

across his breast he seemed to walk as one apart, towering above the ordinary throng – that was what struck me most. On his forehead he had the mark of a true prince among men.

A small incident in that gathering is indelible. In one of the rooms a pundit was reciting some Sanskrit verses of his own composition and explaining them in Bengali to the audience. One of the allusions was not exactly coarse, but somewhat vulgar. As the pundit proceeded to expound this Bankim Babu, covering his face with his hands, hurried out. I was near the door and can still see his shrinking, retreating figure.

After that I often longed to see him, but I could not get the opportunity. At last, when he was deputy magistrate of Howrah, I made bold to call on him. We met, and I tried my best to make conversation. But I somehow felt greatly abashed while returning home, as if I had acted like a raw, bumptious youth in thrusting myself upon him unasked and unintroduced.

Quite soon, within a year or two, I attained a place as the youngest of the literary men of the time; but my position in order of merit remained uncertain. The reputation I had acquired was mixed with plenty of doubt and not a little condescension. It was then the fashion in Bengal to assign each man of letters a place by comparing him with a supposed compeer in the West. Thus one was the Byron of Bengal, another the Emerson and so forth. I began to be styled the Bengal Shelley. This was insulting to Shelley and only likely to get me laughed at.

My established cognomen was the Lisping Poet. My attainments were few, my knowledge of life meagre, and in both poetry and prose the sentiment exceeded the substance. There was nothing on which anyone could base praise with any degree of confidence. My dress and behaviour were of the same anomalous description. I wore my hair long and indulged in what was probably an ultra-poetical refinement of manner. In a word, I was eccentric and could not fit myself into everyday life like an ordinary man.

At this time Babu Akshay Sarkar started his monthly review, *Nabajiban* (New Life), to which I used occasionally to contribute. Bankim Babu had just closed a chapter in his editorship of the *Bangadarshan* and was absorbed in theological writing, for which purpose he had started the monthly *Prachar* (The Preacher). I contributed a song or two to this and an effusive appreciation of Vaishnava lyrics.

Now I began constantly to meet Bankim Babu. He was living in Bhabani Dutt's street. I visited him frequently, true – but there was not much conversation. I was then of an age to listen, not talk. I fervently wished we could warm up into discussion, but my diffidence got the better of my conversational powers. Some days his elder brother Sanjib Babu would be there reclining on his bolster. The sight would gladden me, for he was a genial soul. He delighted in talking, and it was a delight to listen. Those who have read his prose must have noticed how gaily and airily it flows like the sprightliest conversation. Very few have this gift in speech; and fewer still the art to translate it into writing.

This was the time when Pandit Sashadhar rose into prominence. I first heard of him from Bankim Babu. If I remember right, Bankim Babu also was responsible for introducing him to the public. His curious attempt to revive the prestige of Hindu orthodoxy with the help of western science soon spread all over the country. Theosophy had been preparing the ground for some time previously. Not that Bankim Babu even thoroughly identified with the new cult. No shadow of Sashadhar fell on his exposition of Hinduism in *Prachar* – that would have been inconceivable.

I was then coming out of my seclusion, as my contributions to these controversies show. Some were satirical verses, some farcical plays, others letters to newspapers. I descended into the arena from the clouds of sentiment and began to spar in right earnest.

In the heat of the fight I happened to fall foul of Bankim Babu. The history of this remains recorded in *Prachar* and *Bharati* of those days and need not be repeated here. At the close of this period of antagonism Bankim Babu wrote me a letter, which I unfortunately lost. Had I not, the reader could have seen with what consummate generosity Bankim Babu took the sting out of that regrettable episode.

## 41. *The steamer hulk*

Lured by an advertisement in some paper, my brother Jyotirindra went off one afternoon to an auction and on his return informed us that he had bought a steel hulk for seven thousand rupees; all that was now required being an engine and some cabins to make a full-fledged steamer.

My brother must have thought it a great shame that our countrymen had set their tongues and pens in motion, but not a single line of steamers. I have narrated earlier how he tried to light matches for his country, but that no amount of rubbing would make them strike. He also wanted to operate power-looms, but after all his travail only one little *gamcha* was born and then the loom stopped. Now he wanted Indian steamers to ply and so bought this empty old hulk. In due course it was filled not only with engines and cabins but with loss and ruin too.

The latter fell on him alone while the experience benefited the whole country. These uncalculating, unbusinesslike spirits sow and water the country's field of business with their activities. Though the flood subsides as rapidly as it comes, it leaves fertilising silt behind to enrich the soil. When the time for reaping arrives no one thinks of these pioneers; but they who have cheerfully staked and lost their all in life, are not likely in death to mind a further loss – that of being forgotten.

On one side was the British-run Flotilla Company, on the other my brother Jyotirindra. How tremendously the battle of the fleets was waged, the people of Khulna and Barisal may still remember. Under the stress of competition, steamer was added to steamer, loss piled on loss, while income dwindled until printing tickets ceased to be worthwhile. A golden age dawned between Khulna and Barisal: not only were the passengers carried free of charge, but they were offered light refreshments *gratis*! Then a band of volunteers formed up who, with flags and patriotic songs, marched the passengers in procession to the Indian line of steamers. So while there was no dearth of passengers, every other kind of want began to multiply apace.

The accounts were uninfluenced by the fervour. While patriotic enthusiasm mounted higher and higher, three times three continued steadily to make nine on the wrong side of the balance-sheet.

One of the misfortunes which always pursues the unbusinesslike is that, while they are as easy to read as an open book, they never learn to read the character of others. And since it takes them a lifetime and all their resources to discover their weakness, they never get the chance to profit by experience. Others certainly gained – the passengers with free refreshments, the staff who showed no sign of starvation – but it was my brother who gained most, by facing his ruin so valiantly.

The daily bulletins of victory or disaster which arrived from the scene of action kept us in a fever of excitement. But one day came the news that the steamer *Swadeshi* had fouled the Howrah bridge and sunk. My brother had now completely overstepped the limits of his resources, and there was nothing for it but to wind up the business.

## 42. *Bereavements*

In the meantime death made its appearance in our family. Until now I had never met it face to face. When my mother died I was a child. She had been ailing for quite a long time, and we did not even know when her malady took a fatal turn. As we grew up, she used to sleep on a separate bed in the same room with us. Then in the course of her illness she was taken for a boat trip on the river, and on her return a room on the third storey of the inner apartments was set apart for her.

On the night she died we were fast asleep in our room downstairs. At an hour I could not tell, our old nurse ran in weeping, crying: 'Oh my little ones, you have lost your all!' My sister-in-law rebuked her and led her away, to save us the sudden shock at dead of night. Half awakened, I felt my heart sink but could not make out what had happened. When we were told of her death in the morning, I did not realise all it meant for me.

We came out into the verandah and saw my mother lying on a bedstead in the courtyard. Nothing in her appearance showed death to be terrible. The aspect it wore in that morning light was as lovely as a calm and peaceful sleep, and the gulf between life and absence of life was not brought home to us.

Only when her body was taken out through the main gateway and we followed the procession to the cremation ground did a storm of grief pass through me at the thought that Mother would never return by this door and again take her accustomed place in the affairs of the household. The day wore on, we returned from the cremation, and as we turned into our lane I looked up towards my father's rooms on the third storey. He was still sitting in the front verandah, motionless in prayer.

She who was the youngest daughter-in-law took charge of the motherless little ones. She saw to our food and clothing and all other wants, and kept us constantly near, so that we might not feel our loss too keenly. One of the attributes of the living is the power to heal the irreparable, to forget the irreplaceable. This power is strongest in early life, so that no blow penetrates too deeply, no scar is permanent. Thus the first shadow of death which fell upon us left no darkness behind; it departed as softly as it came, only a shadow.

In later life, wandering like a madcap at the first coming of spring with a handful of half-blown jessamines tied in a corner of my muslin scarf, as I stroked my forehead with the soft, rounded, tapering buds the touch of my mother's fingers would come back to me; and I clearly sensed that the tenderness dwelling in the tips of those fingers was the very same as the purity that blossoms every day in jessamine buds. And I felt that this tenderness is on the earth in boundless measure whether we know it or not.

The acquaintance I made with Death at the age of twenty-three was a permanent one, and its blow reverberates with each succeeding bereavement in ever-expanding wreaths of tears. An infant can skip away from the greatest of calamities, but with the coming of age evasion is not so easy. The shock of that day I had to face full-on.

That there could be any gap in life's succession of joys and sorrows was something of which I had no idea. I had seen nothing beyond life, and accepted it as the ultimate truth. When death suddenly came, and in a moment tore a gaping rent in life's seamless fabric, I was utterly bewildered. All around, the trees, the soil, the water, the sun, the moon, the stars, remained as immovably true as before, and yet the person who was as truly there, who, through a thousand points of contact with life, mind and heart, was so very much more true for me, had vanished in an instant like a dream. What a perplexing contradiction! How was I ever to reconcile what remained with that which had gone?

The terrible darkness disclosed to me through this rent, continued to lure me night and day as time went by. I would constantly return to it and gaze at it, wondering what was left to replace what had departed. Emptiness is a thing man cannot bring himself to believe in: that which is *not*, is untrue; that which is untrue, is not. So our efforts to find something where we see nothing are unceasing.

Just as a young plant confined in darkness stretches itself, on tiptoe as it were, to reach the light, so the soul, when death surrounds it with negation, tries and tries to rise into affirmatory light. What sorrow is deeper than to be trapped in a darkness that prevents one from finding a way out of darkness?

Yet amid unbearable grief, flashes of joy sparkled in my mind on and off in a way which quite surprised me. The idea that life is not a fixture came as tidings that helped to lighten my mind. That we are not for ever prisoners behind a wall of stony-hearted facts was the thought that kept unconsciously rising uppermost in rushes of gladness. What I had possessed I was made to let go – and it distressed me – but when in the same moment I viewed it as freedom gained, a great peace fell upon me.

The all-pervading pressure of worldly existence is compensated by death, and thus it does not crush us. The terrible weight of eternal life does not have to be endured by man – this truth came over me that day as a wonderful revelation.

With the loosening allure of the world, the beauty of Nature took on a deeper meaning. Death had given me the correct perspective from which to perceive the world's full beauty, and as I saw the universe against this background, it entranced me.

At this time I had a recrudescence of eccentricity in thought and behaviour. I was being called upon to submit to the customs and fashions of the day as if they were something soberly and genuinely real; instead they made me want to laugh. I could not take them seriously. The burden of stopping to consider what other people might think of me was completely lifted from my mind. I have been about in fashionable book-shops with a coarse sheet draped round me as my only upper garment and a pair of slippers on my bare feet. In heat, chill and wet I used to sleep out on the verandah of the third storey. There the stars and I could gaze at each other, and no time was lost in greeting the dawn.

This phase had nothing to do with any ascetic feeling. It was more like a holiday spree occasioned by discovering the schoolmaster Life with his cane to be a myth, and being thereby able to shake myself free from the petty regulations of his school. If, on waking one fine morning, we were to find gravitation reduced to only a fraction of itself, would we still demurely walk along the main road? Wouldn't we rather skip over multi-storeyed houses for a change, or on encountering some monument take a flying jump and not have the trouble of walking round it? So, with the weight of worldly life no longer dragging at my feet, I could not adhere to the usual conventions.

Alone on the terrace at night I groped like a blind man trying to find some device or sign upon the black stone gate of death. In the morning, the light falling on my unscreened bed as I opened my eyes made me feel that the haze enveloping my brain was really transparent; just as when mist clears, hills, rivers and forests shine anew, so the dew-drenched picture of existence spread before me seemed refreshingly beautiful.

## 43. *The rains and the autumn*

According to the Hindu calendar, each year is ruled by a particular planet. So, in each period of my life, a particular season has assumed special importance. When I look back to my childhood I recall the rainy days best. I can see the wind-driven rain flooding the verandah floor; the row of doors into the rooms all closed; Peari, the old scullery maid, coming from the market, basket laden with vegetables, wading through the slush and drenched with the rain. And for no rhyme or reason I am careering about the verandah in ecstasy.

Something else comes back to me: I am at school in a class held in a colonnade with mats tied across the pillars as screens; cloud after cloud has rolled up during the afternoon, and they are now piled across the sky. As we watch, the rain falls in a dense sheet, the thunder rumbles at intervals long and loud; some mad woman with nails of lightning seems to rend the sky from end to end. The mat walls tremble under the blasts of wind as if they will be blown in. We can hardly see to read for the darkness; the pundit gives us leave to close our books. Letting the storm romp and roar on our behalf, we swing our dangling legs, and my mind flies right away across a distant plateau without end over which the prince of the fairy tale passes.

I remember, too, the depth of night in the month of *Shravan*. The pattering of rain, infiltrating my slumber, produces in me a restfulness more profound than deep sleep. In my waking intervals I pray that morning may see the rain continue, our lane under water, and the bathing platform of the tank submerged to the last step.

But at the age of which I was earlier speaking, autumn, not the rainy season, is on the throne beyond doubt. My life may be seen spread leisurely beneath the clear transparent sky of *Ashwin*. And in the molten gold of autumn sunshine softly reflected from the fresh dewy green outside, I pace the verandah and compose, in the raga Jogiya, the song:

In this morning light I know not what my heart desires

The day wears on, the gong in the house sounds twelve noon, the mode changes; but my mind remains full of music, leaving no room for work or duty. I sing:

What idle play is this, my heart, in the listless hours?

Then in the afternoon I lie on the white sheet on the floor of my small room, trying to draw in a sketch-book – by no means an arduous pursuit of the muse, just a toying with the wish to make pictures.

The most important part remains in the mind; not a line of it is put on paper. And in the meantime the serene autumn afternoon filters through the walls of my room, filling it, like a cup, with intoxicating gold.

I do not know why, but all my days at that time I see as if under this autumn sky, lit by this autumn light: the autumn that ripened my songs as it ripens corn for the cultivators; the autumn that filled my granary of leisure with radiance; the autumn that flooded my unburdened mind with unreasoning joy and fashioned song and story.

The great difference between the rainy season of my childhood and the autumn of my youth is that in the former, Nature closely hemmed me in, entertaining me with her numerous troupe, her variegated make-up and her medley of music; while in the latter the festivity is within me. The play of cloud and sunshine has receded into the background, and murmurs of joy and sorrow have occupied the mind. It is these that lend the blue of the autumn sky its wistful tinge and invest the breath of the breezes with poignancy.

My poems had now reached the doors of men's minds. No longer could they come and go as they liked: there was door after door, chamber within chamber. How many times must we return with only a glimpse of light in a window, only the sound of pipes somewhere within the palace gates – some flute or *shehnai* – lingering in our ears! Mind has to treat with mind, will come to terms with will and many obstacles be surmounted before there can be true intercourse. The cascade of life dashes round these obstacles, splashing and foaming with laughter and tears, dancing and whirling in eddies and never allowing one to form a definite estimate of its course.

## 44. Sharps and Flats

*Kari o Komal* (Sharps and Flats) is a serenade from the streets before the dwelling-place of Man, a plea to be allowed entry and position within that house of mystery.

> This world is sweet – I do not want to die.
> I want to live within the stream of humanity.

This is the individual's dedication of himself to life.

When I started on my second voyage to England, on board ship I made the acquaintance of Ashutosh Chaudhuri. He had just taken his MA degree from Calcutta University and was on his way to England to join the bar. We were together only the few days the steamer took from Calcutta to Madras, but it became evident that depth of friendship does not depend upon length of acquaintance. Within this short time he so drew me to him by his natural simplicity of heart that our friendship seemed always to have been there.

When Ashu returned from England he became one of the family. He had not then had time or opportunity to pierce all the barriers that hedge in his profession and become completely immersed in it. The money-bags of his clients had not yet entirely loosened the strings holding their gold, and Ashu was still an enthusiastic gatherer of honey from various literary hives. The spirit that infused him had none of the mustiness of library morocco, but was fragrant with the scent of unknown exotics from over the oceans. At his invitation I enjoyed many a springtime picnic in those distant glades.

He had a special taste for French literature. I was then writing the poems later published as *Sharps and Flats*. Ashu discerned resemblances between many of them and old French poems. The common element, according to him, was the appeal made to the poet by the play of life, which found varied expression in each and every poem. An unfulfilled yearning to join this larger life was the vital force in both cases.

'I will arrange and publish these poems for you,' said Ashu, and the task was accordingly entrusted to him. The poem beginning 'This world is sweet' was the one he considered the keynote of the series, and so he placed it at the beginning.

He was very possibly right. In childhood, when I was confined to the house, I looked wistfully through the openings in the parapet of our inner roof-terrace and offered my heart to Nature. In my youth it was the world of men that exerted a powerful attraction upon me. I was an outsider, and looked out upon it from the wayside. My mind, on the brink of life, called out to a ferryman sailing away across the waves, as it were, with an eager waving of hands. For my life longed to begin its journey.

It is not true that my marked isolation acted as a bar to plunging into the social stream. I see no sign in those of my countrymen who have been in the thick of society all their lives that they enjoy any more than I do a life-giving touch from such intimacy. The social existence of our country has its lofty banks, its flights of steps, and its cool dark waters shadowed by antique trees from whose leafy branches the *koel* coos its ancient ravishing song. But, for all that, the water is stagnant. Where is its current, where are its waves, when does the high tide rush in from the sea?

Did I receive an echo of the triumphant paean of a river rising and falling in wave after wave, cutting its way through walls of rock to the sea when I looked at the neighbourhood beyond our lane? No! In my solitude I simply fretted for lack of an invitation to the place where the world's festival was being held.

Man may be overcome by profound depression in voluptuously lazy seclusion if deprived of commerce with life. From such despondency I have always struggled painfully to break free. My mind refused to respond to the cheap intoxications of political movements, devoid as they were of any national consciousness, completely ignorant of the country, and supremely indifferent to real service of the motherland. I was tormented by a furious impatience, an intolerable dissatisfaction with myself and all around me. Much rather, I told myself, were I an Arab Bedouin!

In other parts of the world there is no end to the movement, clamour and revelry of life. We, like beggar-maids, stand outside and look longingly on. When have we had the wherewithal to deck ourselves and join in? Only in a land where an animus of divisiveness reigns supreme, and innumerable petty barriers separate one from another, must this longing to express a larger life in one's own remain unsatisfied. I strained to reach humanity in my youth, as in my childhood I yearned for the outside world from within the chalk-ring drawn around me by the servants: how unique, unattainable and remote it seemed! And yet if we cannot get in touch with it, if no breeze can blow from it, no current flow out of it, no path be open to the free passage of travellers, then the dead things accumulating around us will never be removed but continue to mount up until they smother all vestige of life.

During the rains there are only dark clouds and showers. In the autumn there is the play of light and shade in the sky; but there is something else too – the promise of corn in the fields. The rainy season of my career was similarly vaporous and moist with puffy sentiment; my message was misty, my rhythm incoherent. But with my autumnal *Sharps and Flats* not only could colours be seen in the clouds but clearly crops were rising from the ground. There was a definite attempt in variety of both language and metre to establish contact with the real world.

And so another chapter closes. The light-hearted days of mixing freely with the world at will are over. My journey has now to be completed through the dwelling-places of men. And the good and evil, joy and woe which it thus encounters may not be viewed as pictures. What tumult is going on here! What construction and destruction, conflict and conjunction!

I do not have the power to disclose and describe the supreme art with which my Guide joyfully leads me past all obstacle, antagonism and crookedness towards fulfilment of my life's innermost meaning. And if I cannot clarify this mystery, whatever else I may attempt to explain is sure to mislead at every step. To analyse an image is to gather only dust, not the spirit of the artist.

So, having escorted you to the door of my sanctuary, I take leave of my readers.

# TAGORE FAMILY TREE

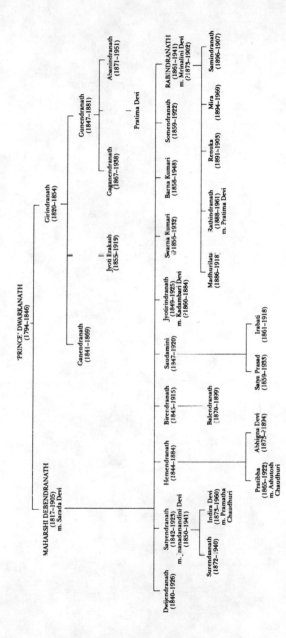

NB: Only those mentioned in *My Reminiscences* are included in this tree.

# Glossary of Indian Words

Agrahayan
: The eighth month of the Bengali year corresponding to mid-November to mid-December

Asharh
: The third month of the Bengali year corresponding to mid-June to mid-July

Ashwin
: The sixth month of the Bengali year corresponding to mid-September to mid-October

Babu/babu
: For example, Naba Gopal Babu. A form of address implying formal/respectful distance from person addressed; a rough equivalent of 'Mr'. On its own, babu means someone from the leisured class or someone with pretensions to it, depending on context

Baishakh
: The first month of the Bengali year corresponding to mid-April to mid-May

Bauls
: Baul means 'madcap'. Bauls reject established religions and believe in primacy of personal communion with the Divine, aided by songs and drugs. Found in northern India, in their dress they resemble Buddhist monks more than Hindu sanyasis

191

| | |
|---|---|
| *Bhadra* | The fifth month of the Bengali year corresponding to mid-August to mid-September |
| *Chaitra* | The twelfth month of the Bengali year corresponding to mid-March to mid-April |
| *choga* | A long-sleeved garment, like a dressing-gown; originally an Afghan form of dress |
| dhoti | About six metres of cloth wound around the lower half of a man's body in various styles in northern India. Gandhi wore a dhoti |
| *gamcha* | A napkin or cloth used as a towel |
| *gayatri* | A verse of the Rig Veda regarded as its most holy passage; comparable to the Lord's Prayer in Christianity. It is addressed to the old solar god Savitri |
| *Jaishtha* | The second month of the Bengali year corresponding to mid-May to mid-June |
| *jhampan* | A litter used for carrying people on hills |
| *kadamba* | A pale yellow mildly fragrant tropical flower with tubular stem, *Ipomea aquatica*. The tree is sacred to Krishna |
| *Kartik* | The seventh month of the Bengali year corresponding to mid-October to mid-November |
| *kathaka* | A bard or reciter |
| *koel* | A cuckoo, the common name in northern India of *Eudynamys orientalis*, taken from its cry during the breeding season |
| *luchi* | A thin, circular bread prepared from refined flour and water and fried in ghee so that it blows up like a balloon. Popular at marriages, feasts and festivals, it is the regular food of the upper class in Bengal |

| | |
|---|---|
| *Magh* | The tenth month of the Bengali year corresponding to mid-January to mid-February |
| *mali* | A gardener |
| *mofussil* | Up-country, the provinces; in Tagore's Bengal anywhere outside Calcutta |
| *pan* | A mildly addictive preparation of arecanut, catechu, lime paste and other condiments, wrapped in a leaf of the betel tree and chewed all over India, especially as a digestive after meals. The combination of ingredients produces blood-red juice |
| *Paush* | The ninth month of the Bengali year corresponding to mid-December to mid-January |
| *payar* | A heroic couplet of Bengali poetry, and its principal medium until the nineteenth century. The rhyming couplet has four feet in each line. It is based on *matra*, the first three feet having four *matras* each and the last foot having two *matras*, hence fourteen *matras* per line |
| *Phalgun* | The eleventh month of the Bengali year corresponding to mid-February to mid-March |
| *pranam* | A form of greeting to a respected older person in which one 'takes the dust of the feet' |
| *puja* | Worship, alone or in a group. Durga Puja is the most important festival in the Bengali year, taking place over a fortnight in September/October: it celebrates Durga's slaying of the buffalo demon Mahisha. The actual ritual lasts five days in the middle of the fortnight |
| *shehnai* | A classical double-reed wind instrument with a sound similar to the oboe, played in |

|  | temples and especially during festivals and weddings |
|---|---|
| *Shravan* | The fourth month of the Bengali year corresponding to mid-July to mid-August |
| *sutra* | Literally 'thread', but used to mean a manual of instruction in the form of brief aphorisms (in Sanskrit) |
| *tanpura* | A four-stringed instrument with sympathetic strings, used as a drone accompaniment for the sitar and other instruments. The player simply plays the same scale over and over again |
| Vaishnava | Pertaining to the worship of Vishnu, generally through ecstatic songs and other practices. Older Bengali literature was powerfully influenced by Vaishnavism, propagated by Chaitanya (1485–1533) |
| *yaksha* | An earth-spirit; a kind of gnome or fairy. *Yakshas* were generally friendly, but their womenfolk, *yakshis*, might be malevolent and sometimes eat small children |
| zamindar | A landlord, originally created by the distribution of land revenue rights by the Mughals and later given ownership of land (*zamindari*) by the British under the terms of the 1793 Permanent Settlement Act |

# Notes

## by Krishna Dutta and Andrew Robinson

In compiling these notes we have depended on many sources in both Bengali and English. Full publication details of books referred to below by author alone are given in the Bibliography.

Rabindranath made several factual errors in *Jibansmriti*, for example, the names of his schools and his order of attending them. The errors have been retained in the text but corrected in these notes.

Rabindranath is referred to below as RT.

## 2. Teaching begins

**page 19** 'We three boys'. The other two boys were each a year and a half older than RT. Somendranath Tagore (1859–1922) was RT's brother and encouraged his early writing and helped to publish it. Satya Prasad Gangopadhyay (1859–1933) was the first child and only son of Soudamini Devi, Debendranath Tagore's eldest daughter, and thus was RT's nephew. He published the first collected edition of RT's poetry in 1896.

'The rain patters'. The line is similar to one in an elementary reader written by Ishwar Chandra Vidyasagar (see note on p. 86) and published in 1855, but RT has transformed it in his memory into something more lyrical than the original.

'*kara, khala*'. These are exercises in two syllables (each word having only two letters in Bengali).

**page 20** 'The rain falls pit-a-pat'. This is a folk-rhyme.

'beginning of my school life'. This was in March 1864, when RT was not yet three, according to Pal, *1*, p. 64.

'elder brother'. See note on p. 19.

'Oriental Seminary'. According to Pal, *1*, p. 64, RT did not attend this school but had a home tutor who was its headmaster. RT's first school was the Calcutta Training Academy, then at 13 Cornwallis Street, which opened its primary section in 1860. He attended it until September 1864.

**page 21** 'Chanakya's aphorisms'. Chanakya is another name for Kautilya, the very able but unscrupulous Brahmin minister of the Maurya king Chandragupta who ruled in the late fourth century BC, around the time of Alexander's invasion of India. The treatise on statecraft attributed to Chanakya, the *Arthasastra*, shows the king as weak and insignificant, the real ruler of the empire being Chanakya, an idea that may have appealed to RT's servants.

'the *Ramayana* of Krittivas'. The *Ramayana* is one of the two great epics of India, the other being the *Mahabharata*. Originally in Sanskrit, and therefore guarded from the common people, the *Ramayana* has been retold in the Indian vernacular languages by numerous translators. Krittivas, a Brahmin born *c.* 1380, was the first to translate the *Ramayana* into Bengali, at the behest of the King of Gaur. The sweetness and simplicity of his retelling have made his *Ramayana* an essential part of Bengali life ever since. 'There is no home in [Bengal] which does not possess a copy of it, no man or woman who does not know some of its verses by heart.' (Ghosh, p. 34.)

Krittivas' *Ramayana* was one of the texts chosen to teach East India Company servants Bengali. It was first printed as a book in 1802 by the Mission Press at Serampore.

'my mother'. Not much is known of Sarada Devi, who bore Debendranath Tagore fifteen sons and daughters (the first and last of whom died in infancy). She married him in 1834 when she was about eight and he was seventeen. Throughout her life she suffered a conflict between her wish to follow traditional Hindu rites and her husband's Brahmo rejection of idolatry: publicly she accepted the latter, but secretly she sent offerings to certain important shrines. She was uneducated in the modern sense but she read Bengali books such as the translations of the epics. As a conventional Hindu housewife she found her second son Satyendranath's liberal views on women hard to accept. But she enjoyed a certain freedom in the management of the house, including the receiving of interest on her own deposit account. She died in 1875 at the age of about forty-nine, when RT was thirteen (see chapter 42).

'her old aunt'. She was probably the widowed second wife of Sarada Devi's uncle, about the same age as Sarada Devi.

## 3. Within and without

**page 22** 'Niyamat, the tailor'. In his seventies RT wrote a nonsense rhyme about Niyamat (published as number 93 in *Khapchhara*).

**page 23** 'the tribulations of Sita'. Sita is left alone in the forest, after Lakshman has gone in search of Rama. Before he went, Lakshman drew a circle around their cottage with the tip of his bow and warned her not to leave it. When she does so, in order to serve a wandering hermit, the hermit, who is really Ravana, captures her and flies off with her to Lanka.

**page 24** 'outer garden'. The outer portion of the house is the men's, and the inner the women's.

'banyan tree'. 'Purono Bat' (The Ancient Banyan) first appeared in the *Bhadra* (August–September) 1885 issue of *Balak* (see chapter 39).

**page 25** 'the poem I wrote when I was older'. 'Dui Pakhi' (Two Birds) appeared in the collection *Sonar Tari* (The Golden Boat), published in 1894.

'a newly married bride'. Kadambari Devi, the wife of RT's brother Jyotirindranath (see note on p. 95), entered the Tagore household in 1868 when she was about ten and RT was eight. Totally uneducated on arrival (and disapproved of by Satyendranath for that reason), she soon became an avid reader of Bengali literature and in due course, especially after the death of RT's mother in 1875, RT's closest companion and critic. She followed her husband's emancipated ways, even to the extent of openly riding a horse in Calcutta. In April 1884 she committed suicide (see note on p. 178).

**page 26** 'Singhi's Garden'. The garden belonged to Kali Prashanna Sinha (1840–76), satirist and literary patron.

'*chai churi chai*'. *Churi* means bangle, and the cry translates roughly as 'Bangles, who wants bangles?'

**page 27** 'the waterworks had just started up'. They were completed in 1870 and the pipes, acquired from Mackintosh Burn and Company, were fitted in 1871.

**page 28** 'a little girl playmate'. This was Irabati Devi (1861–1918), sister of Satya Prasad Gangopadhyay (see note on p. 19) and niece of RT.

**page 29** 'an elder cousin's rockery'. It belonged to Gunendranath (see chapter 18 and note on p. 91), the son of Debendranath's younger brother Girindranath and the father of Gaganendranath and Abanindranath, who became well-known artists in the early twentieth century.

**page 30** '*Magh* festival'. Maghotsab was the annual festival of the Brahmo Samaj which fell in the month of *Magh* (January–February). It celebrated the founding of the Brahmo Samaj with the signing of the Trust Deed of the Brahmo Sabha on 11 *Magh* (23 January) 1830 by Raja Rammohun Roy and his friends.

**page 31** 'pundit'. The science tutor's name was probably Nil Kamal Ghoshal.

## 4. Servocracy

**page 31** 'Slave Dynasty'. This dynasty of Turkish origin, some of whom were originally slaves, ruled in Delhi from 1206–90.

**page 33** 'the literary and spoken languages'. Until 1800, when English education was introduced in Bengal, Bengali was written in *sadhu-bhasha*, a classicised literary language incorporating many words borrowed from Sanskrit, which, unlike Latin, was alive when Bengali was born. Under the impact of English, especially in the second half of the nineteenth century, *sadhu-bhasha* came to be seen as artificial and unsuitable for prose and was replaced by *chalit-bhasha*, or common language, based mainly on the colloquial speech of Calcutta. RT's work enormously assisted this shift.

'the story of Kusha and Laba'. Following the defeat of Ravana in the *Ramayana*, Rama returned to his kingdom with his abducted wife Sita but there he gave way to pressure of opinion that his wife was impure (having lived in Ravana's palace) and sent her away to live in the forest. She took shelter with sage Valmiki, the supposed author of the *Ramayana*, and gave birth to twins, Kusha and Laba. After many years, when Rama invited Valmiki to perform a religious ritual, the twins came with him. Before Rama they sang the ballad of the *Ramayana* – and justly blamed Rama and Lakshman for banishing Sita.

**page 34** 'the quickstep of Dashuraya's verses'. Dasharathi Ray (1805–57), known as Dashuraya, was a singer-songwriter whose main audience was rural (such as the families of RT's servants) but who became fashionable in Calcutta in the mid-nineteenth century. He started a troupe of *panchali* singers, *panchali* being a compromise between the more conventional slower recitation of the epics and *kabiali*, fast story-telling based mainly on folk tunes accompanied by a small drum and metal cymbal and involving a contest between two singers. Besides mythology, earthily handled, Dashuraya's material came to include controversies of the day such as widow remarriage, urban decadence and the perniciousness of English education.

'Bhishma'. Bhishma is the elder statesman of the Kauravas and their commander-in-chief in the great battle with the Pandavas in the *Mahabharata*. As he lies dying on a bed of arrows, he delivers himself of a dissertation on statecraft and ethics.

'contamination'. Orthodox Hindus consider food unclean while being eaten, and also utensils or anything else touched by the hand engaged in conveying food to the mouth.

## 5. *The Normal School*

**page 35** 'Normal School'. RT joined this school in November 1865 when he was four and a half and left in February 1872. The school's official name was Calcutta Government Pathshala or Calcutta Model School. It was founded in 1839 by David Hare (1775–1842) to 'provide a system of national education and to instruct Hindoo youths in literature, and in the sciences of India and of Europe through the medium of the Bengali language'. Originally situated on land next to Hindu College (which became Presidency College in 1854), the school was transferred in 1860 to 83 Chitpur Road.

**page 36** '*Kallokee pullokee*'. The actual lines are 'Follow me, full of glee, singing merrily, merrily, merrily', from *Hymns for Children* by the American writer Eliza Lee Cabot Follen (1787–1860).

**page 38** 'Pandit Vachaspati'. The second master of the Normal School. RT received one of his books as a prize for good behaviour.

'superintendent'. Gobinda Chandra Bandopadhyay.

## 6. *Versification*

**page 38** 'Jyoti'. Jyoti Prakash Gangopadhyay (1855–1919) was the son of Kadambini, the daughter of Debendranath Tagore's brother Girindranath.

**page 39** 'my elder brother'. See note on p. 19.

'Naba Gopal Mitra'. Mitra, an ardent Brahmo nationalist, was appointed the first editor of the *National Paper*, an English newspaper started in 1865 by Debendranath Tagore as a platform for the Adi Brahmo Samaj which he led. The articles in the first few years were written mostly by Dwijendranath Tagore, the eldest son of Debendranath (see note on p. 44), and advocated a national consciousness free of imitation of the British and of western civilisation. In 1867 Mitra started the Hindu Mela (see note on p. 91). His many patriotic activities earned him the sobriquet 'National Mitra'. He died in 1894.

'*dwirepha*'. This encounter occurred when RT was about eight, and was recalled when he was fifty. In between, aged thirty-three, he referred to it by implication in a letter written from the family estates in East Bengal describing some bees that daily disturbed him in his houseboat: 'I often imagine them to be dissatisfied spirits returned from the next world that call upon me in passing to give me the once-over. But I know better really. Actually they are mere bees, honey-suckers: what we occasionally call in Sanskrit twin-proboscideans.' (*Glimpses of Bengal*, 23 February 1895).

## 7. Diverse lessons

**page 40** *Meghnadbadh*. This poem, the title of which means 'The Capture of Meghnad', was written in 1861 and is the earliest blank verse in Bengali literature and the first epic to be written in Bengali. It is based on an episode in the *Ramayana* and attempts to combine the conventions of Sanskrit, Greek and English heroic verse. Its author was Michael Madhushudan Datta (1824–73). A Christian convert, he spent his early life trying to become a great poet in English, including five disastrous years in England and France from 1862 to 1867. Returning to Calcutta, he commenced practice as a barrister, but proved a failure. He died homeless and destitute in a charitable hospital.

'my third brother'. Hemendranath Tagore (1844–84) is known principally for his supervision of RT's early education. Interested in education and physical fitness, he studied medicine for a while and knew French well. He fathered three sons and eight daughters, of whom one,

Abhigna, had a singing voice loved by RT. She died young, like her father.

'Aghore Babu'. Aghorenath Chattopadhyay taught RT English from March 1869 until ?February 1873.

**page 41** 'Vishnu'. Vishnu Chandra Chakravarti (1819–1901) was appointed as a Brahmo Samaj singer by Raja Rammohun Roy in 1830 and remained one for the rest of his life.

'Sitanath Dutta'. RT is in error: the name should be Sitanath Ghosh (1841–83). He was well known for electrotherapy and was closely associated with attempts to weave cloth organised by the Hindu Mela (see note on p. 91).

'skeleton'. The skeleton was kept in the room next door to the bedroom where RT and the other two boys slept. Its bones used to creak at night when a breeze blew but, RT recalled in old age, having handled the bones and learnt their names he no longer felt a sense of fear. He later wrote 'Kankal' (Skeleton), a short story which appeared in 1892.

**page 42** 'Eurasian students'. Nowadays it would be 'Anglo-Indian students', that is, those of mixed British and Indian parentage, but in RT's day the term Anglo-Indian referred to British people, particularly officials, living in India. Relations between native Bengalis and Eurasians were always in a state of tension.

**page 43** 'Peary Sarkar'. Sarkar (1832–75) was a well-known educationist and writer of school texts. He was a professor at Presidency College and editor of the *Education Gazette*.

**page 44** 'eldest brother'. Dwijendranath Tagore (1840–1926) was the most intellectual of the children of Debendranath. His lasting achievement is the allegorical poem 'Swapnaprayan' (Dream Journey), described by RT in chapters 18 and 19. But he was also a mathematician, musician (he introduced the piano to Bengal) and philosopher, besides sketching well, cleverly constructing cardboard boxes, and inventing a Bengali shorthand which he described in a remarkable verse manual. He also hailed Gandhi long before the rest of his countrymen including RT. 'If he did not achieve the fame of his youngest brother, it was largely due to his utter lack of ambition and perseverance. He was too versatile to stick to any one line and too philosophic (in the traditional Indian sense of being unattached) to take anything too seriously.' (Kripalani, p. 35.)

## 8. *My first outing*

**page 44** 'Chhatu Babu'. This was the familiar name of Ashutosh Dey, one of the wealthiest men in Calcutta. Son of the millionaire Ramdoolal Dey, Ashutosh was one of the original directors of the Union Bank, founded in 1829 by RT's grandfather Dwarkanath and, until its crash in 1848, the keystone of the commercial structure of Calcutta. The crash ruined the Tagore family but not Ashutosh (who nevertheless suffered a severe loss). His riverside villa was at Panihati.

## 9. *Practising poetry*

**page 47** 'Baitarani'. This corresponds to Lethe in Roman mythology.

'Satkari Datta'. His *Pranibritanta* (The Story of Life) was published in 1859.

'Gobinda Babu'. Gobinda Chandra Bandopadhyay.

## 10. *Srikantha Babu*

**page 49** 'Srikantha Babu'. Srikantha Sinha first came to Jorasanko in January 1873 when RT was about to leave for the Himalayas with his father (see chapter 14). He became very friendly with the children of the family and took them on visits to interesting places. RT became a favourite of his after his return. Many of the songs he sang to RT inspired RT's own songs. RT immortalised Srikantha Babu in his first full novel *Bouthakuranir Hat* (The Young Queen's Market). Srikantha Babu was the elder brother of the father of the Brahmo Satyendra Prashanna Sinha, later Lord Sinha, the first Indian member of the Viceroy's Council and the first Indian to be raised to the peerage.

'Hindustani and Bengali'. Hindustani was the Indian language most widely spoken by Europeans in India. At the time RT is describing, Hindustani meant 'the language of the Mahommedans of Upper India ... with a mixture of Persian vocables and phrases, and a readiness to adopt other foreign words ...'. This language was for a long time a kind of Mahommedan *lingua franca* over all India, and still possesses that character over a large part of the country, and among certain classes.' (*Hobson-Jobson*, p. 417.) Another name for Hindustani was Urdu, the language of the *urdu* (horde). In the twentieth century, Hindi has grown out of Hindustani by the adoption of Sanskritised vocabulary, and is now the common language of north India.

**page 50** *'Banishment of Sita'*. *Sitar Banabas*, by Ishwar Chandra Vidyasagar (see note on p. 86) was published in 1860. It is a retelling of the story of Sita's banishment to the forests in the *Ramayana*, based on the Sanskrit version of Bhavabhuti.

**page 51** 'Braja'. This is the name of Krishna's playground, the district where he was born and spent his boyhood.

'a hymn had been set'. The person responsible was Jyotirindranath Tagore (see note on p. 95).

'Chunchura' (Chinsurah). It lies about twenty-five miles north of Calcutta on the Ganges. Formerly a Dutch enclave, Chunchura was ceded to the East India Company in 1825 and became a major military centre until the military station was given up in 1871.

'last visit to my father'. This was in *Ashwin* (September–October) 1884.


## 11. Our Bengali course ends

**page 52** 'Akshay Datta's book'. Akshay Kumar Datta (1820–86) joined Debendranath Tagore's Tattwabodhini Sabha, the successor to Rammohun Roy's Brahmo Sabha when it began in 1839, after a youth of desperate indigence. In 1843 he became editor of its journal *Tattwabodhini Patrika*, filling the position with considerable distinction until 1855. His philosophical and scientific writings, to which RT refers, were largely indebted to English works. 'He was the first Bengali writer to employ modern and scientific methods of inquiry, and he shaped the language into a fit instrument of

argument and discourse.' (Ghosh, p. 122.) His most famous
book, which became a school text, is a miscellany of facts
about the world entitled *Charupath*.

'*Meghnadbadh*'. See note on p. 40.

'my grandfather's life by Mittra'. *Memoir of Dwarkanath
Tagore* by Kissory Chand Mittra was published in Calcutta
in 1870.

**page 53** 'my third brother'. See note on p. 40.

## 12. *The Professor*

**page 54** 'Bengal Academy'. This was an English-medium
institution, unlike the Normal School. The principal was
DeCruz. RT went there in March 1872 and left in December
1873, but his attendance was irregular because of his
Himalayan trip with his father (February–June 1873) and
an attack of dengue fever.

**page 55** 'I have a school of my own'. The school at
Shantiniketan was inaugurated on 22 December 1901 with
five pupils including RT's eldest son Rathindranath (1888–
1961).

**page 56** 'separate refreshment room'. Although Debendranath, Rabindranath and Brahmos as a group were in
principle opposed to caste, caste practices persisted in
the Brahmo Samaj. In chapter 15 RT mentions one of his
own unsuccessful attempts to change them. In 1915, when
Gandhi first visited Shantiniketan, he found separate seats
provided for the Brahmin boys in the refectory, a practice
RT tried to justify on the grounds that he would not force
others to behave against their will, whatever he himself might
believe. This practice was later abolished.

## 13. *My father*

**page 59** 'my father took to constant travel'. In fact,
Debendranath Tagore (1817–1905) took to travelling much
earlier than RT implies. According to his second son
Satyendranath: 'Ever since embracing the Brahmic faith
[that is, since 1838], my father had travelled a good deal.
He made it a rule to set out on tour every year when the

Durga Puja festival came round, with a view to keep himself aloof from the idolatrous ceremonies which were still adhered to and practised in his domestic circle, and which he had no power to abolish.' (Satyendranath, p. 10.) In 1856 Debendranath first set foot in the Himalayas. 'He spent a year and a half among the mountains in the vicinity of the Simla Hills, absorbed in intense study and contemplation, and returned to Calcutta shortly after the Sepoy Mutiny, a regenerated soul, full of ardour and enthusiasm, to propagate the holy religion he had found.' (*ibid.*, pp. 10–11.)

'Lenu'. Debendranath brought him from the Punjab in December 1874.

'Ranjit Singh'. Known as the Lion of the Punjab, the Sikh ruler Maharaja Ranjit Singh (1780–1839), was master of a large part of the area. His relations with the British were uneasy, but he supported them in the 1838 war against Afghanistan. The Koh-i-noor diamond was in his possession, and was partly responsible for his reputation as one of the grandest native rulers of his time.

'my sister-in-law'. See note on p. 25.

'the huge Kabulis'. 'These men, who were known as Kabuliwallas, were much dreaded by Bengalis, who looked upon them as uncouth barbarians who lent money at usurious rates and were ready to kill at the slightest provocation, rough characters who might well steal children and carry them away in the big bags that hung on their huge shoulders.' (Kripalani, p. 163.) RT saw the Kabuliwallas differently and wrote one of his best-known stories, 'Kabuliwalla', about the friendship between a Kabuliwalla and a young Bengali girl (first published in 1892).

**page 60** 'my letter . . . to my father'. The exact date is unknown but it probably lies between May 1868 and December 1870. The British government remained worried about the Russian 'threat' throughout the latter half of the nineteenth century.

**page 61** 'sacred thread'. The investiture took place on 6 February 1873. Debendranath was opposed to idolatry and caste but supported what he conceived as the requirements of 'pure' Vedic Hinduism. One of these was the *upanayan*, or investiture with the sacred thread, which Hindus regard as a spiritual second birth comparable to Christian baptism. What was necessary, Debendranath felt, was to cleanse the debased ritual then in orthodox use and replace it with something truer to the original spirit: 'the investiture with the thread, the begging of alms, the Brahmachari, or student, receiving instructions from the guru – these and such other rites as are the essential part of the ceremony, [would all be] retained. After the investiture, the student [would be] initiated into the holy *gayatri*, a Vedic *mantra* handed down to us from hoary antiquity; and the duties of student-life [would be] duly impressed upon him.' (Satyendranath, p. 30.)

'Pandit Vedantavagish'. Ananda Chandra Bhattacharya (?1820–75), known as Vedantavagish, was an *acharya* (minister) of the Adi Brahmo Samaj.

'*Upanishads*'. About two hundred prose and verse treatises on metaphysical philosophy, produced as commentaries on the *Vedas* and dating from around 400 BC. They deal with the nature of Brahman and the soul and are reputedly divinely inspired. They were the chief scriptural inspiration of Debendranath Tagore and of his son RT, though neither man accepted their divinely revealed nature. W. B. Yeats produced a translation of the *Upanishads* in the 1930s, working with Swami Purohit.

'*Brahma Dharma*'. This was the first attempt to codify the beliefs of the Brahmo Samaj. Compiled by Debendranath Tagore, it was published in 1850. The first part of the book is devotional, and contains texts from the *Upanishads* on the existence and attributes of God and how He should be worshipped. 'This part of the book was thrown off in one sitting, and under one spell of inspiration. My father gave vent to the outpourings of his heart in the words of the *Upanishads*, and Akshay Kumar Datta took them down in writing there and then, and in three hours the whole book was composed.' (Satyendranath, pp. 5–6.) The second part of the book consists of moral precepts from Manu, *Yagnavalkya*, the *Mahabharata* and other Hindu scriptures.

'Becharam Babu'. Becharam Chattopadhyay (1834–86) was a friend of Debendranath Tagore.

'three-days' retreat'. Much later RT wrote that during the retreat his sister-in-law Kadambari Devi had brought them the appropriate food: sunned rice boiled in ghee.

'avert his eyes'. It was considered sinful for non-Brahmins to cast glances on neophytes during the process of their sacred-thread investiture before the ceremony was complete.

**page 62** 'Saradwata or Sarngarava'. Two novices in the hermitage of the sage Kanva, mentioned in the Sanskrit drama *Sakuntala* by Kalidas.

'my eldest brother'. See note on p. 44.

'*The Cloud Messenger*'. *Meghduta* (The Cloud Messenger) is one of the best-known Sanskrit poems. Attributed to Kalidas, ancient India's greatest dramatist and poet, it describes in a little over a hundred verses the voyage of a cloud across India. 'It seems to contain the quintessence of a whole culture.' (Basham, p. 419.) Later poets, including RT, were inspired by the poem's conception and imagery to compose their own versions.

**page 63** 'houseboat'. This trip probably took place in 1875. The boat later became an inseparable companion of RT, when he became estate manager in 1889. He named it *Padma*, after the river. According to Rathindranath, RT's son who also travelled in the boat, it was built by Dwarkanath Tagore and remained moored on the banks of the Hooghly near Calcutta during his lifetime and that of Debendranath. In this boat Debendranath probably received the news of the death of his father Dwarkanath in London in 1846, by fast courier sent from Calcutta: Debendranath was then up-river. Some of his river trips went as far as Benares.

'*Gita Govinda*'. This poem was written in Sanskrit by Jayadeva, a Bengali then resident at the court of Lakshman Sen, the last Hindu king of Bengal, who lost his throne *c.* AD 1200 to Muslim conquerors. The *Gita Govinda* has been called the Indian Song of Songs – an apt description in many ways. It sings of the love of Krishna and Radha with an intensity of physical passion, and with a wealth of sensuous imagery and verbal music, of which there are but few equals in the world.

(Ghosh, p. 28.) It has enjoyed great popularity in Bengal ever since its composition.

**page 64** '*Birth of the War-God*'. The lines quoted by RT are from *Kumarasambhava* (*1*, 15). 'The poem describes the courtship and marriage of Siva and Parvati, and the birth of their son, Kumara or Skanda, the war-god. As he grows to manhood Kumara is appointed general of the gods, and he leads them forth to battle with the terrible demon Taraka, who has long been afflicting the whole universe. Taraka hears of their approach, musters his forces, and goes out to meet them; but terrible omens greet the army of demons . . . The poem ends with the death of Taraka in single combat with Kumara . . . With brilliant use of assonance and alliteration Kalidas has wedded sound to sense in a way rarely achieved in the literature of the world.' (Basham, pp. 421–2.)

## 14. A journey with my father

**page 65** 'to the Himalayas?' Debendranath made the offer in January 1873, when RT was eleven. They left Jorasanko on 14 February and arrived in Shantiniketan the same day. RT returned to Jorasanko in May/June 1873.

'the dust of my elders' feet'. This gesture, known as *pranam*, involves bending to touch the feet of the respected person with the fingers, which one then touches to one's own forehead.

**page 66** 'Bolpur'. This was then the nearest railway station to Shantiniketan, as it still is. Debendranath had bought the land nearby on 1 March 1863 from the Sinha family of Raipur (see note on p. 49) after falling in love with the spot. A hut already existed with the name Shantiniketan; this was demolished but the name retained. There was also a *chhatim* tree under which Debendranath pitched a tent and meditated. During the next few years a structure was built and some plants and shrubs brought from Calcutta. Nevertheless, father and son had barely two rooms when they visited in 1873.

'Satya'. See note on p. 19.

**page 67** 'railway carriage'. The first commercially run passenger train in Bengal went from Howrah (Calcutta) to Hooghly in August 1854. The following year a train ran from Howrah to Burdwan, the nearest large town to Shantiniketan. During the 1850s and 1860s the service was widely extended in Bengal.

**page 69** 'Livingstone'. RT was, of course, writing long after Livingstone's expedition to the source of the Nile, but since Livingstone's famous encounter with Stanley took place in October 1871, it is quite possible that it was in the mind of the boy Rabi as he explored the Bengal countryside in 1873.

**page 70** 'estate accounts'. Debendranath appointed his son manager of the family estates in East Bengal and Orissa in June 1889, when RT was twenty-eight.

'Park Street'. Park Street is a fashionable street in central Calcutta several miles from Jorasanko. It was the residence of several Tagores at various times. Debendranath lived at 52 Park Street from 1887 to 1898.

'the new prayer hall at Bolpur'. Known as the Mandir, this striking building is still a central feature of Shantiniketan. Plans were begun in October 1888; RT became a trustee in July 1889; the foundation stone was laid in December 1890; and the first service took place on 21 December 1891. The chief architect was Prashanna Kumar Sarkar. Parts of the building were assembled in Calcutta. It has a wrought-iron frame supporting glass panels of several colours, and a marble floor.

'*Bhagavadgita*'. Book VI of the *Mahabharata* is the famous *Bhagavadgita* (Song of the Lord), in which Krishna, as Prince Arjuna's charioteer, counsels him on his duty to God in time of war, his duty to men, and the nature of God and men.

**page 71** 'Defeat of King Prithvi'. Prithviraj is the bold and chivalrous hero of the Rajputs, whose defeat in 1192 laid the foundations of Muslim rule in northern India. RT probably read of him in James Tod's classic *Annals and Antiquities of Rajasthan* (1829–32). He may also have read the manuscript of his sister Swarna Kumari's (?1856–1932) first novel *Dipnirvan* (The Extinction of the Lamp), based on the story of Prithviraj. The novel was written in 1873–4 and published in 1876.

'Sahibganj, Dinapur'. Sahibganj is roughly north of Calcutta on the Ganges at the point where the river bends west. Dinapur is also on the river, close to Patna. By the time RT reached Amritsar he had crossed northern India from east to west.

**page 72** 'The Golden Temple'. The religious importance of Amritsar dates from the early sixteenth century when Nanak founded Sikhism and built a temple. The present temple – the one RT would have seen – dates from the eighteenth century.

'O Companion'. This is a Brahmo devotional song composed by Satyendranath Tagore in January 1869 and set to music by Vishnu Chakravarti.

**page 73** 'Srikantha Babu'. See note on p. 49.

'*Magh*'. See note on p. 30.

'Chunchura'. See note on p. 51.

'Peter Parley series'. Other books in this series belonging to the family covered the history and geography of the world and a book on plants.

'the advance I had made in Bengali'. A large proportion of words in literary Bengali are derived unchanged from Sanskrit. The proportion was higher in the nineteenth century than in this century.

**page 74** 'Proctor'. Richard A. Proctor was the author of a number of books of popular astronomy, some of which were in the possession of the family.

## 15. In the Himalayas

**page 74** 'Dalhousie hills'. Named after a governor-general of India, Dalhousie is a hill-station on the borders of Jammu and Kashmir state at a height of nearly 7000 feet. In 1873 it was just a small cluster of bungalows.

**page 76** '*Upanishads*'. See note on p. 61.

**page 77** 'the Grand Trunk Road'. This ancient arterial route across northern India links Calcutta, Benares, Kanpur,

Aligarh, Delhi, Ambala, Lahore and Peshawar. RT's fascination with it recalls a similar feeling in the young Rudyard Kipling at about the same time, which found expression in *Kim*. There an old soldier speaks of the 'wonderful spectacle' of the road where 'all castes and kinds of men move . . . Brahmins and chumars, bankers and tinkers, barbers and bunnias, pilgrims and potters – all the world coming and going. It is to me as a river from which I am withdrawn like a log after a flood.'

**page 78** 'Secretary of the Adi Brahmo Samaj'. The appointment was made in *Ashwin* (September–October) 1884. The Adi (Original) Brahmo Samaj was so called to distinguish it from the two further Brahmo Samajes formed from the original Samaj in the 1860s and 1870s.

'Park Street'. See note on p. 70.

'my second brother', Satyendranath Tagore (1842–1923) was a brilliant student of Presidency College who became the first Indian to travel to England and successfully sit the entrance examination of the Indian Civil Service, in 1862. He served in the ICS in many parts of India (he was stationed in Pune when he wrote the letter RT mentions). A fine scholar in Sanskrit, he also wrote well in Bengali and English. His books include verse translations of the *Bhagavadgita* (see note on p. 70) and the *Meghduta* (see note on p. 62), a study of Buddhism, a volume of reminiscences and his fine translation into English (with his daughter Indira) of his father Debendranath's autobiography. '[Satyendranath's] influence, direct and indirect, on the development of his youngest brother, Rabindranath, as a man if not as a poet, was deep, subtle and abiding. It acted as a gentle and healthy corrective to the overpowering moral and intellectual influence of the Maharshi on the young Rabindranath. The Maharshi was radical in his religious convictions but conservative in his social attitudes, though he was big enough to tolerate differences of outlook from members of his family. It was Satyendranath who first asserted his freedom to live as he chose, in accordance with the new values of women's education and their rights

which he had imbibed during his education in England.'
(Kripalani, pp. 35–6.)

**page 79** 'my father sent me back home'. This happened
some time in May/June. On 27 June 1873 Debendranath
wrote from Bakrota to Calcutta: 'I am sending Rabindra
to you all as a live letter' (translated).

## 16. My return

**page 80** 'the youngest bride of our house'. See note on p. 25.

'my youngest sister'. Barna Kumari Devi (1858–1948)
was Debendranath's youngest daughter. She never went
to school and little is known of her life, apart from her
marriage to a medical student.

'Nil Kamal Pandit'. See chapter 11.

**page 81** 'Aghore Babu'. See chapter 7.

**page 82** 'someone who looked small'. RT is referring
to his own name Rabi, which means Sun.

**page 83** 'Dasharathi'. See note on p. 34.

'the god whose role is to puncture pride'. This is
Madhusudhan, one of the many names of Krishna.

**page 84** 'St Xavier's'. The college was established in
1834 and affiliated to Calcutta University in 1862. RT
spent about two and a half months there from February
1875; his name was spelt 'Tagore, Nubindronath' in the
school register. There were three other Bengali boys in his
class.

**page 85** 'Father DePeneranda'. Alphonsus DePeneranda
(1834–96).

## 17. Home studies

**page 86** 'Gyan Babu'. Gyan Chandra Bhattacharya.

'Pandit Vedantavagish'. See note on p. 61.

'*Birth of the War-God*'. See note on p. 64.

'*Macbeth*'. Although the rest of RT's translation was
lost, the 'Witches' Scene' appeared in the *Ashwin* (September–October) 1880 issue of *Bharati*.

'Pandit Ramsarvaswa'. Ramsarvaswa Bhattacharya (1843–
1912) was head pandit of the Metropolitan Institution (see

note on p. 108). He was appointed to teach RT Sanskrit in November 1874.

'*Sakuntala*'. This is the most famous of the three plays by Kalidas, first translated into English by Sir William Jones in 1789. It concerns the love of King Dushyanta for a semi-divine nymph.

'Pandit Vidyasagar'. Ishwar Chandra Vidyasagar (1820–91) was a scholar, educationist, social reformer, philanthropist and the most outstanding Bengali between Raja Rammohun Roy and RT. His major works are versions in Bengali – largely original – of other works in Hindi, Sanskrit and English, including *Sakuntala*, *Sitar Banabas* (The Banishment of Sita), and *Bhrantibilas* (based on Shakespeare's *Comedy of Errors*). With the publication of these works, 'Bengali prose [had] at last arrived . . . The writers before [Vidyasagar] had observed an arbitrary divorce between *chalit-bhasha* (colloquial language) and *sadhu-bhasha* (literary language), and their style had faltered between the coarseness of the first and the pedantic obscurity of the second. But Vidyasagar reformed them both and created a style which combined the naturalness of the one with the strength of the other.' (Ghosh, pp. 125–6.)

'Raj Krishna Mukherji'. RT appears to be in error: he means Raj Krishna Bandopadhyay (Banerji), a friend of Vidyasagar, translator and founder member of the Calcutta Training Academy, RT's first school.

**page 87** 'Dinabandhu Mitra's satires'. Mitra (1829–74) was a highly successful dramatist in the early days of Bengali theatre. His plays are mainly farces abounding in 'crude and crazy mirth'. (Ghosh, p. 150.) The titles give a good idea of the plays' content: *Sadhabar Ekadasi* (Forced Widowhood of a Married Girl, 1866), *Biye Pagla Buro* (Old Man Mad for Marriage, 1866), *Jamai Barik* (The Barrack for Sons-in-law, 1872). His first play, *Nil Darpan* (The Mirror of Indigo, 1860), was more serious and is his most famous because it led to a prosecution of its publisher Reverend James Long by the indigo planters.

**page 88** 'Dr Rajendra Lal Mitra'. He started his magazine *Bibidhartha Sangraha* (Miscellany of Various Matters) in

1851. 'The first serious attempts at a history of the Bengali language and literature appeared in the pages of [this] magazine.' (Sen, p. 170.) See chapter 35 for RT's description of Mitra.

'My third brother'. See note on p. 40.

*'Abodhabandhu'*. This magazine was first published in *Baishakh* (April–May) 1863 and stopped after a few months. It resumed publication in 1867 for three years.

**page 89** 'eldest brother's library'. See note on p. 44.

'Bihari Lal Chakravarti'. Chakravarti (1834–94) was never a scholar but his poetry was profoundly influenced by the *Ramayana* and Kalidas. Lyricism is its keynote and it is 'inward-looking and subjective, but has little of significance to communicate'. (Ghosh, p. 148.) The best-known work is 'Sarada Mangal' (The Divine Song of Poetic Inspiration, 1879), begun in 1870 and published incomplete. It was finished at the instance of Kadambari Devi, RT's sister-in-law. Chakravarti later wrote part of another poem 'Sadher Ashan' (The Cherished Cushion, 1888–9) for Kadambari, in exchange for a woollen cushion she had knitted for him. After her suicide in 1884, he completed the poem.

*'Paul et Virginie'*. The didactic romance *Paul et Virginie*, set in Mauritius in the first half of the eighteenth century, is the best-known work of the French naturalist and writer Jacques Henri Bernardin de Saint Pierre (1737–1814), a friend of Rousseau. The book was first published in 1787, translated into English in 1789, and has since passed through more than five hundred editions in many languages. The Bengali translation by Krishna Kumar Bhattacharya appeared in *Abodhabandhu* in 1868–9.

'Bankim's *Bangadarshan*'. Bankim Chandra Chattopadhyay (Chatterji) (1838–94) was Bengal's first novelist, besides being a formidable essayist. He wrote fourteen novels in Bengali, mostly with historical settings, and was known as the Scott of Bengal. He started *Bangadarshan* (Mirror of Bengal) in 1872 and ran it until 1876. *Bishabriksha* (The Poison Tree, 1873) was the first of his novels to be serialised in the magazine. *Chandrashekhar* (1877) was serialised in 1874–5. For RT's description of his relationship with Bankim, see chapter 40.

'compilations from the old poets'. This series appeared between 1874 and 1876, jointly edited by Mitter (1848–1917) and Sarkar (1846–1917).

**page 90** 'Vidyapati'. Vidyapati lived in Mithila in Bihar in the fifteenth century and wrote in Maithili, a language different – but not fundamentally so – from Bengali. Though not strictly speaking a Bengali poet, he came to be regarded as one. The diction of the Maithili poets strongly appealed to the Vaishnava poets of Bengal in the sixteenth to eighteenth centuries, as it did to RT in the nineteenth.

## 18. My home environment

**page 90** 'Ganendra'. Ganendranath Tagore (1841–69) was the first child of Girindranath, brother of Debendranath. He died of cholera.

**page 91** *'Vikramorvasi'*. This play, the title of which means 'Urvasi Won by Valour', is one of the three plays by Kalidas.

'Hindu Mela'. This annual festival was started in 1867 by Naba Gopal Mitra (see note on p. 39) and others, with the active support of the Tagore family. Its purpose was cultural-cum-political: to turn the attention of city-dwellers to indigenous rather than imported products and to the tradition of village handicrafts in particular; and to boost national pride. It was thus one of the precursors of the Indian National Congress, founded in 1885. The motives behind the Mela were questioned by many (including Dwijendranath Tagore who criticised Mitra's tendency always to invite senior English officials), and it was closed down in 1881 for lack of public interest.

'Gunendra'. Gunendranath Tagore (1847–81) was the father of the artists Gaganendranath and Abanindranath. His granddaughter Pratima Devi married RT's son Rathindranath.

**page 92** 'Satya'. See note on p. 19.

'my eldest brother'. See note on p. 44.

*'Swapnaprayan'*. This poem was written in 1873–4 and published in 1875.

## 19. Literary companions

**page 95** 'Akshay Chaudhuri'. A friend of Jyotirindranath, Chauduri was the first contributor to *Bharati*, the magazine started by the Tagores in 1877.

'my fifth brother'. Jyotirindranath Tagore (1849–1925) is intertwined in the early life of RT, as the second half of *My Reminiscences* shows. Musician, composer, artist, poet, dramatist, translator (from Sanskrit, English and French), Jyotirindranath was 'a genius of uncommon versatility and one of the most accomplished men of his age. Handsome, elegant and daring, he was a Prince Charming of the Indian renaissance and a pioneer in almost every field . . . It would hardly be an exaggeration to say that evidence of Jyotirindranath's genius is to be seen only partly in his own individual achievements; in part it lies hidden in the great fulfilment of his [younger] brother's powe.s.' (Kripalani, p. 37.)

**page 96** '*Bangadarshan*'. See note on p. 89.

**page 97** 'our difference in age'. This was about twelve years.

**page 98** 'to help hold them in our memories'. Systems of notation were not then in use. One of the most popular of the systems used in this century was devised by Jyotirindranath.

'Gyan Babu'. See note on p. 86.

'Braja Babu'. Brajanath Dey, superintendent of the Metropolitan Institution.

**page 99** 'my sister-in-law'. See note on p. 25.

'Bihari Lal Chakravarti'. See note on p. 89.

**page 100** 'Valmiki and Kalidas'. Sage Valmiki is the traditional composer of the *Ramayana*; Kalidas is ancient India's greatest poet and dramatist (see notes on pp. 21 and 62.)

## 20. Publication

**page 101** '*Gyanankur*'. This magazine was first published in ?*Ashwin* (September–October) 1872.

'*Bhubanmohini Pratibha*'. The author was Nabin Chandra Mukhopadhyay (1853–1922).

'Akshay Babu'. See chapter 19 and note on p. 95.

'Bhudeb Babu'. Bhudeb Mukhopadhyay (1827–94) was a scholar, critic and writer of fiction.

## 21. *Bhanu Singh*

**page 102** 'Akshay Sarkar and Sarada Mitter'. See note on p. 89.

**page 103** 'Maithili'. See note on p. 90.

'Adi Brahmo Samaj'. See note on p. 78.

'Bhanu Singh'. The old Vaishnava poets used to bring their name into the last stanza of a poem to serve as their signature. Bhanu and Rabi both mean Sun. The name may have been given to RT by his sister-in-law Kadambari Devi, whom he had named Hecate after the Greek goddess associated with the night. (See Pal, *1*, p. 337.)

'Vidyapati and Chandidas'. See note on p. 90 for Vidyapati. Chandidas probably lived in the fifteenth century, like Vidyapati, but wrote in Bengali not Maithili. There may have been several poets who used the name Chandidas. His songs were later admired by the mystic Chaitanya (1485–1533).

**page 104** '*Bharati*'. The poems were published from 1877 in *Bharati*, the Tagore family magazine.

'Nishikanta Chatterji'. Chatterji (1852–1910) was in Europe from about 1873 to 1882.

## 22. *Patriotism*

**page 105** 'Hindu Mela'. See note on p. 91.

'Naba Gopal Mitra'. See note on p. 39.

'*durbar*'. These grand imperial assemblies at Delhi (following Mughal tradition) took place in 1876–7 (when Lord Lytton was Viceroy) and in 1902–3 (when Lord Curzon was Viceroy).

'Nabin Sen'. Sen (1846–1909) was a minor poet who became famous with a Byronic poem about the battle of Plassey. He wrote a trilogy based on the Krishna story as told in the *Mahabharata*.

'Raj Narain Bose'. Bose (1826–1899) has been described as the high priest of Indian nationalism. He spent his youth as part of Young Bengal, uncritically admiring everything western including alcohol, and then, like many young men of his time, experienced a severe crisis of identity. When he was nineteen he came in contact with Debendranath Tagore and joined the Brahmo Samaj. In 1870, after the first split of the Samaj, Bose became president of the Adi (Original) Brahmo Samaj. His outlook may be expressed by quoting one of his witticisms directed at his own deracinated youth and at others following the same westernised path laid down by Thomas Babington Macaulay: 'I can speak in English, write in English, think in English, and shall be supremely happy when I can dream in English.' (Quoted in Kopf, p. 167.)

**page 108** 'Braja Babu'. See note on p. 98.

'Metropolitan Institution'. RT attended this school briefly from January 1874. The school was founded by Ishwar Chandra Vidyasagar (see note on p. 86.)

'Raj Narain Babu'. See note on p. 105.

**page 110** 'Richardson'. He was Captain D. L. Richardson, a poet and teacher at Hindu College, the precursor of Presidency College, from 1835–43.

## 23. *Bharati*

**page 110** 'earth . . . sober stability.' Earthquakes are not infrequent in Bengal. A particularly serious one occurred in June 1897.

**page 111** *'Bharati'*. The first issue appeared on 29 July 1877.

*'Meghnadbadh'*. See note on p. 40.

'Kabikahini'. This book, RT's first, was published in 1878. The 'enthusiastic friend' was Prabodh Chandra Ghosh.

## 24. *Ahmedabad*

**page 113** 'my second brother'. See note on p. 78.

'a palace of the Badshahs of old'. Shahibagh was a seventeenth-century palace originally built by Prince Khurram (later the Emperor Shahjahan, builder of the Taj Mahal). The house became the official residence of the governor of Gujarat and is now a museum in which

RT's room is preserved. RT later immortalised the house in 'Kshudita Pashan' (The Hungry Stones, 1895).

'Sabarmati river'. It was on the banks of this river at Ahmedabad that Gandhi built his ashram in 1915.

**page 114** 'Dr Haberlin'. The book is *Kabya Sangraha*, edited by Dr John Haberlin, and contains passages by Kalidas and other Sanskrit poets. It was published by the Mission Press at Serampore in 1847.

'Amaru Shataka'. Amaru was an erotic poet, probably of the seventh century AD.

'song addressed to the rose-maiden'. This was published in December 1880 in *Bharati*, after RT's return from England.

## 25. England

**page 115** 'we started for England'. RT sailed on 20 September 1878 with Satyendranath.

'my sister-in-law and her children'. Satyendranath's wife was Jnanadanandini Devi (1850–1941). When she married Satyendranath in 1859 she was more or less illiterate. He educated her not only in Bengali and English but in the accomplishments of Victorian women in England. The occasion when he took her out unveiled in an open carriage in Calcutta, like a memsahib, is said to have caused a major scandal. It was she who later changed the orthodox woman's costume and adapted the sari to present-day styles, and designed the blouse to accompany it. Their children were Surendranath (1872–1940) and Indira (1873–1960), both of whom had a close relationship with RT, including translating some of his writings. (*My Reminiscences* was translated by Surendranath.)

**page 116** ' "a" in warm and "o" in worm'. RT could have offered his own name Rabindranath as an example of the problems of spelling Bengali words in English: it would be better written, for pronunciation purposes, as Robindronath, but this would play havoc with the spelling of the name in Bengali. The accepted spelling in English therefore leaves much ambiguity in the correct pronunciation of 'a'.

'she in Bengal'. See note on p. 25.

'cranium'. There was a craze for phrenology at the time.
**page 117** 'Tarak Palit'. Latterly Sir Taraknath Palit (1841–1914), he was a distinguished lawyer and lifelong friend of Satyendranath Tagore. He later lent RT money to help him run his school at Shantiniketan.
**page 120** 'a refuge in the house of a Dr Scott'. This was probably at 10 Tavistock Square, WC1. Apart from Dr and Mrs Scott, there were four daughters, two sons, three maids, and a dog Toby. The youngest Scott children called RT Uncle Arthur!
**page 122** 'Anglo-Indian'. See note on p. 42.
**page 123** 'University College'. RT attended lectures in the faculty of arts and laws for only three months. With Henry Morley he read *Religio Medici*, *Coriolanus* and *Anthony and Cleopatra* – an experience he recalled with pleasure.

## 26. *Loken Palit*

**page 127** 'Loken Palit'. Lokendranath Palit was the son of Taraknath Palit (see note on p. 117). He, RT and Satyendranath Tagore visited England in 1890. In the 1890s RT tried to involve his friend in writing for his new magazine *Sadhana*, but Palit preferred only to write letters to RT. He pursued a career in the Indian Civil Service and died young.
**page 128** 'Indian Civil Service'. The first Indian to gain entry into this élite was Satyendranath Tagore (see note on p. 78).

## 27. *'The Broken Heart'*

**page 128** 'The Broken Heart'. The book was dedicated to 'H', whom RT admitted was Hecate, his name for his sister-in-law Kadambari Devi (see note on p. 25). RT did not allow it to be reprinted in his collected works. Many aspects of his relationship with Kadambari Devi are found in his novella *Nashtanir* (The Broken Nest, 1901). (For a recent translation of this, see *Selected Short Stories* in the Bibliography.)
**page 131** 'Akshay Chaudhuri'. See note on p. 95.
**page 132** 'songs of Shyama'. Devotional songs in praise of the goddess Kali, known as *Shyamasangit*, have a long and powerful tradition in Bengal deriving from the most

famous composer of them, Ramprashad Sen, who lived in the eighteenth century.

## 28. European Music

**page 135** 'Madame Nilsson or Madame Albani'. Christine Nilsson (1843–1922) was Swedish, Dame Albani (1852–1930) was Canadian.

## 29. Valmiki Pratibha

**page 137** 'Moore'. Thomas Moore (1779–1852).
'Akshay Babu'. See note on p. 95.
**page 138** *'telena'*. Some Indian classical melodic compositions are designed on a scheme of accentuation, for which purpose the music is set not to words but to unmeaning notation sounds representing drumbeats or plectrum impacts, which in Indian music are of a considerable variety of tone, each having its own sound symbol. *Telena* is one such style of composition.
'Two English tunes ... and an Irish melody.' These were probably among those taught to RT by one of the daughters of Dr Scott in London.
'my niece, Pratibha'. Pratibha Sundari Devi (1865–1922) was the eldest daughter of RT's brother Hemendranath.
**page 139** 'some work of Herbert Spencer's'. This was 'The Origin and Function of Music',. in *Essays Scientific, Political, and Speculative*, Vol. 1.
'King Dasharatha'. This killing eventually leads to Dasharatha's son Rama having to leave the kingdom, and hence to the epic of the *Ramayana*.
*'Mayar Khela'*. This was published in *Agrahayan* (November–December) 1888.
**page 140** 'Bihari Chakravarti'. See note on p. 89.
**page 141** *'Alik Babu'*. Alik Babu (The False Babu, 1900) was the revised title of Jyotirindranath's second farce, originally entitled *Eman Karma Ar Karba Na* (I Won't Do It Again, 1877).
'Shelidah'. In the 1890s RT spent much of his time at Shelidah, while managing the family estates. It was in the back of beyond, reachable only by boat. According to Pal, *1*,

p. 286, the name Shelidah derives from Shelley, the name of the indigo planter who ran a factory there, and *dah*, a word describing a bay cut off from a river that has created it – in this case two rivers, the Padma and the Gorai, which meet at Shelidah.

## 31. *An essay on music*

**page 144** 'father had recalled me home from England'. RT returned to India in February 1880 aged eighteen.

'second voyage'. RT left in April 1881 with his newly married nephew Satya Prasad Gangopadhyay (see note on p. 19). They returned because Satya was missing his wife.

**page 145** 'Mussoorie'. This is a hill-station in the western Himalayas.

'Bethune Society'. John Drinkwater Bethune was a social reformer particularly dedicated to the education of Bengali women. He founded a school for women in 1849 and a society in 1851, just before his death. In 1879, a college for women bearing his name was also founded. RT spoke at the society on 19 April 1881.

'K. M. Banerji'. The Reverend Krishna Mohun Banerji (1813–85) was a well-known Brahmo missionary.

**page 146** 'classic style of Hindustan'. RT is here distinguishing the style from different provincial styles, but chiefly from the Dravidian style prevalent in the south of India.

'Nidhu Babu'. Ramnidhi Gupta (1742–1839) introduced into Bengali song the *tappa*, a light, semi-classical type of song from the Hindustani tradition.

**page 147** 'Bolpur'. See note on p. 66.

## 32. *The riverside*

**page 148** 'Chandannagar'. Chandernagore, twenty miles north of Calcutta, was first settled by the French in 1673. It remained a French enclave until 1951, when a referendum made it part of India.

'I went to stay with them.' This was in mid-1881.

**page 149** 'Puravi . . . Behag'. Many of the Hindustani classical ragas are supposed to be best in keeping with particular seasons of the year or times of the day. Thus Puravi is an early-evening, Behag a late-evening raga.

'Moran's Garden'. Moran was an indigo planter.

## 33. More about Evening Songs

**page 151** 'Ramesh Chandra Dutt'. R. C. Dutt (1848 –1909) was a distinguished historian, a novelist and translator, and a social reformer. Besides a career in the Indian Civil Service, he was also president of the Indian National Congress.

## 34. Morning Songs

**page 152** *'Bibidha Prabandha'*. This was published in *Bhadra* (August–September) 1883.

**page 153** *'Bauthakuranir Hat'*. This was published in *Paush* (December–January) 1883–4.

'a house in Calcutta, on Sudder Street'. It was 10 Sudder Street, off Chowringhee in central Calcutta, in the European quarter. Jyotirindranath was in the house from about April to June 1882.

**page 154** 'Awakening of the Waterfall'. This was published in the *Agrahayan* (November–December) 1882 issue of *Bharati*.

**page 159** 'Mohit Babu's edition'. In 1903–4 Mohit Chandra Sen, a professor of philosophy in Calcutta and a lover of RT's poetry, edited a collection of his poems and plays, rearranging them in sections according to content and labelling them with headings that do not always follow the titles of the constituent books. The poet wrote a new prefatory poem for each section in which he attempted to indicate the significance of the new heading. (See Sen, p. 266.)

**page 160** *'Bibidha Prabandha'*. See note on p. 152.

*'Alochana'*. These were published in ?April 1885.

## 35. Rajendra Lal Mitra

**page 161** 'Sahitya Parishad'. At a public meeting in July 1893 a resolution was passed to set up a Bengal Academy of Literature. Towards the end of the same year the name was changed to Bangiya Sahitya Parishad. The first president was Ramesh Chandra Dutt (see note on p. 151); RT was a vice-president. The first proposal for such a body dates to 1872.

'Pandit Vidyasagar'. See note on p. 86.

'Bankim Babu'. See note on p. 89.

**page 162** *'Bharati'*. See chapter 23.

**page 163** 'Krishna Das Pal'. Pal (1838–84) was a celebrated editor and a politician known for his close relationship with the government.

'Asiatic Society'. Founded in 1784 by Sir William Jones, throughout the nineteenth century it published some of the most significant research on all aspects of Indian history, arts and sciences. Rajendra Lal Mitra was one of the first Indians to become involved with the Society.

'death' [of Mitra and Vidyasagar]. Vidyasagar died two days after Mitra in July 1891.

## 36. Karwar

**page 163** 'Karwar'. RT went there in March 1883 and returned to Calcutta in the autumn.

**page 164** 'my second brother'. See note on p. 78.

'Shivaji'. Shivaji (1627–80) was the founder of the Maratha dynasty and a formidable opponent of the Mughal emperors.

'Mohit Babu's edition'. See note on p. 159.

## 37. Nature's Revenge

**page 167** 'Mother, leave your darling boy to us'. This song is addressed to Yashoda, mother of Krishna, by his playmates. Yashoda used to dress up her darling every morning in his yellow garment with a peacock plume in his hair but when it came to the point, she was nervous about allowing him, young as he was, to join the other cowherd boys at the pastures. It often required a great deal of persuasion before they would be permitted to take charge of him. This is part of the Vaishnava tradition of Krishna's early life.

'I was married.' The suddenness and brevity of this comment fits well with the nature of RT's marriage, though it may surprise a western reader. Efforts to find a bride for RT had, in fact, been made earlier: once, he and his brother Jyotirindranath had been invited to a principality in neighbouring Orissa to meet a young lady, only to find two young ladies present, one exceedingly plain, the other exceptionally attractive. Sadly for RT, the first turned out to be the prospective bride, the second her stepmother!

His new wife was an almost illiterate ten-year-old, the daughter of one of the family employees on the Tagore estates in the district of Jessore in East Bengal. She was chosen by the wives of Satyendranath and Jyotirindranath – themselves equally uneducated at the same age – simply because she was one of the few girls of the right Pirali Brahmin caste. Debendranath Tagore, the head of the family, was conservative in such matters, whatever his other views. His youngest son RT – the great romantic in poetry – fell in obediently with his father's wish.

The wedding took place at Jorasanko, instead of the bride's home as was usual, on 9 December 1883. RT had sent out invitations in which he wrote that 'his intimate relative Rabindranath Tagore was to be married'. On the day itself he sang one of the songs written by his sister Swarna Kumari Devi, while looking at his bride to embarrass her. The traditional Hindu rituals were mostly observed but there was very little fuss and few people attended – not even RT's father and second brother Satyendranath were present. The family does not appear to have taken the occasion very seriously: the main intention seems to have been to anchor RT's wayward personality.

The bride's name was Bhavatarini, a name that was old-fashioned even at the time. It was changed to Mrinalini, probably at RT's own suggestion.

## 38. Pictures and Songs

**page 168** '*Chhabi o Gan*'. This was published in *Phalgun* (February–March) 1884.

'*busti*'. The original sense of the word was an inhabited quarter or village. In Tagore's day, according to a note in the first edition of *My Reminiscences*, 'A *busti* [is] an area thickly packed with shabby tiled huts, with narrow pathways running through and connecting it with the main street. These are inhabited by domestic servants, the poorer class of artisans and the like. Such settlements were formerly scattered throughout the town even in the best localities, but are now gradually disappearing from the latter.' Since then, the *bustis* of Calcutta have grown enormously and the word is now synonymous with slum.

## 39. An intervening period

**page 169** '*Kari o Komal*' This was written in 1884–6 and published in 1886.

'*Balak*'. The first issue appeared in *Baishakh* (April–May 1885) It was the idea of Jnanadanandini Devi, the wife of Satyendranath (see note on p. 115).

'Raj Narain Babu'. See note on p. 105.

**page 170** 'Deoghar' A town off the railway line from Calcutta to Patna, some fifty miles south of the Ganges near Bhagalpur.

'*Rajarshi*'. This was published in instalments in *Balak* in 1886–7 and then as a book in 1887.

## 40. Bankim Chandra

**page 172** 'Bankim Babu'. See note on p. 89.

'Calcutta University'. Hindu College was founded in 1816 and in 1854 became Presidency College. This was the nucleus of Calcutta University, founded in 1857.

'Chandranath Babu'. Chandranath Basu (1844–1910) was the librarian of the Bengal Library. RT met him in September 1884 and they remained friends until Basu's death. Basu reviewed a number of RT's works.

**page 173** 'Howrah'. This is the name of the area on the opposite bank of the Hooghly from Calcutta. It is now a sprawling suburb of the city.

**page 174** '*Nabajiban*'. This was first published in *Shravan* (July–August) 1884. See note on p. 89 about Akshay Sarkar.

'*Bangadarshan*'. See note on p. 89.

'Sanjib Babu'. Sanjib Chandra Chattopadhyay (1834–89)

wrote several novels but is best known for his travel sketches *Palamau* (published serially 1880–2).

'Pandit Sashadhar'. He visited Calcutta in 1884. Sashadhar Tarkachudamani (?1851–1928) sought to justify every Hindu practice – from child marriage and *sati* to the most trivial superstitions – by reference to Hindu scriptures, bolstered with pseudo-science. He claimed to find the roots of all scientific knowledge in Hinduism and dismissed western civilisation as inferior. This had an immense appeal to Hindus bruised by the colonial encounter.

**page 175** *'Prachar'*. This began publishing a fortnight after *Nabajiban*. The editor was Bankim's son-in-law.

'happened to fall foul of Bankim Babu'. The argument began when RT criticised Bankim's role as a 'preacher' in one of his novels, which in RT's view made the novel's characters unreal. It developed into a debate between the Hindu and Brahmo view of lying. Bankim commented, with reference to an episode in the *Mahabharata*, that there are occasions when a departure from *satya* – truth – may be justified. RT criticised this apparent approval of lies. In his reply Bankim claimed that the English translation of the word *satya* as 'truth' had distorted its Sanskrit meaning. He went on to argue that by adopting English terms and concepts Bengalis were in danger of adopting English vices too – hypocrisy in particular.

## 41. The steamer hulk

**page 175** 'auction'. Jyotirindranath saw the auction advertised in the *Exchange Gazette* and paid Mackenzie Lal and Company 7000 rupees for the hulk. After an engineer, Mr Bushby, had gone over it, the hulk was rebuilt by the Kelso-Stewart Company. It was not ready as soon as expected, and so the Flotilla Company was able to get started first. The steamer was called *Sarojini*.

**page 176** 'Khulna and Barisal'. These are two towns in the southern part of East Bengal (now Bangladesh).

**page 177** 'Howrah bridge'. the first bridge across the Hooghly connecting Calcutta and Howrah was built in 1874. It was a pontoon type, so constructed that its central portion might be raised for a certain period each day to permit passage of vessels of more than normal height. The present steel bridge dates from 1943.

## 42. Bereavements

**page 177** 'my mother died'. Sarada Devi died on 11 March 1875 when RT was thirteen.

'my sister-in-law'. See note on p. 25.

**page 178** 'she who was the youngest daughter-in-law'. See note on p. 25.

'at the age of twenty-three'. RT's sister-in-law Kadambari Devi died in April 1884, so RT was actually twenty-two. She committed suicide, possibly by taking an overdose of opium on 19 April and probably died on the morning of 21 April after being attended by several eminent doctors. The police were informed but the body was not sent to the morgue; instead a coroner's court sat at Jorasanko. Its report appears to have been destroyed, along with a rumoured letter in which Kadambari explained the reasons for her suicide, and all her other letters – presumably at the request of Debendranath, to avoid scandal. Her death went unreported in the newspapers of the time. (The family account book, according to Pal, *2*, p. 272, has the following entry: 'Expenses towards suppressing the news of the death to the press Rs 52.')

**page 179** 'ever-expanding wreaths of tears'. In the period after Kadambari's death up to 1911, when RT wrote *Jibansmriti*, the following close relatives died: Hemendranath, RT's third brother, 1884; Abhigna Devi, a niece, ?1894; Balendranath, a nephew, 1899; Mrinalini Devi, RT's wife, 1902; Nitindranath, a nephew, 1902; Renuka, a daughter, 1903; Debendranath, RT's father, 1905; Samindranath, a son, 1907.

## 43. The rains and the autumn

**page 182** 'What idle play is this, my heart'. Both this and the song on p. 184 are from *Kari o Komal* (Sharps and Flats).

## 44. Sharps and Flats

**page 184** 'my second voyage to England'. See chapter 31 and note on p. 144.

'Ashutosh Chaudhuri'. He later became Justice Sir Ashutosh Chaudhuri (1860–1924), of the Calcutta High Court.

'one of the family'. Ashutosh Chaudhuri married Pratibha Devi, daughter of Hemendranath Tagore (see note on p. 138).

**page 186** 'Arab Bedouin'. RT is quoting himself: the line is from 'Duranta Asha' (Wild Hopes), a poem he wrote in 1888. It is one of several from that time in which he satirises the so-called patriots of Bengal.

# Select Bibliography

Banerji, Sumanta, *The Parlour and the Streets: Elite and Popular Culture in Nineteenth Century Calcutta*, Calcutta, Seagull Books, 1989

Basham, A. L., *The Wonder that was India*, pbk edn, London, Sidgwick and Jackson, 1985

Brough, John (trans.), *Poems from the Sanskrit*, London, Penguin Classics, 1968

Coulson, Michael (trans.), *Three Sanskrit Plays*, London, Penguin Classics, 1981 (includes *Sakuntala* by Kalidas)

Ghosh, J. C., *Bengali Literature*, 2nd edn, London, Curzon Press, 1976

*Hobson-Jobson: A Glossary of Colloquial Anglo-Indian Words and Phrases, and of Kindred Terms, Etymological, Historical, Geographical and Discursive*, Calcutta, Rupa, 1986 (first published 1886)

Kopf, David, *The Brahmo Samaj*, Princeton University Press, 1979

Kripalani, Krishna, *Rabindranath Tagore: A Biography*, 2nd edn, Calcutta, Vishva Bharati, 1980

Narayan, R. K., *The Ramayana*, London, Heinemann, 1972
*The Mahabharata*, London, Heinemann, 1978

Robinson, Andrew, *The Art of Rabindranath Tagore*, London, Andre Deutsch, 1989

Sen, Sukumar, *History of Bengali Literature*, 3rd edn, New Delhi, Sahitya Akademi, 1979

Tagore, Rabindranath, *Creative Unity*, London, Macmillan, 1922

    *Gitanjali*, London, Macmillan, 1913

    *Glimpses of Bengal*, London, Macmillan, 1921 (2nd edn, 1991)

    *The Home and the World*, London, Macmillan, 1919 (2nd edn, Penguin, 1985)

    *Nationalism*, London, Macmillan, 1917 (2nd edn, 1991)

    *Selected Poems*, trans. by William Radice, London, Penguin, 1985

    *Selected Short Stories*, trans. by Krishna Dutta and Mary Lago, London, Macmillan, 1991

Tagore, Satyendranath, 'Introductory Chapter' to *The Autobiography of Maharshi Devendranath Tagore*, trans. by Satyendranath Tagore and Indira Devi, London, Macmillan, 1915

## *In Bengali*

Pal, Prashanta Kumar, *Rabijibani*, Calcutta, vol. 1, Bhurjapatra, 1982; vol. 2, Bhurjapatra, 1984; vol. 3, Ananda Publishers, 1987; vol. 4, Ananda Publishers, 1988; vol. 5, Ananda Publishers, 1990; (further volumes expected)